FIC
DOB

Dobyns, Stephen

A boat off the
coast

$16.30

DATE		

A Boat off the Coast

Books by Stephen Dobyns

NOVELS
A Boat Off the Coast (1987)
Saratoga Snapper (1986)
Cold Dog Soup (1985)
Saratoga Headhunter (1985)
Dancer with One Leg (1983)
Saratoga Swimmer (1981)
Saratoga Longshot (1976)
A Man of Little Evils (1973)

POETRY
Cemetery Nights (1987)
Black Dog, Red Dog (1984)
The Balthus Poems (1982)
Heat Death (1980)
Griffon (1976)
Concurring Beasts (1972)

A Boat off the Coast

Stephen Dobyns

Viking

VIKING
Viking Penguin Inc., 40 West 23rd Street,
New York, New York 10010, U.S.A.
Penguin Books Ltd, 27 Wrights Lane, London W8 5TZ (Publishing & Editorial)
and Harmondsworth,
Middlesex, England (Distribution & Warehouse)
Penguin Books Australia Ltd, Ringwood,
Victoria, Australia
Penguin Books Canada Limited, 2801 John Street,
Markham, Ontario, Canada L3R 1B4
Penguin Books (N.Z.) Ltd, 182–190 Wairau Road,
Auckland 10, New Zealand

First published in 1987 by Viking Penguin Inc.
Published simultaneously in Canada

LIBRARY OF CONGRESS CATALOGING IN PUBLICATION DATA
Dobyns, Stephen, 1941–
A boat off the coast.
I. Title.
PS3554.02B6   1987   813'.54   87-40033
ISBN 0-670-81668-X

Printed in the United States of America by
Arcata Graphics, Fairfield, Pennsylvania
Set in Primer
Designed by Quinten Welch

For Frederick Wiseman

A Boat off the Coast

one

Lowell Perry wanted a new car. Even though his Camaro was hardly a year old, he wanted something bigger and faster. He wanted one of those new Corvettes with a 5.7 liter V8 engine that could do zero to sixty in 5.6 seconds. He'd get a red one, like his Camaro, and he'd paint the name on its side in gold letters: Red Mischief or maybe Midnight Marauder. Then he'd find a pretty little girl to go riding with him.

At the moment, the Corvette seemed so close that Lowell Perry could smell the leather of its dark red seats. The knob on the gearshift of both the Camaro and the Corvette was covered with black leather and had a plastic button in the center, but the Camaro's knob was round while the Corvette's was square and Perry could almost feel the difference, feel the square knob pressing against his palm, that's how close that Corvette was. Thirty-two thousand, fully loaded.

Next to him was the man who could give him the money, Harry Nixon, a lieutenant in the Tactical Enforcement division of the U.S. Customs Department out of Portland, Maine. Dressed in dark blue coveralls and a matching baseball cap with a U.S. Customs insignia, Nixon stood seemingly without breathing, like a machine with a little switch in his back waiting to be set in motion. The two men were leaning against a yellow Caterpillar parked at the railway tracks. In front of them a rusty freighter was being nudged into the slip by a pair of tugs that signaled back and forth with short toots.

It was mid-afternoon on a Thursday in early August and the freighter, which they had heard approaching through the fog for a good half hour before they saw it, was bringing 25,000 tons of solar salt up from Brazil and maybe a little cocaine. That was why Harry Nixon was here, along with ten other U.S. Customs and Coast Guard officers. The Customs men were all in dark blue coveralls and looked like a Swat team. "The Black Gang" was what sailors called them. With them were two dogs, a golden retriever and a German shepherd, that could not only smell out drugs but probably judge the quality and even sniff their way back to the farmer who had originally grown the plants in Bolivia or wherever.

Lowell Perry knew there was cocaine on that ship. He was good at knowing things. He made it his business. Perry had worked the docks here in Searsport for about eleven years, ever since getting out of the army. Normally, he operated the middle of the three hoists, which looked like a red caboose sitting sideways on an old trestle and topped by a tilted oil derrick. Sprague dock was the freighter's first port of call, and Perry guessed he'd be working from seven to seven all the next day scooping the salt out of the hold, salt which would be used to make the Maine roads driveable throughout the winter. Several salt boats made about a dozen trips from Brazil during the year, mostly in the summer and fall. After getting rid of the salt in Searsport, the freighter would continue to Canada to pick up a load of grain, then head back down to Brazil.

The dogs kept barking and Lowell Perry didn't like that. The German shepherd in particular seemed high-strung and tugged at its leash. Looking up, Perry saw sailors staring over the railing as the ship was moored to the pier. The Customs people should have hidden someplace or boarded the ship when it took on the pilot off Monhegan Island. Maybe just hide the dogs. Even though all ships were met by Customs and Immigration officers, the dogs were only used if drugs were suspected. These damn salt boats had been bringing up drugs for more than a year. Lowell Perry knew all about it.

"Those dogs are too obvious," said Perry. "It's like waving a red flag." To the left of the freighter, he could just make out the shore of Sears Island rising out of the fog.

Harry Nixon shook himself as if just waking up. "What can you do?" he asked. "Shoot them?" He was a big man in his mid-forties, at least six inches taller than Lowell Perry, who knew that Nixon didn't like him, despite all that Perry had done for him. One time he'd heard Nixon refer to him as a ferret but Perry hadn't minded. Ferrets were hunters; they were small and quick and sharp-eyed. If it hadn't been for Nixon's tone of voice, Perry would have felt complimented.

But then Perry stopped thinking of the Customs lieutenant as he noticed the sailors preparing to lower the gangplank. He felt his body tensing itself, all his muscles getting ready. Perry had been on these searches before and knew what to expect. Hicks would go first, get the store's declaration and ship's manifest, then have the captain sign the Master's Oath. Nixon would be right after him with the dogs as he led the search, splitting his men into two groups to get both the officers' quarters and crews' quarters at the same time. On a ship this size there were hundreds of places to hide drugs, but Nixon usually knew the favorite ones and anyway Perry would be there to help out. This, however, was just a small operation. Whoever was doing the smuggling probably kept the stuff with his personal gear, a suitcase of coke. Well, he was in for a surprise.

The gangplank hit the pier with a crash. Hicks ran up it with Nixon a few feet behind him. The dogs were right on

3

Nixon's ankles, prodding him, almost tangling him up in their leashes. Turning to kick the dogs away, Nixon noticed Lowell Perry following him.

"Not this time," said Nixon.

"Why not?"

"You're too eager," said Nixon. Then he turned and ran up the gangplank before Perry could say anything. At the top, Hicks was already talking to the captain. Nixon hurried around him as if he wasn't there.

Perry pressed himself to the side as the rest of the Black Gang squeezed around him. Then he made his way back down to the pier, cursing Nixon and his dogs. Damn cops were all the same. The moment they knew you wanted something, they did their best to see you didn't get it. Nixon needed him for the simple reason that Perry could smell out drugs that no dog could find.

Instead of waiting on the pier, Perry ran toward the three hoisting towers, climbed over the conveyor belt, then went up the ladder of the middle hoist, working his way around the steam engine and rolls of cable and up into the cabin where he spent most of his days. From here he could look down on the ship and see something of the search. The fog was so thick that even the pier was a blur and he could barely pick out the yellow Caterpillar which he had been leaning against earlier.

The ship was the *Andrade*. Lowell Perry figured it had come into Searsport about twenty times since he'd been working the docks. He even recognized some of the crew. What a wreck it was, as if rusted into junk by its own cargo. Looking down from the cabin of the hoist, Perry saw some of the Black Gang and two Customs officers in the wheelhouse. Down on deck men were shouting in Portuguese. Perry didn't trust any of them. A million dollars of cocaine, the sailors could pass it around the ship as Nixon and the others searched uselessly. It had happened before. Name a trick and Perry

4

had seen it already. It would be just like Nixon to miss the cocaine and rob Lowell Perry of that new Corvette. After all, it had been Perry who had done most of the work. He had found out about the cocaine just like he found out about everything. He should be on the TV getting a fucking medal instead of stuck up here in the tower.

Perry remained in the hoist as the afternoon grew darker and the big lights were turned on. Even though he'd run out of cigarettes and had to take a leak, he kept his eyes on the ship as if he might see something important, like one of those dagos hiding something or throwing something over the side. But there was nothing to see except sometimes Nixon as he led the search through the ship from the wheelhouse down into the engine room, the fo'c'sle, the lifeboats and even down into the hold itself, while the crew stood around getting more and more impatient. As soon as they were let off the ship, they'd go find themselves a local whore or hitch a ride into Belfast six miles away or go buy Levi's up at Epstein's on Route 1 in Searsport. The young ones would do all three.

It got dark and still the search continued. Perry was just level with the ship's bridge and a sailor by the wheel kept looking over at him and grinning, until Perry was sure that he knew all about the cocaine and was making fun of him. On deck he saw one of the dog handlers being dragged by the German shepherd toward another lifeboat. It was like the dog was their boss, thought Perry, ordering them around with its lousy nose. Anyway, it showed no excitement. Usually the damn things got hysterical if there was any trace of drugs. Perry looked back at the bridge and again the dago was grinning. He'd like to pop him one, break those shiny white teeth into junk.

By nine-thirty the search was over. Perry saw the Black Gang making their way back to the gangplank and he began to climb down out of the hoist, trying not to get grease on his clothes. He was almost certain they hadn't found anything.

Still, he was sure it had been on the boat. He guessed that whoever was bringing it up had managed to dump it when he saw the Black Gang waiting on the pier. If he was really greedy or just gutsy, he might have hidden it someplace else. But probably he didn't have time. Probably the whole package had gone over the side.

Perry waited by the railway tracks as the Black Gang and Customs men descended the gangplank. One of the dogs was barking. Nixon came last. Several of the officers and crew were grinning and calling out in Portuguese. Nixon didn't look up.

Lowell Perry bummed a cigarette from Hicks, then lit it as Nixon approached. Noticing that Nixon's shoes and the legs of his blue coveralls were spotted with white powder, Perry experienced a rush of hope until he realized it was dust from the salt down in the hold. Anyway it was too dirty for cocaine, which sparkled and always looked clean.

Nixon took off his cap and slapped it against his leg. "Nothing," he said.

"You're kidding," said Perry. "Damn." He was certain that Nixon liked disappointing him.

"It'd been there though," said Nixon. "The dogs smelled it. An officer had had it in his cabin." He seemed frustrated but not particularly angry. Lowell Perry, however, was furious. He felt if Nixon had let him come onto the ship, then he would have found the cocaine, no matter where it was, even down in the water where it was probably lighting up the fish and making the lobsters go crazy.

Lowell Perry stared up at the salt boat. Under the yellow lights, it looked filthy and the streaks of rust on the white paint reminded him of blood. He wished he could take it apart bolt by bolt and send it to the bottom. He wished he could find the bastard who had cheated him out of his Corvette and hang his ears on a necklace like he had known guys to do in Vietnam. He'd almost bought one once but the price was too

high: twelve ears on a dogtag chain looking like dried fruit.
"Maybe you didn't look hard enough," said Perry.

Nixon didn't even bother to answer.

"Don't kill them, don't kill them!" shouted Brian Davis, even though that was what he always shouted and hardly anyone paid attention.

Hank Jackson ran at Brian and shook ten chickens in his face. "Yah!" he yelled.

Brian turned away, pretending not to care. He knew Jackson had no doubt that Brian would fire his ass if he kept acting up. He also knew that Jackson hated guys like him, guys he had grown up with who were now foremen and bosses and store owners. Even though Brian tried to treat him fair, Jackson would be happy to see him fall down and break a leg. And minutes earlier when Brian had cracked his head on one of the feeders that was pulled up to the ceiling, Hank Jackson had laughed so hard he nearly choked.

As Hank Jackson ran to the pickup door, Brian stood back, trying not to open his mouth to let in the chicken dust and keeping his eyes squinched half shut. His father had owned a chicken barn in Belfast and Brian had grown up in them. That didn't make him like them any better. Often he wore a face mask, but this was just a short job, a small order of eight thousand roasters, and if he worked too, they'd be back in Belfast by eleven. He had a gray railroad hat pulled down to his ears but even so the dust would get in his hair, as it had already gotten into his short beard and mustache. It was now nine-thirty. After he finished with these damn birds, he'd go down and check the oil level on his boat. Maybe he'd get four hours' sleep before he went out to haul his lobster traps.

Brian watched Jackson as he grabbed up five more roosters in each hand, letting them hang by their crusty yellow legs—left, right, left, right—watching them flap their wings and try to crank out another squawk before he shoved his arms out the pickup door where either Lou or Sam-Sam would slide his fingers under Hank Jackson's, taking the chickens so Hank could go back for ten more—eighty pounds of birds. Brian knew a guy once who could carry seven roosters in each hand, but that wasn't so great because he broke their legs and even killed some. But five was nothing; even though Brian could only manage four, most guys could do five after a while: five roosters and up to seven pullets, which were half the weight. It was like grabbing a bunch of pencils covered with warts. The trick was in how fast you could do it, slamming into a pen of two thousand birds, jamming the chickens between your fingers, trying not to break their legs or minding how they wriggled on you, then trying not to slip in the mixture of sawdust and bird shit which after twelve weeks was slicker than a hockey pond. Jackson was fast, almost faster than anybody, and Brian admired him for it. If you did it enough, it became a game and the slow guys had to buy beer for the winners. That made slamming chickens out the pickup door something you could just about stand.

Right now they were having a race in a chicken barn out toward Swanville, hitting the first pen on the first floor, half drunk, half stupid, half choking on the dust, half knocked out by the heat and stench of ammonia. Five men running and shouting like crazy people as the chickens squawked, and Brian tried to keep up even though he knew he had no chance. Mostly Brian didn't work the chicken barns but he'd promised his wife a new washer-dryer combination, and anyway they always seemed to come up short at the end of the month, so he'd volunteered to fill in as foreman for someone who was out sick. During the day Brian worked as a foreman on the processing floor of the poultry company in Belfast. "Downstairs" was how it was called, and most everyone in Waldo County knew what that meant.

As they picked up the last few roosters in the first pen, Brian got ready to set up the second. The process was the same: turn out the lights, then go to the far end with a flashlight, flick it on and frighten the chickens so they ran down to the pickup door, while you hoped they didn't suffocate or have heart attacks. Then, once they were packed tight, you surrounded them with the portable pen, screwed in the blue light and the birds would lie down, thinking it was night and time to go to sleep. That's when you got them. The floor had four pickup doors in an area of about ten thousand square feet.

Brian rubbed his head where he had hit it on the feeder as he made his way through the darkness to the far side of the next pen, sliding his boots in the slime so he wouldn't tromp down on a chicken. Behind him in the dark, Hank Jackson was shouting about pussy and how he wanted some. Brian was sick of telling the men to be careful. If they got too rough, he'd start shouting, but he figured if he was tired, then they must be exhausted. Of course some chickens got suffocated but still you had to watch out. Several of the men were drinking and had a hard time even seeing the chickens. It was the feathers that Brian hated, the little feathers you got in your mouth and stuck in the back of your throat.

Brian flicked on the flashlight and let out a yodel that rose above the whir of the ventilating fans. There was a sudden rush of wings as maybe two thousand roosters began squawking and running toward the pickup door. Poor things couldn't even crow. As a kid Brian used to teach them to crow, by crowing once or twice himself every time he entered the barn. After a week or so, some of the roosters started crowing back. It almost made him like them, even though that was the same summer they had eaten his favorite cat. Brian moved forward as Jackson and Bodo began setting up the pen. The beam of the flashlight picked out a dead rooster a few yards ahead. When they keeled over with heart attacks, it was always onto their backs, Brian didn't know why. He picked it up and tossed it into the pen. All the birds went into Belfast, both living and dead. The dead ones went to the reclamation plant where they were ground up and sent back to the chicken barns as part of the medicated feed. Brian guessed that some of these birds had been through here a hundred times.

Brian screwed in the blue light and all the roosters settled down. Even after all these years he was amazed by their stupidity. He began grabbing the birds, letting them hang from his hands by alternating feet. His cotton gloves were already wet from the gunk on the floor. Most of the pickup crew used their bare hands. Most didn't even wear boots. Wading through the birds to the pickup door, he reached out his hands to Sam-Sam, who took the eight roosters and jammed them into a coop, a white plastic crate that held up to fourteen birds. Sam-Sam stood on the back of the flatbed tractor-trailer truck parked out in the yard lit by twin arc lights. The truck was an old Ford that whined on the hills. The three men outside packed the coops onto the platform—twenty rows of four, eight crates high, with ropes attached to the rub rail to tie them down. At least you could breathe out here. The air was cool and Brian could smell the ocean. A dog was barking over near the house. Hank Jackson dropped a rooster and it scurried away, then settled down under the front wheel of the truck.

"Try not to lose any," called Brian. Jackson ignored him. The men were all poor and took the job either because they couldn't find another or because they liked getting drunk and doing it fast so the whole thing became crazy. Anyway, Waldo County wasn't a place where you could pick and choose your line of work. The choice was usually between a bad job and no job at all. If you were lucky, it was just bad paying, like a job at a gas station. Otherwise, it was bad all around, a job to bust your pocket and your body. Brian had already been working for the poultry company for fifteen years, ever since high school, and he'd been a foreman for five. At least it was better than the fertilizer plant out in Monroe.

"Come on, Jackson," shouted Sam-Sam, through the pickup door. "I want to get home."

Jackson shoved another ten birds at him. "You gotta date with the widow and her four daughters?"

"Nah," said Lou, "he's finished his pint bottle and wants another."

"Hey, I'm tired," shouted Sam-Sam. "I need female companionship."

Another rooster fell to the ground, this time on its head. "You gotta be gentle," shouted Brian. The bird had a broken neck and flopped around in the dust. Sam-Sam threw it up on top of the truck. That's where they put some of the busted ones. Already along the road a dozen people were waiting for the truck to get moving and the chickens to blow off. Living near a chicken barn almost paid for itself if you could stand the smell.

Lou had another crippled chicken. "Hey, Brian, watch this." He tossed the chicken into the air and then kicked it lightly onto the top of the truck. Brian refused to acknowledge him. "You like football," shouted Lou. "I thought you'd appreciate that."

"I haven't played football for fifteen years," said Brian. Lou had been in high school with him, as had some of the others. Except for tourists, Brian hardly ever saw anyone he hadn't known all his life. But even as he thought that, he questioned it. Since the late sixties, a lot of flatlanders had moved into Waldo County to take up homesteading or build a summer place. Brian didn't know any personally, although he saw them at the food co-op in Belfast and maybe the movie theater.

By ten-forty-five they were done. Hank Jackson claimed that was a record but Sam-Sam disagreed. Now the farmer would have fourteen days to turn the barn around, clean it, disinfect it, put down fresh sawdust, before getting another load of 44,888 chicks, some with bits of egg shells still stuck to them.

The pullets and broilers would go in seven weeks, the roasters in twelve. All told it cost the company fifty-one cents a pound to raise a bird and process it.

As the last coops were tied down, the men began drifting over to the blue passenger van that Brian had driven in from Belfast. The pickup crews always worked at night and a full barn of forty-four thousand birds could take them till morning, which made it even harder because in the daylight the birds were awful to catch. But now it was still early and, while some of the crew would go home, others would continue drinking at Clara's or Rollie's Cafe. Brian pulled himself up into the driver's seat of the van. Hank Jackson was beside him and everyone was ready to go. Brian started up, revving the motor a couple of times, then waited for the chicken truck to pull ahead of him.

As the truck lurched onto the road, Brian saw some people get out of the cars parked at the side. There was a general squawking and commotion as the maimed and damaged chickens blew off the top of the truck. One old guy in a red hat grabbed, up five chickens by their necks, giving each a swing to make sure it was dead. Then he ran to an old Buick of an indeterminate color, yanked open the rear door and threw the birds in the backseat.

The truck, with the van right behind it, turned onto Blake Curtis Road, past Smart Cemetery, then across the small bridge over the Goose River to Smart Road. Many of the houses were dark, cheap ranch houses mostly, some mobile homes, a few big houses but not many, a Pentecostal Church—all scattered along the edge of the woods. After a few minutes, the truck turned on to Route 141 toward Belfast. The van was so noisy that conversation was impossible. Hank Jackson was shouting something about what he'd had for lunch and how it had disagreed with him, but Brian was too tired to ask what the hell he was talking about. After a few minutes, they crested the hill by Holmes Greenhouse and could see Penobscot Bay and the lights of Belfast ahead of them. At the bottom of the hill, Brian turned right onto Route 1 and began crossing the high bridge over the Passagassawakeag River and Belfast Bay. Brian looked to his left, trying to spot his own boat, an old thirty-five-foot lobster boat built on Vinalhaven. But the fog was too thick and his mooring was on the other side of the city wharf.

Belfast in the fog was more of a compact glow than a set of individual buildings. But he could make out the wharf, although the tugs were out, probably over in Searsport. And he could see the lights going up the hill on Main Street. Beyond Main Street, the chicken processing plant was a gray blur. Brian had promised his five-year-old, Jimmy, that he'd buy him a Transformer robot but he'd have to do it tomorrow. His wife, Margaret, got pissed off when he spent money like that. Buying junk for the kids, she said. But it made them happy and made him happy, so what was the harm?

At the end of the bridge was the sign BELFAST BROOKS FREEDOM and an arrow pointing to the right. An old high school teacher of Brian's had once told their class that the sign could be read not just as the names of three local towns but as a sentence with Brooks being the verb: Belfast permits freedom or tolerates freedom. And Brian liked that, even though he didn't believe it much. The truck made the turn. Caught up in its wake, a thin stream of white feathers spun and cavorted, blew against the van's windshield, drifted into the gutters, spotted the lawns of the Victorian houses, the mansions of sea captains whose names were forgotten except for maybe a grave in the cemetery or attached to a disintegrating tintype or frock coat hung up in a glass case at the local historical society.

Tucker Morgan didn't feel like dancing. He felt like getting laid. He felt like getting one of these girls and taking her back to his place or to the Belfast Motor Inn and working on her body till she screamed. Not brutally, you understand. There was nothing mean about Tucker. He wanted her to scream with the pleasure of it, to scream and help take his mind off himself, his troubles, his lack of money and the fact that his wife had moved out three weeks ago taking his kid, Jason, age two, who was the only human being he liked in this whole shithole state.

But the girls at Clara's Place were either too fat or too skinny or too fucked up. He was tired of girls with a lot of past history, girls who had more troubles than he had. But the more he drank, the more his ugly quotient went down and down, until even the porkers he'd disdained when he walked into Clara's two hours before were beginning to look good. That's what happened when you drank tequila—the ugly girls got cute. Liquid socialism, he called it.

The band was a group called the New Kentucky Stompers. Tucker doubted if any of the four had ever set foot in Kentucky, but they had bounce and most of their notes were the right ones and in any case the twenty people jumping up and down on the small dance floor hadn't come looking for some recital or artsy concert. This wasn't Camden, after all, and even the band's equipment squeaked and was staticky.

The smoke was thick and Tucker stood at the end of the bar, which at least got a draft from the open door. He was tall and thin and wore jeans and a white cowboy shirt under a Levi's jacket. He had long, thin hands that used to throw perfect passes back in high school. Later, in the army, they had thrown all sorts of things. He kept glancing around the room. There were no vacant tables or empty seats and the clientele looked one hundred percent local. Few tourists came to Clara's, although they might show up for lunch. Instead, they were next door at the Belfast Cafe drinking frozen drinks and eating sandwiches called "melts" and salads with bean sprouts and maybe tofu.

The room was long and low and dark. On the opposite wall

was a mural of the *Osprey,* a big power boat that Clara once owned a piece of that made little tours of the bay. Tucker knew most of these people, which didn't make him like them much. Not that he necessarily disliked them, he just felt impatient. He'd been born in Belfast and had gone to school here, even though his father, a dentist, had moved to Maine from Philadelphia. But Tucker had been away for a little over eleven years—the army, bumming around, then college. Now he'd been back three years and was getting sick of it. Not enough he didn't know what. Maybe it was just a shortage of cute girls, although at the moment his ugly quotient had fallen so low that he hardly cared who he went home with. That girl over there with those three chicken guys, for instance. They were ignoring her and she looked bored to death. There must be some way to cut her off from those fellows if he could just catch her eye.

But even as he mapped out his strategy, Tucker realized the three men were wise to him. Tactfully, he pretended to take an interest in the band. One of the guys he knew, Hank Jackson, a local fuck-up whom Tucker had played softball with a couple of times. The other two were just faces. Maybe the girl was with Jackson, although that showed pretty bad taste. Tucker was just turning to sneak another look when he saw Jackson lurch to his feet and begin making his way toward him. He wore coveralls over a flannel shirt despite the heat and had white feathers stuck on his clothes as if he'd just come from work. Tucker braced himself. But Jackson didn't seem angry. In fact he was smiling, some combination of half leer, half sneer intended to show good humor. He was also drunk.

Jackson slapped a big hand on Tucker's shoulder and mumbled something that Tucker couldn't hear over the music.

Tucker pulled back, making Jackson drop his hand. His eyes looked like red pinwheels. "What was that?" Tucker asked.

Jackson leaned toward Tucker's ear. "You got any more of that stuff?" he shouted.

Uh-oh, thought Tucker, he's going to make himself a scene. "I don't know what you're talking about."

Jackson bent closer and raised his voice. He was a big man with a thick brown beard. He smelled like chicken dust and when he spoke he shot little drops of spit onto Tucker's neck. "That cocaine, mister, you got any more of it?"

He was speaking loud enough for other people to hear. Tucker shook his head and started to walk away. "I don't know what you're talking about."

Jackson took hold of Tucker's arm and tried to look sly. "We got money, how much do you want?"

Tucker wanted the floor to open up and a big pair of hands to drag Mr. Jackson away. Five months earlier he had peddled a little cocaine, but he hadn't done any since and didn't want to. It got you all messed up with assholes like Jackson. Tucker pulled away. "Get the hell outta here," he said.

Jackson seemed not to notice and again lurched forward. Tucker felt that people were watching. "What do you want?" said Jackson. "Just tell me what you want."

I've got to stop this, thought Tucker. "Your wife, asshole," he shouted, giving Jackson a shove.

Jackson looked surprised and Tucker could almost hear the synapses drunkenly clicking within Jackson's brain, slowly leading him toward indignation and anger. Jackson stepped back and lifted his fist, but ponderously, almost as if he found it heavy. "You . . ." he said, then paused as if searching for the exact word.

Tucker didn't give him a chance to finish but hit Jackson in the stomach with all the strength he could muster. He had drunk too much tequila and the room was bobbing round. He knew if he got hit like he was hitting Jackson, he'd puke his guts out. He was sick of the racket. It was time to go home.

Jackson stumbled backward, holding his stomach and his

lips forming a perfect *O* of pain and surpise. All his gestures continued to be slow and thoughtful. His two friends, however, responded more quickly, pushing back their chairs and hurling themselves the ten feet or so toward Tucker. Stepping away from the bar, Tucker shoved a bar stool in front of one man and tried to kick the other in the groin, but missed and hit his hip, knocking him aside. Then Tucker punched his ear. The first man was still tangled up in the bar stool and by the time he got to his feet, a bouncer had grabbed him. But now Hank Jackson was coming to life. He dove toward Tucker, who dodged to his left and hit him in the stomach again. There wasn't time to do much else because the bouncers and bartender and manager were all shouting and flinging themselves into the fight, dragging Jackson back as Tucker gave him a kick. Arms were wrapped around Tucker from behind. The band had stopped playing and people were yelling. Tucker braced himself and bent forward quickly, heaving someone over his shoulder. But then some other guy grabbed his legs. He got an arm free and took hold of someone's hair, had the pleasure of hearing him shout. Tucker was being carried toward the door. Violently twisting himself, he got loose and fell to his knees, then he punched someone, he didn't know who and didn't care. He was into the game of it now and it hardly mattered who he hurt or how much he got hurt himself. He grabbed someone's shirt and again found himself being carried. He supposed he was shouting. Everyone was. Obscenities mostly. Kicking and shouting. Someone pinned his free arm. Someone else rabbit-punched him. Everything was jerking around like crazy.

The door was being held open. Hank Jackson and one of his friends had already been dumped out onto High Street. Then Tucker was through the door and being thrown against the side of a parked car. He was ready for that, however, and sprang back at the bouncer, Fat Frankie, kicked him in the leg for all he was worth, then slugged out at someone else but missed. The manager dragged Frankie back inside and the door was slammed shut and all Tucker could think about was that one way or another he had separated that pretty girl from the three drunken assholes and here he was stuck with the assholes. For a second they all looked at one another. The street was foggy and the air felt cool and moist. Tucker took a deep breath. About a dozen people stood around yelling. Tucker dodged back into the street, swinging at Jackson and missing.

It was time to find his truck and get out of town. These guys were sloppy but they could still hurt him. He tried to keep Jackson and his friends in front of him, but one circled around and another grabbed him around the waist. Tucker swung up his feet, kicked someone, then grabbed the hair and beard of the guy who was holding him and yanked until he let him go. Then he broke free and ran toward the parking lot in front of Brooks Drugs where he'd stashed his truck.

Up the block Lowell Perry was parking his Camaro. He liked to drive it real slow in town so the motor barely rumbled and the people stuck behind him got pissed off. But now the streets were nearly empty and driving around wasn't worth the gas. Besides that, he was in a bad mood. His red Corvette with its Z51 Performance Handling package, 4-speed manual overdrive transmission and 3.07:1 axle ratio had drifted back into fantasy land, and what he wanted now was a couple of beers at Clara's and the opportunity to check out the girls.

As he locked the car door, Perry heard shouting up the street. He turned and saw the fight. He knew those guys. Dopes, every one. And there was Tucker. Why had he bothered to come back to Belfast, that's what Lowell Perry wanted to know? Even though Tucker had grown up in Belfast it wasn't like he was from here. Not only that but his old man had already left again, gone to Florida or some such place. Tucker had been in Vietnam about the same time Lowell Perry had been there. Then he'd gone off to college. And here he was fighting in the street, despite his college degree and all that crap. Perry couldn't imagine making such a display of himself. If anybody came after him like that, he'd stick a knife in him.

Without looking again at Tucker and the others, Lowell Perry pushed his way through the edge of the crowd to the door of the bar. He had to hammer on it hard before they would open. Fat Frankie was bent over on a chair pissing and moaning and a couple of older women were clucking around him like nervous hens. With a grin, Lowell Perry realized that one of those guys fighting had been Hank Jackson. He had a pretty girlfriend or wife, Perry didn't know what. If she was inside, then maybe she'd like some company.

Brian Davis had made it as far as the Depot, the newsstand right across from Clara's where the Greyhounds stopped, before giving the fight any attention. There were lots of fights and this was just one more. He'd already recognized Hank Jackson and was faintly impressed that Jackson had managed to get drunker and in major trouble in the half hour since Brian had dropped him off in front of the bar. Even as Brian looked over at him someone put his fist smack in the center of Jackson's face. The country music from Clara's seemed to be keeping pace with the fight. Brian was carrying his toolbox and he switched it from his left hand to his right as he approached the door of the Masonic Temple. It was eleven-thirty and he still had to check his boat. He had no time for distractions.

But that tall guy was doing a good job holding his own, even though it was clear that pretty soon, unless the cops showed up, he'd get the shit kicked out of him. Brian glanced at him again, sensing something familiar about him, something about his shoulders or the way he held his head. Then he stopped.

19

He knew that man. Even before Tucker's name sprang into his head, Brian knew it was someone he loved, someone he hadn't seen for years.

At that moment Tucker took another swing at Jackson, missed, then ran across the street toward the parking lot by Brooks Drugs. Jackson and the other two—one of them was Willie Pierce but Brian couldn't remember the other guy's name—took off after Tucker, staggering a little. They were all drunk, Brian realized, although Tucker less so. Brian took a step after them, then another. He knew Jackson and his friends would think nothing of pounding Tucker's head to a red pulp. Brian began to run, following the crowd of spectators toward the parking lot. It was a Thursday night and people were bored. A good fight took the edge off. It was something to talk about.

His toolbox banging against his leg, Brian ran into the parking lot just in time to see Tucker haul off and kick Willie Pierce in the balls. Immediately, Jackson tackled Tucker from behind, knocking him down so they slid along the pavement in a confused jumble. Then Jackson tried to bang Tucker's head against the concrete.

"You fuckin' leave my wife alone, you hear me?"

Tucker twisted away. "Hey, man, you wanted a price and I gave you one." He was breathing so hard that he spoke in gasps. The other man kicked at him and missed as Tucker pulled himself up by grabbing onto a car door.

Brian shoved a path through the crowd. "Tucker," he shouted, "is that you? Hey, Tucker!" He put down his toolbox, then jumped forward and took hold of Willie Pierce's shoulder, yanking him back so he fell down. "Leave him alone, what're you doing?" The last time Brian saw Tucker, fourteen years earlier, there'd also been a fight. Tucker had been home on leave before being sent to Vietnam and was strutting around town in his new uniform. Some guys hadn't liked it and tried to take it off him and Tucker had objected. Brian helped him then too.

Going after Hank Jackson, Brian pulled him away by the straps of his coveralls, as Tucker hit the other guy, whatever his name was.

"Break it up!" shouted Brian.

Jackson peered at him in surprise, then swung at him. Brian blocked his arm, then hit him in the shoulder, knocking him away. He turned back to Willie Pierce, who looked hesitant. Not only was Brian strong and a good fighter, he was sober.

"I don't have no quarrel with you," said Pierce. He held his hands in front of him as if preparing to catch a ball.

"Then get outta here," said Brian. The fog dampened the noise, while across the street Clara's Place was almost invisible. A dozen people watched from the edge of the parking lot, so gray and blurry they seemed like ghosts.

Jackson was also backing away. Tucker and the third man were still fighting. "Why do you have to be so serious about everything?" shouted Tucker. He swung at the man, missed, then got knocked down himself as the man hit him in the chest. Brian grabbed the man's hair and dragged him back. Then he kicked his leg. Even as the man fell, Brian realized his name was Parker and that he used to date his wife's cousin. Parker scrambled to his feet. All three looked at Brian. There was a siren from someplace. Jackson and his friends ran off through the fog.

"Too tough for you?" shouted a woman and the man next to her laughed.

Brian bent down over Tucker, who was on his hands and knees next to the front bumper of a VW. His shoulders were shaking as if he were crying.

"Tucker, are you all right?"

Tucker lifted his head. He was laughing. There was blood on his face. He wiped it with his hand, then looked at the hand. "I bet I look like a fucking goony bird," he said. Both men paused. From up the street the siren was louder. "Let's get the hell outta here," said Tucker.

two

Jumping to his feet, Tucker sprinted down High Street past the Depot and the entrance to the Masonic Temple. Brian started to run after him, then remembered his toolbox. The dozen onlookers had dispersed. The street was again empty. The siren was going someplace else. Brian grabbed his toolbox, then ran after Tucker. "Hey," he shouted, "hey, Tucker, wait up." Even as he said the words, he realized it was a phrase which, for many years, he had said almost daily. And, as before, Tucker didn't wait. As Brian ran with Tucker barely visible ahead of him, it was like they were back in high school with Brian again helping him in some escapade or folly.

By now Tucker had turned right at the corner. In the fog, the stoplight was a dull green glow, which switched to yellow, then red. It was the only stoplight in Waldo County, the only light for about forty miles: Rockland to the south, Augusta to the west, Bangor to the northwest, Ellsworth to the north. When the law had been changed to allow a right turn on red, Brian had known several people who had driven twenty miles to Belfast just to do it.

Brian turned the corner. A souped-up Plymouth Duster rumbled past and pulled up in front of Clara's, where the music was still blaring. Brian could just make out Tucker's back halfway down the hill in the fog. He tried to run faster, passing some kind of new art gallery for the tourists, then past where Hall's Hardware used to be, then across the street, his legs pumping so fast that he wondered how he'd stop. He couldn't get over seeing Tucker, couldn't get over running like this as if the last fourteen years had been just swept aside.

He ran past the bingo hall crowded with older women seated at long tables and staring silently at the boards in front of them. At the end of the room, a thin man in a white shirt and black suspenders withdrew a Ping-Pong ball from a wire basket and said, "B-twelve, B-twelve." The women rustled in their chairs. Then past Rollie's Cafe where he could hear the jukebox and laughter and click of pool balls. Glancing through the window, he saw many people he knew—friends or acquaintances from his thirty-four years in Belfast. Seeing them, he felt their stories pass through his mind. Perhaps not the stories themselves but an awareness of them: a man recently widowed, another recently divorced, Charlie Evans celebrating the birth of twins. Then they were gone as he ran past the Homeport Grocery, past an empty lot, past Mathew Brothers which sold window casings and doors.

Then the hill got steeper and Brian could hardly keep his balance. But he was gaining on Tucker and given another quarter mile, he'd beat him. They ran into the parking lot by the Weathervane Restaurant, then to the wharf where a local schooner was moored, a red light blinking from the top of its foremast, like a warning to keep them from galloping into the harbor.

By the time they reached the end of the wharf, Brian was only ten feet behind Tucker, who was still laughing, bending over as he ran and holding his stomach as he burst out with one laugh after another, deep thick-sounding laughs that seemed to burst from way down in his body. Tucker came up short against the railing above the water and leaned over, balancing, until Brian was afraid he would fall in and reached out to grab his sneaker should he need to catch him. Tucker rocked back and forth on his belly and just kept laughing.

"She was just sitting there, man, with these three assholes. I knew she wanted to play. I mean, I could see it. She was ready to boogie and there she was stuck with three drunken assholes."

Brian stared at Tucker balanced on the railing. "Tucker, where've you been?"

"Clara's, man, they just kicked me out." He pushed himself off the railing and turned around, breathing hard. There was blood on his lip and chin and some had dripped onto his white shirt. The fog lay so thick that the tugboats looked towering and prehistoric.

"But where you been?" persisted Brian. "I haven't seen you for years."

Tucker squinched his eyes at Brian, then opened them wide. "Brian, you old dog, is that you? I wondered who was rescuing me." Tucker grabbed Brian's hand and shook it. "Where you been keeping yourself?"

Brian felt slightly hurt that he had known Tucker right away, while it had taken Tucker all this time to recognize him. Still, he clung to Tucker's hand and squeezed it. "I been right here in Belfast, what about you?"

"I been around. I been out in Brooks now for a while." Tucker coughed several times and spat into the water.

"But why didn't you call me?" Brian asked. "We were buddies." He wanted to add that they were best friends. How could Tucker be right here in the county and not call him?

"Fourteen years, man, I don't even know who I was back then. I was tending bar at the Cafe for a coupla months. I thought I'd see you. Either that or you'd moved away, just like I did."

It struck Brian that Tucker was embarrassed: the way he

stood back and had quieted down. "I don't go out much at night," said Brian. "I got to be up early."

"Then what're you doing out now?" said Tucker, and grinned as if he had caught Brian in some deception.

"I was going out to my boat to check the oil. It's got a leak somewhere. Come out with me."

Tucker hesitated, then followed Brian down the ramp to the float where the dinghies were tied. Once below the level of the dock, their voices became flat and muffled.

"You got yourself a yacht?" asked Tucker.

Brian untied the dinghy and climbed in. "Yeah, a yacht for lobsters."

He waited for Tucker to get in, steadying the dinghy by holding on to the float. Tucker got in clumsily and the small boat rocked. Once Tucker was settled in the stern, Brian slipped the oars into their sockets and began to row out into the fog.

"So what are you doing in Brooks?" asked Brian.

Tucker glanced over his shoulder at the wharf, which was already disappearing. Just the streetlights were visible, glowing yellow circles suspended in the air. "I been building a house. I got some land and been building the place myself." He described where it was in relation to Brooks, a little south of town near Skyscraper Hill.

Brian couldn't imagine why Tucker would want to live in Brooks. And he thought too of the Tucker he had known in high school whose one desire had been to leave Belfast, leave Maine completely. That, after all, was why he joined the army. As for building a house, Tucker used to pride himself on being the only kid in high school who consistently flunked shop. Dumb people used hammers and nails, he used to say. Smart people hired somebody to do it for them.

"I been doin' some carpentry work as well," continued Tucker, " 'though right now I'm cutting cord wood for a guy, Ezra Phelps, maybe you know him."

Brian shook his head, although he recognized the name. It was as if a whole new Tucker Morgan had appeared. He was silent a moment, then asked, "How do you like it out there?"

But he knew the answer when Tucker raised his face to look at him. "To tell you the truth, I'm pretty sick of it."

The dinghy bumped up against the lobster boat, called the *Margaret* after Brian's wife. Brian fished the painter out of the bow, then tied it to a cleat on the port quarter of the lobster boat. He steadied the dinghy as Tucker climbed awkwardly over the side, then he followed him. The engine was just inside the cabin, three-fourths of it rising above the floor. Ducking into the shelter, Brian opened the door of the cabin, then took his flashlight from the work chest beneath the bunk on the port side. Looking back, he saw Tucker sitting on a lobster pot in the stern with his head in his hands.

"Here," said Brian, going to him and handing him the light, "come hold this." Tucker followed him into the cabin and sat down on a bunk. As Tucker held the light Brian found the dipstick, wiped it on a rag, reinserted it, then removed it again. Down two quarts. He guessed the oil was leaking into the bilge.

"What a lousy time for an overhaul," he said.

"How many traps d'you have?" asked Tucker. The cabin was about eight by ten feet and smelled of salted herring.

"About a hundred. I haul 'em in the morning before I go to work."

"How far out can you go?"

"Far as I want depending on the weather. I got a twenty-gallon tank and it takes about a gallon an hour. Two tanks, forty hours. The motor's an old six-cylinder Chevy with a marine transmission and a water-cooled manifold."

"Could you go out past Matinicus?"

"Sure, there're people out there all the time." Brian thought how Tucker had always asked questions. It was like a nervous tic. Then he thought how he had spent years in high school wondering why Tucker did this or that, what made him work, and Brian's inability to come up with adequate answers was one of the reasons he had stayed fascinated by Tucker.

"Not me though," added Brian. "All my pots are right here between Belfast and Bayside."

"Take it to fuckin' England, man."

"Let's get back," said Brian. He took the flashlight, stuck it in the toolbox, then put the box back in the work chest. He had a couple of quarts of oil at home. If he got the time, maybe he could work on the boat this weekend. He climbed over the gunwales into the dinghy, then steadied the boat as Tucker took his place in the stern. The fog had a yellow glow from the lights on the pier.

As Brian began to row, he looked at Tucker, who was rubbing his chin. The blood around his mouth had dried into a dark smudge. It amazed Brian to see him again and to begin talking as if their long conversation had been interrupted only by a day or so instead of fourteen years.

"I still can't believe you didn't bother looking me up," said Brian. "It pisses me off."

"Actually, I was going to give you a call once we got settled and the house was in decent shape. Just never got settled, that's all."

"You married?"

"Separated."

"Recently?"

"About a month ago."

They reached the float and Brian tied up the dinghy. He waited for Tucker to say more but he didn't. The two men stood on the float, which rocked slightly. The fog seemed even thicker.

"What happened?" asked Brian.

"I don't feel like talking about it." His voice was not so much aggressive as grieving. Tucker turned and walked up the ramp to the parking lot. At the top, he turned again, waiting for Brian. He still seemed a little drunk. Stepping forward, he slapped Brian on the back. "Jesus, it's great to see you."

"Your lip's bleeding some," said Brian. "I live just up the street. Why don't you come over and I'll fix it up?"

"Nah, it's fine."

"It'll just take a minute." Brian felt that Tucker wanted to talk but maybe he was wrong. Even as kids Tucker had played tough with his feelings, never admitting having them, never talking about his family even though he didn't get along with them. Tucker's father had seemed nice enough for a dentist, although Brian hadn't gone to him. His own father had preferred another dentist who wasn't from out of state.

"You have any beer?" asked Tucker.

"Maybe a six-pack."

Tucker grinned but only his lips moved. The rest of his face stayed frozen. "Well, all right then," he said.

Brian and Tucker began climbing back up the hill. The streetlight in the fog looked like a disembodied eye, reminding Brian of bankers and store owners and landlords—all those people to whom he owed a little money. Beside him, Tucker was silent. Brian thought he might be depressed and asked about his parents. Both were still alive, living in St. Pete. His mother had recently been diagnosed a diabetic but was doing okay. There was also a sister who had married a veterinarian and lived in Portland. Tucker answered the questions as if talking about strangers.

They retrieved Tucker's pickup from the lot at Brooks Drugs. Tucker's dog was waiting in the cab, a big black long-haired mongrel by the name of Rooster. The dog was half hysterical with pleasure and licked Brian's face about twenty times. Instead of a collar he had a red bandanna tied around his neck.

"This dog," said Tucker, "this dog's a fuckin' saint. I swear he's the only person I can talk to."

They drove to Brian's house a block from the library with Rooster sitting between them. The truck was an old Dodge and seemed to be running on three cylinders. The cab smelled of beer and was littered with white Styrofoam cups, wrappers from Baby Ruth candy bars and empty beer cans. Brian found himself sitting on a rusted hacksaw and gingerly pulled it out from under him. The muffler was half gone and Tucker revved the motor to make as much racket as possible. Then he looked at Brian and winked as if the noise made him feel better.

When they pulled up to his house, Brian said, "Be quiet now, my wife's probably asleep."

Tucker coasted to a stop, but then slammed his door when he got out. Rooster stayed in the truck. Brian's house was a small two-story Victorian with a large front porch and a lot of gingerbread trim along the gables and dormers.

"Not a bad crib," said Tucker. "You own this place?"

"Rent it." The door was open and Brian led the way around the kiddy debris of tricycles and stuffed animals. Margaret was still awake, watching Johnny Carson with her young sister, Cindy, whom she had practically raised, bringing her into the house when Cindy was three. Now at seventeen Cindy was entering her senior year of high school. Blond, slender and with a quick tongue, it sometimes seemed that she was the one who ran things and not her older sister, who was quieter and seriously involved in the Congregational Church. Both looked up at Tucker.

"Guess who I ran into?" said Brian, and began to explain about seeing Tucker downtown. But even without mentioning the fight, Brian realized he'd made a mistake. Margaret disliked interruptions in the routine of their life and one look at Tucker with his ripped shirt and blood on his chin caused her face to get that flat expression.

"I remember you talking about him," she said. She stared at him a moment before turning back to the television. Margaret wore a blue terry cloth robe of Brian's and as she turned away she pulled the lapels together at her neck.

But Tucker didn't help any, standing by the door and leafing through a *TV Guide* that had been on the hall table. He nodded to Margaret, gave a little smile to Cindy, then returned to the magazine. Brian was hurt by this, wishing that his wife and his old friend would like each other, that Tucker would see his wife as beautiful and strong, that she would see Tucker as charming and handsome. Instead, they seemed to see each other as interferences, hardly better than stones in their paths.

"Let's sit in the dining room," said Brian. "I'll get you a beer."

"Remember the time, Brian," said Margaret, not looking up.

From the refrigerator, Brian got a couple of cans of Narragansett, what Cindy called Nasty Gansetts. The kitchen clock said midnight. At four-thirty he'd leave to tend his lobster traps. Then, at eight-thirty, he had to be at the poultry plant.

But he still felt excited. Here was his buddy, returned after fourteen years. He looked at Tucker as he sat at the table, leafing through the *TV Guide*. He was clearly older but was still handsome, still in good shape. His brown hair was short, like they cut it in the army, and with only a little gray. His face, which had always been thin, seemed thinner and the contours harder—a long, thin face with no softness in it. And despite the half grin, he had a wary quality, as if trying to make sure he couldn't be taken by surprise. Brian set the beer in front of him. The table was covered with kids' drawings done in bright crayons—pictures of houses, dogs, a burning boat. More drawings were taped to the walls, giving the dining room a look of genial foolishness.

"So you went to college in Portland?" asked Brian.

"Yeah, got a degree in education. Can you see me as a teacher? Taught a year in Skowhegan, then quit. I don't know why the fuck I thought I'd ever like it."

"You mean you spent all that time learning to be a teacher, then threw it over?" Brian glanced at his wife to see if she was listening, but she was smiling at the TV and her face appeared kind and tranquil. He noticed that Cindy's red bathrobe had fallen open to expose part of her thigh and he wished she'd close it, even though Tucker couldn't see it from where he sat.

"Those kids hated me, man. If I'd been the fuckin' Viet Cong, they couldn't have hated me worse. Like they figured they already knew all the stuff they needed to know forever. They were poor and came from bad homes. You know the story."

Brian again glanced toward Margaret. He wished Tucker would keep his voice down. Going into the kitchen, Brian poured some water in a bowl and got a wad of paper towels. "Couldn't you have gotten them to like you?" he called as he turned off the water. He returned to the dining room and handed the towels and bowl of water to Tucker. "Here, you got blood on your chin."

Tucker began dabbing the towels at his face, missing most of the blood. "It was already too late. If you'd grabbed them hot from the womb, then maybe you'd have a chance."

He went on to talk about the school and the antagonisms between the teachers and students and how he'd been caught in the middle. Brian kept seeing little changes in his friend. He felt there was a fragility about Tucker, as if his insides, his psychology or soul or whatever, matched his torn shirt and the blood on his cheek.

"No, it was more than that," continued Tucker. "I looked at the kids, then I looked at the assholes who ran the place and I thought, these guys are crazy, they're treating the kids like the enemy. So I figured I'd be on the kids' side. You know, be their pal. Well, they didn't want me."

Brian got up again and took the paper towels away from Tucker. "Here, let me do it," he said. He wiped the blood off Tucker's chin as Tucker looked up at him with gray eyes that gave nothing away. His face was bruised in several places and Brian guessed it must hurt. "Maybe if you'd stayed at the school longer," said Brian, returning to his seat.

Tucker didn't seem to hear. "One day in the spring, I'd been having trouble with this class and I gave them a quiz, just to punish them a bit. So I'm sitting at my desk watching them and I start imagining I had a weapon, I mean an M-16, and I just start blasting them, blasting them out of their fuckin' seats, bodies flying all over the place, blood and guts. I just wiped out the whole class. Shit, I was supposed to be helping them and here I was pretending to kill them. After that, I just went in the office and quit."

"That's when you moved to Brooks?"

"More or less. There was a guy there I know in Vietnam. I was going to build my own house, grow my own food. Now me and him are cutting cord wood together." Tucker laughed, a crow-like sound that lacked humor. Then he held up his beer can to show it was empty. Brian went into the kitchen to get him another.

"So you're working at the chicken plant after all?" said Tucker as Brian handed him the can of Narragansett.

"Foreman, that's not so bad." Brian paused, thinking of those years in high school. It had been like a time without consequences. "You remember in school when you collected those chickens and stuck 'em in the coach's office? You could hear them all over the building."

Margaret stood up. She was a tall woman with shoulder-length brown hair that had some gray in it. Giving Brian what he thought of as a long look, she turned and went upstairs, probably to check on the kids.

"I'm a little vague about that," said Tucker.

"Don't you remember? You were pissed at Coach Holmes for keeping you on the bench. He said you weren't a team player." Holmes had since retired, but Brian still couldn't see him on the street without feeling dislike. Tucker could have been all-state if Holmes had backed him instead of being spiteful.

Tucker had taken one of the kids' drawings and was folding it into a paper airplane. "I'll take your word for it," he said carelessly. Then he glanced toward Cindy. Brian tried to get back his attention.

"You'd pass that ball and I'd snag it outta the air or you'd run and I'd block for you. Holmes hasn't had a team that good since."

Tucker looked up from the paper airplane and grinned. "I remember those chickens. They were a bitch to collect. They kicked me outta school, didn't they."

"Just for a few days. That big Waterville game was the next Friday and without you we didn't stand a chance."

Tucker lifted the paper airplane and inspected it, his long fingers moving across the colored paper in the way fronds of seaweed can move underwater. Then he tossed it toward Cindy. The plane glided over the table, through the archway and into the living room, where it settled in Cindy's lap. "We win or lose?" he asked.

Brian stared at Tucker. He knew that he could probably describe every play of that game, and at least a third of the plays of all the games during those last years in high school. "You kidding? You ran a sixty-seven-yard touchdown. We won by three points."

"All those games sort of blend together on me."

Brian heard the floor squeak and turned to see Cindy standing in the archway. She had turned off the TV and seemed about to go upstairs. "Can I have a sip of your beer?" she asked Tucker.

Tucker tilted back his chair and squinted up at her. "Aren't you a little young for this stuff?" he said in a cowboy drawl.

"A sip won't hurt."

Cindy's bathrobe was slightly open and Brian could see a white nightshirt underneath. Normally he liked how Cindy seemed so unself-conscious, as if she had no idea how attractive she was.

Margaret came down the stairs and paused above her younger sister. "Cindy, you should be in bed. You too, Brian, if you plan to be up at four."

Tucker had made another paper airplane and was holding it up for inspection. "You get up that early for your lobsters?"

Brian nodded. He knew Margaret was angry. Even her breathing sounded angry.

Cindy stepped away from her sister. "He wants to buy Margaret some frilly nightclothes and maybe a Cadillac car."

Margaret put her hands under Cindy's ribs and squeezed, making her laugh and gasp for air "I want you in bed, young lady."

Cindy pulled herself free, then came around the table to give Brian a kiss on the cheek. Going back to the hall, she waved to Tucker. " 'Night all," she said. Then she disappeared, her feet making a rapid sound up the stairs. Margaret went into the kitchen. Tucker tossed the paper airplane after her but missed. Brian could hear the refrigerator door open and guessed she was pouring herself a glass of milk.

"What's it like living with two sexy women?" asked Tucker.

Brian felt both pleased and disconcerted by the question. He had a sudden wish to go upstairs and see his children, Caroline and Jimmy, ages four and five, to tuck them in their beds. He wanted to tell Tucker about them and how much he'd once worried he'd never have kids, and how much he loved them.

"Cindy's a little advanced, that's all."

"They're all advanced these days. You're lucky they don't get you for bigamy."

"Cindy's been with us since she was a baby."

"Well, you watch yourself." Tucker finished his beer, then squeezed the aluminum can so that it crackled. "Isn't it pretty hard to keep up two jobs?"

"We're hoping to buy a bigger house," said Brian, glad to change the subject. "Margaret's working at the Shop & Save." He went on to say how they had only three small bedrooms upstairs, and about an eight-room house they were looking at, how the lobster boat meant only another six thousand even though he did it six months of the year. Tucker was looking at a calendar on the wall with a picture of the lighthouse in Rockland. It occurred to Brian that he was counting the days since he and his wife had separated.

Margaret again appeared in the door. "Brian, you've got to go to bed. It's late." She looked at Tucker, then glanced at Brian and raised her eyebrows.

Tucker didn't notice. "You hauling traps this morning?"

"Sure, I do it every morning."

"You mind if I come along?"

Brian felt surprised, then touched. "That'd be fine if you want to. I gotta be up in a couple of hours. It's no treat." He tried not to look at his wife.

"I'm too drunk to drive back to Brooks and the place is too lonely with nobody there except me and Rooster. I'll sleep on your couch. A little sea air will wake me right up."

Margaret came the rest of the way into the dining room and began collecting the kids' drawings from the table. "Do you have a wife?" she asked, without looking at Tucker.

Tucker folded his beer can back and forth until it broke in two. "She took off about a month ago," he said. "We got a little boy, Jason, a nice little kid. She swiped him on me."

"She just ran out on you?" asked Brian.

Tucker scratched his scalp and grinned in a way that made him look about thirteen. "She said she was tired of living in a rural ghetto. Her folks live in Camden and she moved in with them. But I'll get him back, don't worry."

Margaret put the kids' drawings up on the sideboard out of Tucker's reach. "How could you take care of a little boy?"

"I could do it. Man, I'm the best daddy in all the world." Tucker held up the demolished beer can, indicating that he wanted another, but Brian didn't move.

"Then why aren't you with him?" asked Margaret.

Tucker glanced at her as if suddenly aware of Margaret's hostility. It seemed to Brian that they'd never like each other.

"I will be soon enough," said Tucker. "It'll just take some figuring, that's all."

Margaret had picked up the two paper airplanes and was unfolding them, smoothing them out on the table. "I bet you got lots of plans," she said, her voice at the very edge of sarcasm.

Tucker stood up and stretched, linking his fingers behind his head. Then he grinned. His split lip had turned purple, as had the bruise on his cheek. "That's right, lady, I be planning all the time."

three

Tucker was crouched behind the wheel of the _Margaret_ with one hand braced against the roof of the shelter and the other steering the boat, which roared like a farm animal in heat. The sun was still low in the east, reflecting off the water and turning the islands and distant Castine into a blur of light. Tucker's dog, Rooster, stood on the foredeck with his nose into the wind and appeared to be chewing the air.

"_Ooowee,_ how fast does this baby go?" said Tucker, grinning. The bruises on his mouth and face looked like blue smudges.

Brian laughed, started to reach for the wheel, then restrained himself. The boat veered to starboard. The chain steering was tricky and Brian imagined capsizing and going to the bottom even though the bay was calm and the water without a ripple. To the northeast he saw a freighter waiting to dock in Searsport about six miles away.

"Maybe twelve knots."

Brian took over the wheel and the boat resumed its steady course. It was an older boat, built in the early fifties, with a shelter closed on the port side and open to the stern and starboard, the working side of the boat. Covering part of the deck was a fragment of blue carpet that Brian and his wife had received as a wedding present. The oil from the bait got over everything and without the carpet, the wooden deck grew too slippery. The boat was white with red trim. Brian had repainted it at the beginning of the summer and the paint still shone. Its name was written across the transom in black letters, then in smaller letters, BELFAST, MAINE. A dozen square lobster pots were stacked in the stern along with a basket with wet seaweed for the lobsters and several five-gallon plastic barrels—one for bait and the others for crabs and any fish that might have found their way into the traps. Half of the traps had been recently repaired and, along with new netting or knit heads, they had new yellow slats interspersed between the weathered ones. About fifteen other lobster boats were also visible on the bay, some heading out to their traps, others moving between their buoys in the way that a bee goes from flower to flower. A small black-headed laughing gull drifted behind the *Margaret,* swooping from side to side while hardly moving its wings.

"Which are your markers?" asked Tucker, staring ahead through the window of the shelter. Under his Levi's jacket, he still wore the white cowboy shirt from the previous night which was torn and spotted with blood. Brian had offered him oilskins and an extra pair of boots but Tucker said he couldn't be bothered. It was too warm for that stuff. Brian wore rubber boots and yellow rubber overalls.

He pointed south toward Bayside. "Those orange Day-Glo ones with the blue stripe. Same as what's up on the roof." All boats had to display their buoys so the fish warden would know if they were hauling someone else's traps. "There's the first straight ahead."

As Brian spoke, he heard the high whine of a diesel engine growing louder. Even as he turned, he knew what he'd see: Herbie Pendergast up to his tricks.

"Hey!" shouted Tucker.

Pendergast's lobster boat, the *Milkmaid*, surged toward them on Brian's port side, seemingly intent on ramming them. Herbie had painted his boat black and red, to make it look threatening, although that seemed pure foolishness when your boat was a twenty-eight-foot Cape Dory trawler. Brian was tempted to throw out a grappling hook and see if he could rip off Herbie's transom. Instead, he held his course and looked bored.

At the last moment, Pendergast swerved aside, sending a spray of water into the *Margaret* and splashing Tucker, who had moved into the stern. Tucker stumbled toward Brian as Pendergast veered off toward Brown's Head with a big rooster tail of water rising from the back.

"What's his trouble?" said Tucker, wiping the water off his face and jean jacket with his hands. Tucker's dog jumped back into the shelter. He was wet and shook himself, his long black fur briefly sticking out like a porcupine's quills.

Brian took a yellow towel from the cabin and tossed it to Tucker. "That's Herbie. You remember him? Herbie Pendergast. He was a couple of years ahead of us in high school."

"Doesn't ring a bell," said Tucker. He dabbed at his jacket with a towel, then knelt down to dry off. "Why's he want to sink you?"

"He thinks I'm crowding his territory. There're not so many lobsters as there used to be, so things get competitive."

"You ever pull up someone else's pots?"

"Not unless I want to get killed. A lot of guys carry shotguns out here."

"Ever use them?" Tucker tossed the towel back to Brian, then stared after the *Milkmaid*, holding up a hand to shield his eyes from the glare off the water.

"A guy was shot and killed off Isleboro not long ago." Brian described how a lobsterman from Castine had been raiding lobster cars, the large storage crates, just off Isleboro, when Pete Owens, the legal owner, caught him and shot him. Owens said that the Castine man had threatened him with a rifle but there was no sign of a rifle on board. According to Owens, it had fallen in the water.

"This guy go to jail?" asked Tucker.

"Overnight, maybe. Cops took away his shotgun. That's his boat over there, that green one." Brian pointed to the boat which was moving toward Isleboro. Across the water they could hear the whine of its diesel motor.

"You're a rough bunch of fellows," said Tucker. Rooster sniffed at the salted herring and sneezed.

Brian cut the engine and the boat drifted up to the first of his buoys. Reaching over the side with the gaff hook, he snagged the rope or pot warp, fed it over the wheel on the davit and wrapped it three times around the niggerhead: the brass drum of the pot hauler which was about five inches across and pointed up toward the wheel at a forty-five-degree angle. It was connected to a pulley on the motor and turned constantly. Several times Brian had had to warn Tucker to stay away from it, since if it caught hold of your clothes you could be in real trouble. The davit rose five feet over the washboard by the wheel like an upside-down yellow J. Because of the rocky ledges, Brian was fishing doubles, meaning there were only two pots on a string. If the water had been deeper and the bottom sandier, he could get maybe eight pots on a string, but this close to shore he was taking a chance that even two might get tangled. Along here the water was between thirty and thirty-five feet deep.

As the first pot broke the surface, Brian heaved it onto the washboard kitchen end first and slipped the warp off the niggerhead. Two lobsters were in the parlor, along with a pair of bricks for ballast. One lobster looked small. Taking his brass gauge, Brian measured the carapace, the length of the shell between the eyesocket and the tail. Anything under three and three-sixteenths inches or over five inches had to go back in the water. This lobster was barely under three inches, so

Brian dropped it overboard. A pollock had got itself tangled up in the hake mouth of the head and Brian tossed it in one of the plastic buckets. Chicken one night, fish the next. These days he dreamt of steak where once he had dreamt of girls. Removing the second lobster, he saw it was big enough but had a V cut in its rear flipper, showing that it was a female with eggs. To keep it could mean a fifty dollar fine from the fish warden. Damn thing had already eaten his bait. Brian heaved the lobster out into the water, then began to rebait the traps.

"That herring in those bags?" asked Tucker.

"That's right. I get it straight from the sardine factory. Have to salt it down though. It's funny. Lobsters don't mind the salted fish. Crabs do."

"Just like people," said Tucker. He was balancing on the washboard and had his feet stretched out in front of him. Rooster growled at the pollock that was flopping back and forth in the plastic bucket.

"How d'you mean?"

"They're different, that's all. Like me and your old lady. Lobsters and crabs."

Brian had wondered if Tucker would mention Margaret and her sharp tongue. "You shouldn't mind her. It was getting late and she worries a lot."

Margaret had been asleep when Brian got to bed last night and she'd been asleep when he dragged himself up at four. Later he expected a lecture about bringing people back to the house. Not that Tucker was people.

Tucker started to speak, then shrugged. Brian had pulled up the second pot. A medium-sized lobster was in the parlor. Lifting it out, Brian took the rubber-band pliers and slipped the small white rubber bands over the claws. Then he tossed the lobster into the basket. Whatever he caught, he sold at the Weathervane on the Belfast wharf for $2.50 a pound. Brian tried to think what was going through Tucker's mind.

He wondered if he should plan a dinner or set aside a night when they could all go bowling so Tucker and Margaret could maybe get to know each other. But he knew it wouldn't work. Even in high school Tucker liked to pretend that nothing of conventional value meant anything to him. As for Margaret, what she saw in Tucker was a general disrespect for everything she believed important.

"So you finish your house out in Brooks?" asked Brian.

"Not quite. You know how it is, you work on everyone's house except your own."

"Is that what pissed your wife off?"

"Among other things."

Brian finished rebaiting the pots and dumped them overboard. Then he steered toward the next buoy. Tucker was leaning against a stack of lobster pots squinting into the sun. His short brown hair made a sharp wedge shape, like a garden trowel, in the center of his forehead. "But you don't like living out there anymore?" asked Brian. As the *Margaret* drifted up to the next buoy, he reached over the side for the warp, hooked it, fed it over the davit, then wrapped it around the niggerhead.

"I need something that makes money," said Tucker. "Also I'm no good at building houses. Some guys love hammering nails. I just bash my thumb. Jesus, I've even thought of going back to school."

"What about your wife, you still like her?"

"Sure, man, I even love her. We just don't get along, that's all. Lobsters and crabs again."

Brian pulled the first pot onto the washboard. It was empty but the bait was gone. Sometimes little fish could eat the bait in a couple of hours. He rebaited the trap. In summer the bait would sour after a day, so he was always replacing it. The second pot had two lobsters and they looked the right size, maybe two pounds each. He took them out and plugged them. Without those rubber bands, the lobsters would eat each other up. He noticed that several slats on the door were cracked and coming loose. Brian heaved the pot onto the aftdeck. Then he replaced the trap with one stacked in the stern. New pots needed seven bricks for ballast since it took a couple of weeks for the oak slats to become waterlogged.

"I still can't believe you studied to be a schoolteacher and then quit."

"I couldn't take it, that's all."

"You could have gone to another school." Brian couldn't see why anyone would throw over a perfectly good job. Even in high school Tucker had talked about being a teacher, despite or maybe even because of his lack of respect for his own teachers.

"I mean the whole fuckin' thing wasn't worth it," said Tucker. "Students, teachers, they seemed like foreigners to me. I just didn't fit in and it depressed me."

"How long were you in Vietnam?" Brian asked, dumping the second pot into the water.

Tucker had knelt down and was scratching Rooster's ears. The dog's red bandanna looked brand new. "I did a tour in seventy-one. Then I was in the States after that."

Brian had a high number in the lottery and missed going. He thought of the war as just one of those things that can happen, something which had occupied a lot of attention and was now a shadow back there in the past, vaguely summoned up by words like fragging and wasting, M-16, slicks, grunts, fire fight.

"Where were you?" asked Brian.

"In Vietnam? Up in the Central Highlands. Then I was teaching in the Special Warfare School in North Carolina. Ambushes and shit like that."

Brian nodded. Of course he had heard of Saigon and Hanoi and other cities like Hue and Phnom Penh, Khe Sanh, Danang and a delta, the Mekong Delta, but the Central Highlands meant nothing to him. "What was it like?" he asked.

"Just what you might expect."

"What's that supposed to mean?"

Tucker continued scratching Rooster's ears as if he hadn't heard. Brian waited for him to say more, but he didn't. Steering toward the third buoy, Brian pulled back the throttle. On the CB radio someone called Dinknose was yammering about trap thieves. This time Tucker leaned over the side and hooked the warp. For years Brian had felt so close to Tucker that part of him wanted Tucker to describe every minute he had spent in Vietnam, every minute he had spent since they had last seen each other during that year following high school when Tucker was hanging around Belfast trying to decide what to do. He hoped that Vietnam hadn't been hard for him and he recalled other men he knew who'd been there and never even fired a gun.

"I got another friend who was in Vietnam," said Brian. "Lowell Perry, maybe you remember him from high school. He spent the whole time at a rest place on the coast. He even learned to surf. Says it was a picnic. Air-conditioned quarters and lots of girls and big meals. You have that?"

Tucker had managed to get the warp on and off the nig-gerhead and was balancing a lobster pot on the washboard. Water was dripping down his jeans. "Not me, man, I thought I was going to die. *Bam, bam,* just like that. I thought I was going to die lots of times."

Brian felt embarrassed. "You ever hurt?"

"Just some shrapnel."

Brian wanted Tucker to pull up his shirt and point to something specific just like President Johnson had done that time in the newspaper. Tucker gingerly removed a lobster from the parlor of the lobster pot. Brian thought how he had spent the past thirty-four years in Belfast and that his only injuries were a sprained ankle and a little frostbite.

There were two lobsters in this string. Brian baited the pots and threw them back in the water. Then he steered toward the next buoy. The morning was warm and his legs were hot in his rubber overalls. Sometimes he wore a rubber apron but he'd offered it to Tucker, who had turned it down, preferring to get wet. He felt a little uncomfortable with Tucker, almost shy with him. It was about five-thirty and off toward Marshall Point on Isleboro he saw his first sailboat of the day, a ketch probably out of Camden and rigged with a red jib.

"So what would you do if you had a lot of money?" asked Tucker.

"Buy a house, like I said. We'd like to own something." As Brian drew up to the next buoy, Tucker leaned over the side to catch the warp. By now his jeans and sneakers were sopping, but he didn't seem to notice.

"You ever suddenly make a lotta money, like winning at the track or in a poker game?" asked Tucker, attaching the warp to the pot hauler.

"One time I made some money," said Brian. "It was a real break. I was out here one morning and I saw something like a suitcase bobbing along. This was about five years ago. Anyway, I snagged it with the gaff hook and you know what it was?"

"What?"

"A whole bale of marijuana, just like a bale of hay." Brian felt pleased when he saw Tucker look at him with interest. The first lobster pot broke the surface and Tucker dragged it onto the washboard.

"What'd you do?"

"First I couldn't decide whether to dump it overboard or give it to the police. Then I called this guy I know who smokes dope and we just split it, fifty-fifty. He took the bale and a couple of weeks later he showed up with five thousand dollars."

Lowell Perry had said he sold the bale in Boston, after having dried it out in his stove. Brian never asked him how he'd known who to sell it to.

"What'd your wife say about it?" asked Tucker.

Brian pulled the second pot onto the washboard. He guessed he had about forty strings left. Margaret had been scared and for months she worried he'd be arrested. Luckily by the time Brian told her, the bale was in the hands of Lowell Perry. Otherwise she would have wanted to turn it over to the police.

"When I got the money, it made her feel better," said Brian. "Bills got paid and we bought a new TV. Then we all went to the dentist."

"That makes you a smuggler," said Tucker, taking a lobster out of the pot.

"That's what Margaret said, but it wasn't as if it belonged to anyone or anything. I didn't even smoke any. Makes me sick in the stomach. Even regular cigarettes make me throw up." Brian stopped talking and looked back at Tucker, who was staring at him with a slight smile. He was still holding the lobster, which was frantically waving all its legs and claws. Rooster kept jumping at the lobster and barking, while wagging his tail. It occurred to Brian that he didn't have the slightest idea what was going through Tucker's mind.

Harry Nixon had the stubborn persistence of a seagull trying to open a clam. He felt tricked but not beaten. He never let himself be beaten if he could help it and just because the cocaine hadn't been on the salt boat was no reason to be upset. People were greedy. They'd try again.

It was early Friday morning and he was in the office of the Belfast police chief. Normally, he didn't like confiding in the local talent because there was no telling who their friends were and if they'd keep their mouths shut. But he liked this guy Foley, and anyway, he needed his help.

It was a small office, a quarter the size of Nixon's back in Portland, and with only one small window which looked out at the back of a bank, for Pete's sake.

"Takes awhile for the tugs to get the freighter into the slip," said Nixon. "Whoever had the stuff could have seen us and dumped it overboard." Moving away from the window, Nixon gently prodded his stomach. He had overeaten the night before out at the Mariner and he felt bilious and full of gas. He took another Tums from the roll in his hand and popped it in his mouth.

"You sure it was there?" Foley sat at his desk with his big red hands folded on the blotter.

"Positive. The dogs smelled it. I got divers in the water right now. It's only thirty to forty feet. Maybe they'll find it." The trouble was, thought Nixon, they could have dumped it out by the four-second bell. And there was always the chance he'd missed it, that it had been on the ship and he'd just missed it. Ideally and with the right budget, they'd do these jobs with helicopters.

Foley lifted a paper with some names written on it. "And you want us to watch out for these guys?"

Nixon chewed another Tums, then worked some of the chalky bits out from between his teeth with his tongue. "That's right, but don't bother them. They've had a sweet operation for about a year. Now they gotta quit or find a new way to bring it in."

"Maybe they'll just quit," said Foley.

Nixon's office was right on Portland harbor with four windows taking in much of Casco Bay, and his desk chair was real leather, none of this Naugahyde crap. Actually, he'd spent five years as a cop in Boston before deciding it was crazy work and that he'd better go back to school. Now, as a lieutenant, there were lots of places to go so long as he didn't fuck up.

"A million bucks a shot," said Nixon. "Would you quit?"

The long track through the woods to Tucker's house was a mass of ruts and Tucker liked to take it at high speed so his pickup bounced as if it might bounce off the face of the earth. The entrance was hardly noticeable from the road and Tucker liked that. He had even considered pulling branches across the opening so no one would know it was there. Yet even as the idea passed through his mind, he would think, "That's a stupid fuckin' plan, you gotta stop that kind of shit." What he really wanted was a twelve-foot brick wall around his fifty acres, but he didn't have the money to make it or skill to build it. But he'd think about his brick wall, then say to himself, "That's a stupid idea too."

The truck with its broken muffler roared through to the end of the driveway and skidded to a stop in the yard, brushing against a couple of Jason's beach balls and sending them bouncing toward the chicken pen where there was a sudden flurry of activity. Tucker jumped out of the truck and slammed the door, then slammed it again when it bounced back open. Rooster was in the back and jumped out over the tailgate. Then he ran around barking. He was glad to be home.

The house was a narrow, two story house. About a third of the front was covered with wooden shakes and the rest with tarpaper. Tucker told himself that if he ever got some extra money, he'd buy more shakes. He had hacked the yard and driveway out of the woods and this summer, because he had been depressed or too busy, he hadn't had time to take care of it and the woods were creeping back. Among the overgrown weeds were stacks of lumber, bales of shingles, a rusty cement mixer, a pile of bricks, rakes, shovels and a small mountain of wood that still needed to be cut, split and stacked for the coming winter. In a weedy garden grew several stunted tomato plants. Tucker glanced over to see when he'd get a fresh tomato and decided it might not be this year after all.

Pausing by the chicken coop, Tucker tossed some grain to the hens. "Chicken soup, man, you kids are going to be chicken soup." Then he continued toward his front steps which were a stack of cinder blocks tilting to the left. Scattered through the underbrush were many of Jason's toys: a red plastic wagon, a yellow plastic three-wheeler and the various pieces of a large toy garden set. It occurred to Tucker that for every tool he had, Jason had a toy one, thanks to a pair of wealthy grandparents. These tools too were scattered around the yard as if to mimic Tucker's disorder.

Entering the house, Tucker poured some kibbles into Rooster's bowl from a fifty-pound bag, then gave the dog fresh water. Rooster nosed Tucker out of the way to get at his food. Tucker watched him appreciatively for a moment, then began a perfunctory cleaning: picking up beer cans, empty cereal boxes and containers of milk and orange juice. He had liked seeing Brian and he felt balanced on the brink of something new, some necessary change in his life. He looked around the room at the bare Sheetrock and exposed studs, the wiring hanging from the ceiling, the muddy pine floor which he had hoped to cover with maple or oak. He'd be the first to admit the place was a wreck: sawdust, beer cans, tools, bits of wood, bags of trash by the back door, dishes in the sink.

It wasn't that Tucker was lazy, but ever since he had realized that his marriage was busting apart, he'd been unable to work on his house, to push it forward to where it was vaguely civilized. That image of a finished house belonged to the future and now he didn't have one. At least not here at any rate. It seemed impossible to drive a single nail, knowing that all this would be sold or even given away, for who would want the wreckage of a half-built house buried in the depths of Brooks, Maine? Calamity Acres, that's what he called it.

But those were bummer thoughts. Better to neaten the place up so it wasn't so depressing. Maybe he should get another pet, a kitten, or one of those canaries that were always singing their hearts out. On the kitchen table were two pictures, one of his son by himself seated on his yellow plastic tricycle, the other of his wife, Sarah, holding Jason as she stood on the front steps managing a smile. The sight of his child made his heart ache. Tucker picked up the picture.

"That's my kid, lady, and I want him back. We'll go join

the circus. Become trapeze artists. Little Jason and his Flying
Daddy. Fuckin' Rooster can be the clown." He turned to the
dog and thumped him on the back. "You like that, Rooster?"
The dog barked and wagged his tail as if he were ready for
anything.

Tucker went to the refrigerator and took out a beer and a
blackened banana. Peeling the banana, he took a great bite
and cracked open the beer. He'd clean up a little more, then
do something else. He thought again of Brian and wondered
why he'd never called him. Tucker had told himself that he
just hadn't gotten around to it, but it was more than that.
After all, Brian thought he was a hero. Maybe he hadn't wanted
Brian to see his life in such disrepair.

He was just finishing the banana when the phone rang.
Having a telephone was one of the compromises he had made
with Sarah. She had refused to live out here without one, but
since she left Tucker hadn't paid the bill and soon his service
would be cut off, or interrupted, as he'd been warned.

Tucker picked up the phone. It was Phillip calling from
Camden. Good old Phillip, the man who always landed on his
feet.

"What's on your mind?" asked Tucker. Then he listened
as Phillip said how he wanted to see him, how he had a
business proposition for him.

"I told you," said Tucker, "I don't want to deal any more
drugs."

"Just come down," said Phillip. "I need to talk to you. Can
you make it tomorrow?"

"Maybe the first part of the week."

"When?"

"You set the time."

"Two o'clock Tuesday afternoon at the Garage."

"And this has nothing to do with drugs?" asked Tucker.

"Of course not," said Phillip. Then he hung up.

Tucker replaced the receiver. "Liar," he said. Then he took

a sip of beer. Back in the spring when he had been stone broke, Tucker had agreed to sell a little cocaine for Phillip, who'd been doing him a favor. He'd even gone to Phillip and asked if he could do something like that to earn a little money. So Phillip had given him ten grams, then another ten about a month later. But Tucker hadn't liked it. He didn't trust the people he sold it to, even though they were mostly locals, and he didn't like the attention it brought him: strange men showing up at his house at three or four in the morning to see if they could score. And Sarah had hated it. Really it had been at that point that she began to talk of moving out.

But Phillip knew how he felt so maybe he had something else in mind. Phillip was a man with many projects, many schemes. When Tucker first met him in Saigon fourteen years before, Phillip was working in the kitchen of an officers' club, supposedly supervising the Vietnamese kitchen help, but actually buying drugs for the officers and selling steaks on the black market. Even though he was only a sergeant, Phillip had an illegal apartment, several mistresses and a narcotics business that made him a small fortune. The only hardship he experienced during his entire tour was being sent home.

On the day they met, Tucker had been drinking in a Saigon bar, pushing away the girls and feeling generally unhappy that he would soon go back up north. It always seemed he was more scared when he was on leave and away from his unit than when they were out on patrol or being flown into some LZ.

The bar was in a back alley away from the constant buzzing of the motorized rickshaws. It smelled of spicy food and garlic and perfume and spilled beer all mixed together. Tucker had been sitting on a stool while the girl next to him kept putting her hand in his lap and he kept shoving it away. A door leading to the right had a curtain of glass beads and, looking up, Tucker saw a man backing through it with his hands above his head—an American, even though he wasn't in uniform.

Following the man was a small dapper Vietnamese in a suit and tie. He was holding a large black .45 automatic that looked so big that Tucker had checked twice to make sure it was real.

The two men were so intent on each other that Tucker doubted they saw him. He was half drunk and couldn't think of any good reason why a Vietnamese should point a pistol at an American, so he had turned and smashed his beer bottle across the side of the man's head. Then everything speeded up as one of the girls started screaming and people ran for the back door. The American had grabbed the .45 and kicked the Vietnamese in the belly, knocking him back against the bar.

"Let's go!" he shouted to Tucker.

So Tucker had followed him, running down one tiny street after another through crowds of people and vegetable vendors and motor scooters, until they ran through a tailor shop and up a flight of back stairs to Phillip's little apartment.

Phillip wouldn't say that Tucker had saved his life, but he had appreciated the help. Apparently, Phillip had been getting drugs from the man with the .45 who for some reason had refused to give him any more. Phillip was vague about that. He was always vague when it came to reasons, justifications, explanations. Instead, he had given Tucker some good whiskey, then sent out for food. They both came from Maine and that struck them as significant, although Phillip had grown up in Brunswick, a college town. After that, they saw each other about four more times, with Phillip being the good host and giving Tucker whiskey or marijuana to take back to base.

"Why aren't you wearing a uniform?" Tucker had asked.

"I find I can move more freely without one."

"Aren't you afraid of getting in trouble?"

"Who'd ever bother about me?" Not only was Phillip evasive, but he enjoyed being evasive. Even if asked the day of the week, he'd lie. In any case, Tucker, who knew there were hundreds of Americans squirreled legally and illegally around Saigon, was no longer surprised by anything in that benighted country.

Tucker stood up to get another beer and another blackened banana, then took his rifle from the corner and began cleaning it. The rifle was a semi-automatic Remington .22 and could fire about twenty-four shorts or fourteen long rifles as fast as he could pull the trigger. It was too small to be a real gun, he thought, but he liked fooling with it. He poked an oiled swab through the barrel and saw that it came out clean. He imagined suddenly having a lot of money. Maybe he could rob a bank or win the lottery or write a best-seller. He sighted the rifle at the picture of Sarah, then lifted the barrel to an empty beer can and clicked the trigger. He used to think that once you got accustomed to shooting people it might be hard to stop. Now he either no longer felt that or he had grown hardened to those fantasies where he solved a problem by putting a bullet in a person's head. At least they couldn't jail him for his thoughts.

Looking around at his house he knew he no longer wanted to live here. He felt at the very edge of a decision and would have made it sooner if the alternatives weren't so unattractive. He hated Camden and its seagoing yuppies. He felt too old to go back to school. If he had money, then at least he could go someplace and support himself while he made up his mind. He found himself wondering what Phillip wanted. He didn't so much mind breaking the law as getting in trouble and sometimes he wondered if that attitude was partly due to Vietnam. He felt no regret about Vietnam and in no way victimized. Laws, he thought, were used by the Haves to keep the Have Nots in line, and they could be changed, bent, put aside, applied without cause any time the Haves felt it necessary. He hardly minded this and, despite the thirteen years he'd been back in the States, he still had that sense of law he had acquired on his single tour of duty. It wasn't an intellectual or verbal sense. In his mind's eye he would have an image of a peasant in black pajamas being pushed out of a helicopter hovering a hundred feet off the ground. There would be a moment as he and several other soldiers and the lieutenant looked down to see where he'd hit. Then they would turn back to the second peasant, the survivor, the one they were hoping to make talk. Maybe he would, maybe he didn't know anything, maybe they would push him out too.

Tucker began loading the rifle, sliding the shorts down the tube in the stock. He knew that Vietnam was different. He knew that for society to function there had to be a rule of law. But he didn't feel it. It always seemed that next time he could be the one pushed out of the helicopter, as if he were both the pusher and the pushee. It was strange knowing what he should do but not caring or not being able to do it, like reaching for something and having his whole nonverbal self rise up and stop his hand in midair, to leave his hand quivering in space unable to move forward or back. He was caught in that place and the only comfort became the game of it, like stepping sideways into a fantasy world, not crazy or deranged, just the game, as if games were a time-out period from the daily travail.

Tucker stood up and crossed the room, balancing the .22 in his right hand. For a moment, he stood by the door, then he kicked open the screen, dropped to his knees and peered out into his driveway. Abruptly, he sprang over the cinder-block steps and landed in the grass. He looked around. No sound or movement except from the chickens. The fucking chickens were hysterical. Tucker slithered through the weeds to the shelter of his truck, being careful to stay away from the gas tank. He'd seen people roasted in gas fires. Pausing by the front bumper, he raised himself to a crouch. The sunlight shimmered on the white trunks of the birches. Leaping forward, Tucker zigzagged toward the trees, diving again onto his stomach.

With his rifle balanced across his arms, Tucker crawled
forward from tree to tree, pausing at each and listening or
lying motionless and thinking, "I am a log, I am a mound of
dirt. They cannot see me." Then he'd crawl forward again.
The sun through the leaves made the air green and bright.
About fifty yards from the house, Tucker slowly raised himself
with his back pressed against a large maple. He held the rifle
vertically in front of him and moved without breathing. Once
he was standing, he got a tight grip on the barrel and trigger
guard. Then he counted to ten, listening and breathing as
shallowly as possible.

When he reached ten, he leapt to his left and fell to his
knees, firing as he fell. The semi-automatic made a staccato
snapping noise. Twenty feet ahead was a large oak set off in
a little clearing. From its lower branches hung dozens of cans,
mostly beer cans, dangling from strings. On a sawhorse to
the left of the tree stood ten plastic milk jugs with faces
drawn on them with black crayon. As Tucker fired, the beer
cans danced in the sunlight and one by one the milk jugs
were knocked off their perch. In less than fifteen seconds it
was over.

four

People were cheering. Tucker heard them as he ran. They were shouting his name. But the hit was a lousy little grounder that popped off the edge of his bat and dribbled toward third as Tucker tried to beat it out, pumping his legs and swearing at himself, faster, asshole, faster. He was wearing a blue uniform which was torn and hadn't been washed all season. Across the back was the team name: DIEHARDS. His cap had fallen off and his shirttail flapped. The third baseman grabbed the ball and threw it toward first. But he threw it too high. Even though Tucker knew he'd be safe, he swore at their lousy third baseman, then at himself again for being a sucker for a bad pitch. Coming to a stop several yards past the bag, he trotted back as the first baseman retrieved the ball from where it had banged against the fence. People shouted to him to run to second, but Tucker knew he wouldn't make it.

"Lucky hit, lucky hit," shouted a man by the dugout.

"Hey, I'm here, aren't I? What's it matter how it happened?"

It was Saturday afternoon and hot and dusty and there were black flies, even though they were often gone by August. It was supposed to rain that evening and the air had a thick feeling. Tucker was bent over with his hands on his knees trying to catch his breath. Along the low chainlink fence were about seventy-five people watching the game, drinking beer and generally horsing around. Some reefers were being passed from hand to hand. One guy had a jug of wine. Tucker's dog ran onto the field and play was stopped as the catcher shooed it away from home plate. About a dozen little kids were shouting and having their own game with rocks and sticks. Now and then some kid would get clunked in the head by a rock and there'd be a howling, and each mother would turn to see if her own kid was all right.

Ernie Daniels batted after Tucker. He had the strangest batting stance in Waldo County, bending over and twisting like a corkscrew, shrinking his six feet four inches to under four feet. People always stopped to watch, wondering if he could hit the ball. Mostly he couldn't. Some guys at the fence were shouting at him to strike out. Ernie hated people being negative at him and he took two swings, missing by a foot each time.

"Good eye, good eye," shouted somebody.

At least if Daniels struck out, thought Tucker, then Peterson would be up and Peterson could be counted on for a hit. The other team was a Belfast team called the Home Wreckers. They were mostly locals, kids who'd been in trouble or had the reputation of being tough. There wasn't a milk drinker in the lot. Hank Jackson sometimes played left field for them but today he must be off nursing his bruised face. Tucker's team, the Diehards, was made up of kids from Brooks and a lot of guys like himself who had moved to Brooks from someplace else. Many had been in the service, even in Vietnam. It wasn't so much a bond as a connection. And although they rarely talked about it, they had a sense of familiarity with one another's pasts.

Daniels took three balls and looked pleased with himself. Tucker stood up. He was getting bored. People were shouting at Daniels to swing and the Home Wreckers pitcher looked exasperated. Another dog ran onto the field and had to be chased off. A baby began to cry. Off behind home plate someone kept revving the motor of a pickup with a busted muffler.

The pitcher threw Daniels the easiest pitch in the world, more of a toss than a pitch, an ironic pitch. Tucker knew that he personally would have knocked the ball over the fence, no trouble. Daniels swung and connected—a piddling little bouncing ball toward third, almost the same hit that Tucker made himself. Tucker felt disgusted. Even as he ran, straining his muscles till they shouted back, he knew he wouldn't make it. The third baseman threw the ball, this time carefully, to the second baseman for the force and Tucker was out. Daniels reached first and stood there with a little self-satisfied smile, the silly asshole.

Tucker walked back across the diamond. "That's the second damn time you've done that to me," he shouted to Daniels, then stopped near the base line to pick up his cap.

Daniels bowed his head and covered his eyes in fake shame. He had a thick bushy beard like that guitar player in ZZ Top and Tucker wanted to give it a yank.

Going into the dugout, Tucker took a Rolling Rock from the large Coleman cooler and cracked it open. Someone slapped him on the back and he shrugged as if to say, "What can you do, what can anyone do?" Rooster was waiting for him, glad to see him back so quickly. Tucker scratched the dog's ears.

Pete Talbot offered him a Marlboro and Tucker took it.

"You were lucky to get on base at all," said Talbot. His Diehards uniform was cleaner than Tucker's and not quite so torn, mostly because he took the game less seriously. He had a black beard and his black ponytail hung down from under his baseball cap. It was Talbot who had originally convinced Tucker to move to Brooks. Talbot took a Marlboro for himself and broke off the filter before touching a match to the tobacco.

"Short-lived glory," said Tucker. "Like a moth I flicker and go out."

"You ready to play a little paintball next Saturday?"

"I guess so. You planning another war?"

"Hey, I got the equipment. I got to rent it out. Anyway, I thought you liked it."

About one Saturday a month, Talbot would convince large groups of men to rent compressed-gas pistols from him that could fire pellets of yellow or red gelatin paint. The men would be divided into two teams spread out across Mt. Waldo. Then, at exactly 10:00 A.M., they would begin to play a game closely resembling Capture the Flag, but if you got shot, and those pellets could hurt, you were out. In fact, you were dead. To offset the physical discomfort, Talbot supplied the beer, and for twenty-five dollars one could play and drink as much as one could stand. In this way, he picked up another six hundred to a thousand dollars a month. Just about what Brian got with his lobster boat, thought Tucker.

The last time, however, it had rained and was boring and there'd only been twenty people and Tucker made enemies with a lot of head shots—smack in the back of the noggin. A bunch of guys thought he had an unfair advantage and knew fuckall about ambushing from being on LURP patrols. Tucker hadn't said anything about Vietnam one way or the other, because the game was nothing like the war and anyway that was years ago, but he had done all he could to make people think he was death on wheels.

"You need more guys," said Tucker. "What's the point of crawling all over Mt. Waldo if there's only a few of us?"

Talbot tossed his cigarette on the ground and crushed it with his running shoe. "Then help me get them. I got ninety pistols. You can have one to keep if you get me twenty guys."

Tucker liked those pistols, which looked like black automatics with a double barrel, one on top of the other. They had a nice weight. Talbot had bought them used after selling a whole shitload of marijuana that he had grown right here in Brooks from good seeds. Even so the pistols had cost about one-fifty each.

Out on the field Ernie Daniels had advanced to second when Peterson hit a single. The score was tied four-four in the bottom of the fifth inning. Slider Fredericks was up, spitting on his hands and twisting the balls of his feet in the dirt. Tucker watched him take a couple of swings, then wandered over to the fence to see if he could interest anyone in the paintball game. Over near the drinking fountain half a dozen little kids were having a water fight.

"Tucker, hey Tucker!"

Tucker looked to see Frank Pendleton by the fence near first base, then winced slightly.

"Hey, Tucker, you got that fifty bucks?"

Tucker strolled toward him, trying to look apologetic. He'd borrowed the money a month ago to keep his electricity from being turned off, but then had used the money to buy a new mitt, a Wilson, which was maybe the best mitt he'd ever had and just about broken in.

"I'm a little short right now," said Tucker, leaning against the fence. He nodded to several other people, who either nodded back or didn't. A woman smiled at him, then looked away. Slider Fredericks took a ball and people booed.

"You said you'd pay it last week," said Pendleton. He wasn't angry, but neither was he happy. Pendleton was several years younger than Tucker and assistant manager of a hardware store in Belfast. People spoke of him as having a future.

"Look, I'll pay you as soon as I can. I'm supposed to start some bartending work in Searsport in a week or so. I'll pay you then." Tucker had been hoping not to take the job but now he'd have to. Slider Fredericks hit a long fly to left field and all conversation stopped.

"Home run!" shouted someone.

But it wasn't. Ratty Jacobs snatched the ball out of the air right at the fence. Then he kissed it and heaved it to the third baseman. Daniels and Peterson hurried back to second and first. Two outs. Ratty Jacobs's girlfriend kept cheering after everyone else had shut up. Then she laughed and looked around.

"Tucker," said Pendleton, "I need the money."

"What can I say, I'm doing the best I can. Hey, Frank, there's a big game next weekend on Mt. Waldo. You want in on it?"

"That's where you vets run around shooting paint at each other?"

"Not just vets, man, all kinds of folks. Drink a little beer, smoke a little dope, shoot a little paint. I might have your money by then."

"How much does it cost?"

"Twenty-five bucks for the pistol, paint pellets, goggles and all the beer you can drink."

"I won't get hurt or nothing, will I?" Pendleton tried to say this jokingly. He was a big overweight man and Tucker imagined popping him in the head with a paint pellet.

"Nah, it's as safe as falling off a log."

Billy McMichaels hit a long ball into right field over the head of whoever was out there. Tucker had forgotten his name—some guy who fixed cycles. Daniels came in to score and Peterson went to third. The score was five to four. Diehards fans cheered. Home Wreckers fans made animal noises. Tucker chose the moment to drift away from Pendleton toward Bob Eggers, who, he realized, had a bone to pick with him. Rooster followed, now and then nuzzling Tucker's hand.

"Hey, Tucker, where were you yesterday?" said Eggers.

"What d'you mean?" asked Tucker, although he knew.

Eggers spat tobacco juice toward Tucker's feet. "You were supposed to help me Sheetrock." He was a man in his forties who had moved up from Massachusetts twenty years ago to raise sheep. Now he ran a little TV and lawn mower repair service.

"I'm sorry, Bob, I forgot all about it. I was out on a lobster boat." He was supposed to have been at Egger's house at eight the previous morning. Tucker hated hanging Sheetrock and Eggers had wanted to do the ceilings of four rooms—pull down the old ceilings, then put up Sheetrock. Tucker guessed he was being hired mostly for the demolition part, which was nasty work. The old plaster was filled with horsehair to hold it together and the dust got in your skin and hair and clothes and kept your eyes red for a week.

"You told me you'd be there. Can you make it tomorrow?"

"Tomorrow's Sunday."

"So what, d'you want the work or not?"

He didn't, but if he slaved all day, then he'd have fifty bucks and could go out that night and find some nice young lady, as long as she didn't mind his red eyes and hair like steel wool.

"Sure, I'll be there. Hey, Bob, we're playing a little paintball next weekend. You want to come?"

Eggers looked depressed and spat another stream of tobacco juice over the fence. "Last time I near fuckin' broke my ankle. Couldn't walk for a week. Besides that, those paint pellets sting like crazy."

"But you had fun, didn't you?"

"Is Talbot supplying the beer?"

"Damn right."

Eggers spat again and transferred the wad of tobacco from one side of his mouth to the other. "I'll think about it. Just be there tomorrow, okay?"

"Sure thing."

There was another hit and Peterson scored. Tucker continued along the fence. It was beginning to seem possible that he'd bat again this inning. Next time he'd knock the ball all the way to Swan Lake. As he moved along, he talked to other men about the paintball game, getting commitments from two and maybes from a couple more. Then he tried chatting up Susie Vendler. She had breasts so pretty that Tucker could feel his palms itch. She was engaged. He congratulated her. Spanky Skoyles hit a fluke single over Bruce Maria's head and Harry Giovanni scored. People were getting excited. There was a steady shouting and stream of friendly abuse.

Tucker talked to Louie Hawkins about the paintball and got a maybe, then got a positive from Sullivan; mostly, he knew, because Sullivan wanted to get even for Tucker's popping him in the ear in a game back in June. Tucker bought himself a lime Popsicle from the ice cream man and a Fudgsicle for Rooster. Just as he was heading behind home plate, Tucker saw Brian leaning over the fence and waving to him. Cindy was with him, wearing shorts and some violent rock and roll T-shirt with lightning zigzags. Tucker thought she looked good enough to eat.

"Tucker," said Brian, "how you doing?"

Brian was standing near the Home Wreckers dugout. Tucker joined him, giving a big smile to the Home Wreckers players who responded with ugly looks.

"Hey, Brian, what's up?" Brian was wearing slacks and a blue dress shirt. Maybe he's just been to church, thought Tucker. Or maybe it was because he was a foreman and had some social status to protect. His little beard surrounded his jaw like a black strip of rubber around a lawn mower wheel. Tucker was tired of feeling guilty that he hadn't contacted him and was prepared to be hostile. But then Brian seemed so pleased to see him that Tucker gave him half his lime Popsicle instead. Brian looked at it and laughed, not knowing what to do with it. Then he gave it back. Tucker shrugged.

"You said you were going to play so I thought I'd come out and watch. You remember Cindy, don't you?"

Tucker tipped his baseball cap and Cindy smiled. "She'd

be hard to forget." He gave her the Popsicle half that Brian had rejected. She licked it once or twice, then showed him her green tongue. Rooster jumped up and put his paws on the top of the fence. Patting his head, Cindy called him a handsome dog and Rooster made a contented growl in the back of his throat.

"Who's ahead?" asked Brian.

Tucker glanced out at the game in time to see Maxwell hit a little pop-out to shortstop, stranding three men on base. Well, he'd be up next inning. The Home Wreckers came running off the field and there was general movement among the Diehards as they grabbed their mitts and left the dugout. Diehards fans applauded, Home Wreckers fans honked like geese.

"We're winning," said Tucker, "by two or three runs. You want a beer?"

"No, thanks. You the captain?"

It occurred to Tucker that Brian wanted him to like him. "Nope, I'm one of the noble soldiers out in the field."

Talbot came running toward him across the diamond. "Hey, Tucker, here's your mitt." He threw it in a high arc and Tucker snagged it by turning and grabbing it behind his back with one hand. Then he winked at Cindy, waved a salute to Brian and followed Talbot out toward right field in a slow jog. Rooster ran after him.

"Pay attention, Pete," warned Tucker. "Don't fall asleep."

"It's a game, man."

Tucker took his position in center field and looked over at Talbot in right. Talbot had a fantastic arm, could hit the ball anywhere he wanted and still he treated baseball as a joke.

"Yeah, and while I'm doing it, it's the most important thing in the world," said Tucker.

Joey Norman, the Home Wreckers left fielder, came up to the plate. Norman was one of those guys who could hit the ball through a basketball hoop, if he wanted, one hundred yards away. "Just pay attention," said Tucker, bending his knees and getting ready. Rooster stayed about ten feet be-him.

Talbot bounced up and down and let his arms hang at his sides monkey fashion. "You can't let these things dig into you, Tucker. You got to make your own rules."

"Hey, this isn't life," said Tucker. "It's softball. Softball's more important." Why the fuck did Talbot have to get philosophical at the worst possible time?

Joey Norman swung at the first pitch, a slow looping ball, and hit it high toward right field. Almost as if he had heard Talbot's blasphemy, thought Tucker. Looking at Talbot, he saw his friend tossing his mitt in the air.

"Catch it, Pete," shouted Tucker, "catch it, don't fuck up."

Talbot managed to put on his mitt and position himself under the ball. He was good enough that he could have caught the ball in his hat had he wanted. He stepped forward and reached up. Then, at the last moment, he spread his arms apart, letting the ball hit the ground at his feet. It bounced away. Talbot looked at Tucker and grinned.

"See what I'm saying, you gotta rise above it."

Tucker sprinted after the ball. "Damn you, Pete." He snatched it up and threw it toward third. Joey Norman was already rounding second. The entire Home Wreckers team and fan club were doing their yodeling and Rebel-yell routine.

Still running, Tucker tackled Pete Talbot, ramming him into the ground. He wouldn't hurt him much, just enough to make him remember. No pain, no gain. He shoved his head into the grass with his new Wilson mitt, then rabbit-punched him. Talbot yowled. Tucker rabbit-punched him again for good measure. Rooster scrambled onto Tucker's back and began chewing on his ear. My own damn dog, thought Tucker, and he bites me.

———

Pete Talbot was pissed off. He was sitting on an oak log stabbing a small hunting knife repeatedly into the bark. So what if it messed up the blade? It was lunchtime Monday and he had just finished a bologna sandwich with sprouts. Next to him on the ground was his Partner chain saw with a pair of tattered leather gloves draped across the fifteen-inch guide bar.

Sitting across from him on another log was Ezra Phelps, the man he worked for as a chopper. He was a red-faced, white-haired, heavily built man in his sixties with scars on his upper arms from where the muscles had busted through the skin. At the moment he was making a chuckling noise that sounded like a motor when it's idling.

"But my kids were born here," Talbot was saying. "So what if I'm from Oregon? They were born right here in Brooks. They're Mainers." He'd like to give Ezra a smack, even though Ezra could probably throw him twenty feet if he had a mind to. Flies were after Talbot's oatmeal cookies and he brushed them away.

Ezra scratched his nose. "But they're not *from* here."

"The midwife delivered them in our bedroom. Both conceived and born here. How much more *from* do you want?"

"Just because the cat has her kittens in the oven doesn't make 'em muffins," said Ezra, finishing the last of the coffee from his Thermos.

Talbot saw Tucker laughing and he began to smile himself. He was always getting into these damn discussions with Ezra. A fourth man, Curtis Miller, was sitting by Ezra and nodding solemnly. Miller was in his early twenties and a real dope. Why else would he be working in the woods? The three of them were cutting pulpwood for Ezra who sold it to St. Regis in Bucksport for $54.50 per cord. The cutters made twelve dollars per cord, just dumping the trees, sawing them up, then letting Ezra load them onto the wagon. If Talbot busted his ass, he could make thirty-six dollars per day. Tucker rarely made more than thirty dollars.

"So how long does it take?" asked Talbot. "My grandchildren, great-grandchildren?"

Ezra shook his head and got to his feet. He was stiff and moved slowly. Sometimes it amused Talbot that Ezra didn't believe anything south of Rockland existed. Around them the stumps and piles of underbrush looked like some huge ruminant had chewed up the forest, then spat out the splinters.

"Even Tucker's a flatlander," said Miller. His voice had a mocking quality and Tucker looked up sharply.

"Don't give me that shit, boy. I was born here, my father worked here, I went to school here, but I'm sure not going to be buried here." Then Tucker grinned and winked at Talbot.

Miller closed his black metal lunchbox and began pulling on his gloves. He was a thin, red-haired man who had been cutting wood ever since he'd quit high school. Once, in a race, he had cut six cords in a day. Usually he cut four. "But you don't belong here," he said.

Tucker leaned back and stretched out his legs. The sun through the leaves put mottled shadows on his face. Talbot couldn't tell if he was angry. That was one of the troubles with Tucker, you never knew what was going through his mind unless he told you. And even then, you wondered.

"Why?" said Tucker. "Because I don't get drunk in cars and fuck my sister and shoot moose that wander into the backyard and eat ten pounds of potatoes and five pounds of beans every week and write stupid things on my arm with a Bic pen, like 'Betty Lou forever' or 'I love my sheep'?"

"No call to get rude," said Miller, standing up. "I'm just saying this isn't where you belong."

"What do you like about this place?" Talbot asked before Tucker could say anything else. Tucker's dog could feel the tension and had gotten to its feet. Damn black thing could bite anybody, thought Talbot.

"It's just mine, that's all," Miller said. "Been mine as long as my family can remember. I like country and how the hills are. I shot two bucks last year and my dad got another."

Tucker nudged Miller's ankle with his foot. "People, man, you should try hunting people. None of this wasting a poor little animal. In Vietnam, we'd catch some gook, then let him escape and sneak after him with blowguns, creeping through the jungle, snakes and leeches and shit. Get 'em with that blowgun, puff-puff. That's real hunting, none of this shit about twenty guys waiting on a power line for Bambi."

Miller stood looking down at Tucker. "You never shot nobody with no blowgun."

Tucker scrambled to his feet. Like a spring, thought Talbot. "What the fuck do you know about it, asshole?"

Miller's face grew red. Taking a step toward Tucker, he raised his fists almost in a parody of the classic stance of a prizefighter. "I don't allow people to talk to me like that."

Tucker grabbed a four-foot branch from the wagon. "Watch it, or I'll bop your head like a baseball." He crouched down and held the branch over his shoulder as if he were expecting a ball to be pitched. Talbot stood back by Ezra's rusted old tractor. At any single moment Tucker seemed to have equal amounts of anger and a willingness to joke. Talbot had no doubt that Tucker would club Miller if Miller took a swing at him.

Without appearing to move quickly, Ezra inserted himself between them. "Come along, Curtis. We got to get back to work. You boys go dump some more trees, if you feel so peppery." Ezra smiled slightly. It seemed to Talbot that Ezra wouldn't mind fighting them both just for exercise.

Ezra walked off with Curtis Miller. Nearby a woodpecker was hammering on a stump. Talbot watched Tucker toss the branch back on the wagon. "Weren't you a little hard on him?" he asked.

"He's ridiculous." Tucker picked up his chain saw and began

walking through the brush to where they had stopped cutting before lunch. Rooster trotted after him. The sun was hot and the air full of bugs.

"But you can't just jump at him," said Talbot, hurrying to catch up. "You been jumping at too many people lately." Talbot felt uncomfortable bringing up a personal subject.

"Guys like Curtis Miller have been in my way all my life," said Tucker. "They're the guys who know nothing and think it's everything. What's he mean saying I'm not from here? I bleed here. Home is where you bleed."

"Hey, if you hadn't been so rude, he might have come to the game on Saturday."

"Sure and I'll shoot him with a real gun. None of this paint shit. Hell, I should have let Rooster bite him." He bent down to pat the dog on the head.

Talbot followed silently for a moment as they worked their way through the brush. The ground was still damp from the rain over the weekend. Ezra had bought the stumpage on a hundred acres in north Brooks. So far he had cut three-fourths, taking out seven thousand cords, selling about a third as pulpwood and the rest as cordwood. Talbot hated the work, hated the constant little pains and bruises and how he was busting himself for so little money. This was partly why he had begun his paintball operation, just to pick up a few more bucks.

"What's bothering you anyway?" Talbot asked.

"I don't want to talk about it."

"Your wife?"

Tucker stopped and turned around. Talbot thought that he had the thinnest lips he'd ever seen, like a pink line drawn on a sheet of paper. The idea occurred to him that Tucker could hit him as easily as he might hit Curtis Miller, or he might just break out laughing. "I don't want to talk about it," repeated Tucker.

"Why act so tough?" said Talbot. "I'm your buddy."

72

Tucker turned again and began walking. Talbot wanted to throw something at him, maybe just a pine cone. What was the point of pretending you didn't have feelings? But Talbot didn't want to make him mad. He wanted to talk to Tucker about that cocaine he'd sold in the spring and if he could get any more. Talbot knew that Tucker hadn't liked selling it, not because of the illegality but because being a salesman had interfered with his loner status. It meant being nice to people, telling jokes, flattering people. Tucker hadn't been good at it. But recently it had occurred to Talbot that if Tucker could get the cocaine, then he could sell it. He, after all, was a born salesman. Mr. Charm himself. The problem was in introducing the subject. That was the main trouble with Tucker these days. You never knew how he'd react.

They reached the spot where they had left off cutting before lunch. Before them stretched a stand of poplar and pine, as well as some maple and birch. The bugs swarmed thicker in the shade and Talbot kept batting at them. Then he picked up a red gas can and shook it.

"By the way," said Talbot, "I been wanting to ask you, d'you think you can locate any more of that coke?"

Tucker had taken a rag and was wiping the sawdust from around the gas tank of his chain saw. "I doubt it. I mean, I only had it that one time." He answered casually, hardly interested in what Talbot was saying.

"Where'd you get it?"

"From a friend in Camden."

Talbot wiped off his chain saw, then handed the can of gasoline to Tucker. "Would he have any more?"

"Maybe. He gave me a call the other day, he wants to see me. I guess there's some stuff coming in." Tucker paused and looked up at Talbot. "I don't know, maybe I can get you a little, but I'm not dealing it."

Talbot held a plastic funnel to the opening of the gas tank of Tucker's saw and Tucker began pouring the gasoline. A couple of blue jays were kicking up a racket in the poplar right above him. "Can you get me half a key?" asked Talbot.

Tucker stopped pouring. "You kidding? I don't want any part of it."

"If you get me that much, I'll take care of the selling. That's a lot of money, man. Over thirty thousand depending on how much it's been stepped on."

Tucker went back to pouring the gasoline. "How long would it take to sell it?"

Talbot pretended to do some simple calculations. The jays were still squawking. They probably knew he was about to cut down their tree. "A couple of days," he said, wondering if that was possible. But sure it was. He knew lots of people who'd buy it. Look at all those guys at St. Regis making fifteen bucks an hour. "I thought you wanted the money to get out of here. Can't you get it?"

Tucker put the gas can back on the ground and again wiped his saw with the rag. Then he began pulling on his gloves. "I just don't have that kind of access. I mean, he gave me the stuff before as a favor because I was broke. But a pound, that's something else again."

"When were you planning on seeing him?"

"Tomorrow. You're getting to be a real businessman, aren't you? Reefers, paintball and now you want to deal cocaine."

Talbot wiped off his saw, then picked up his gloves. His yellow hard hat lay in the grass at his feet and Rooster was sniffing it. "It's what I don't want to do that counts. I don't want to cut any more cord wood or hang any more Sheetrock or do any more cheap carpentry jobs or raise sheep or fix people's cars or tend bar."

Tucker began pulling on his gloves "I know the feeling. But what do you know about dealing cocaine?"

"It's easy, man. That's what I did in the service. Go back and forth between Saigon and An Khe. I'd supply the whole company, coke, smack, you name it."

Tucker had been in the same regiment, but another company. When Tucker had shown up in An Khe, Talbot had been a short-termer and was gone in a month. They had played some basketball together but that was it. When Talbot met him a couple of years later in a bar in Portland, Maine, he at first hadn't recognized him, so different did he seem. No more jokes, no more funny times. It had taken a few years for that to come back. Talbot didn't know much about what Tucker had done in An Khe except that he was on a LURP team, which meant creeping around and wearing black pajamas just like the gooks.

"I smoked a lot of dope over there but that was it," said Tucker. He pulled the cord on his chain saw. It sputtered several times, then caught. He revved it, holding it away from him. It was smoking a lot. He shut it off, took a small screwdriver from his pocket and began fiddling with the feed screw.

Talbot wanted to get away from talking about dealing coke. He'd bring it up later, dribble the idea into Tucker's brain bit by bit. "Dope weighed too much," he said. "If you were doing the supplying for the whole fuckin' platoon, it could be a real nuisance. I remember one time we hit a hot LZ. This black dude had about two keys in his pack. Fuckin' got torn apart as soon as he hit the ground. Pack ripped open and the rotors blew the reefer all over. There we were watching our stash blow into the trees. Could of wept."

Tucker put away the screwdriver. "We used to roll these big reefers before we went out, you know, great big stogies, and if we got a kill, we'd leave the gook propped up against a tree with a stogy stuck in his mouth." Tucker again yanked the cord on his chain saw and revved it a couple of times. The noise tore the silence like tearing a sheet of paper. He notched a poplar, or "popple" as Ezra called it, then he stood back and shut off the saw. Talbot thought it was still acting up.

"But you know, one time we got stuck out overnight," said Tucker, "and I was smoking dope with a guy and we went to sleep. Next morning I woke up and his throat was cut. Blood all over the place. I couldn't figure if it was a VC joke or they just didn't know I was there, you know, hidden in the elephant grass. His fuckin' blood was all over my boots. Couldn't sleep for shit after that."

Lowell Perry had gotten off work at eleven that morning and didn't have to be back until three when he had to replace the shivs, the wheels holding the cables, on the long arm of the trolley of the number-two hoisting tower. That night a barge of iron oxide was due in, which meant using the smaller bucket because of the extra weight. They'd be unloading it all the next day. Perry liked being a hoisting engineer. He liked the name. It sounded sexy. Hoisting engineer. And he liked how he worked at odd hours so today, if he wanted, he could just enjoy the sun and drive around Belfast checking out the local action.

He'd been down in Northport talking to a friend who had a garage, asking his opinion of those new Corvettes. His friend liked them and said how the anti-lock braking system was a real plus. Lowell thought so too. It meant you could slam on the brakes at some speed in excess of one hundred miles an hour and not wrap yourself around a tree. He was glad the Corvette was built right, as well as looking right.

He was now driving back up High Street in Belfast and had just passed the hospital. It was lunchtime but he didn't feel hungry. He didn't eat much as a rule. Maybe he'd stop at the McDonald's later. His windows were down and he drove real slow. For a moment, he considered taking a turn through the City Park to see who was there, then he changed his mind, which was just as well because a little farther up High Street he saw Cindy Long, Brian's sister-in-law, walking toward town swinging a string bag. Her blond hair looked wet and Lowell guessed she'd been swimming at the outdoor pool and was now walking back to the drugstore where she worked. He'd give her a ride. She wore a light yellow dress and was some cute. Cindy Tagalong he'd called her when she was little because of the way she hung around him and Brian.

Lowell Perry slowed the Camaro and pulled over on the dirt shoulder by the sidewalk. Just up ahead was Jack's Grocery. Maybe Cindy'd like a soft drink. Perry leaned across his seat and called out the window on the passenger's side, "Hey, Cindy."

She turned and looked at him for a moment without expression and he thought she didn't recognize him. Then she smiled. "Hello, Lowell."

"You want a ride in the rest of the way?" He began to open the door.

She shook her head and smiled again. "It's only a couple of blocks. I'd rather walk. It's too nice a day."

Perry took his hand away from the door handle. "You sure?"

"I'm sure."

"Some other time then."

Cindy smiled again, gave him a little wave and walked off. Lowell Perry leaned back in the seat and drummed his fingers on the burgundy-colored plush fabric. On the corner was Mrs. Houghton's Guest House and he could see Mrs. Houghton in the backyard picking some yellow flowers. Lowell Perry felt disappointed enough that he was ready to plow his Camaro straight across Mrs. Houghton's garden. Wouldn't she have a cat fit. Then he saw Tucker Morgan driving toward him in his rusty pickup, a truck that any normal person wouldn't want to be seen dead in. Tucker had a beer in one hand and appeared to be singing. His fool dog was sitting next to him as if he were singing too. Lowell Perry felt disgusted. Brian had mentioned running into Tucker and how Tucker had been out on his lobster boat. Tucker tapped his horn and raised his beer can to Cindy in a salute. Cindy waved back and Perry was struck by how cheerful she looked. He hadn't realized that they knew each other. After Tucker had driven by, Perry started the Camaro and pulled a U-turn. He'd follow Tucker. No telling what cheap goods like that was up to. He might learn something.

Around one o'clock Tuesday afternoon Tucker drew his truck to a stop in front of his father-in-law's house in Camden. His brakes made a loud screeching noise and he liked that. It was a hot breezy day and the bright sun made the white paint on the house shine. It was a huge house, maybe twenty-five rooms, and the lawn in the back went down to the water where Tucker could see a small sloop moored at the dock. The house had once been owned by a ship's captain, Tucker had been told, although it seemed that every big house on the coast of Maine had been owned by a ship's captain and that made Tucker suspicious. Just how many of those guys were there? Now the house was owned by Sarah's father, a New York stockbroker who had retired early to come up to Camden to make even more money in real estate. The house was an ornate Victorian affair with bay windows and sloping dormers and side porches with Grecian friezes and a widow's walk from which one could see even more of the bay. In front, borders of yellow and red flowers lined the walk and a gnarled birch with a rope swing and a red baby seat stood off to the left of the front steps.

In contrast, Tucker's truck with its rust and aluminum patches and its bumper stickers saying EAT MORE POSSUM and

WHEN GUNS ARE OUTLAWED ONLY OUTLAWS WILL HAVE GUNS
seemed like a violation of the neighborhood and Tucker was
amused by that. He revved the motor several times, then shut
it off and got out, telling Rooster to stay and promising him
a long walk later. Under his arm he carried a Fischer-Price
farm set gift-wrapped in purple paper. Even on sale it had
cost what he got paid for cutting a stack of wood eight feet
by four feet by four feet. Not that he gave a shit.

For all his rebellious feelings, Tucker walked rather sedately
up the front walk and felt like a trespasser. His jeans were
clean and he wore a clean white T-shirt under his Levi's
jacket. Slowly he climbed the front steps and rang the bell.

When his wife came to the screen door, Tucker felt oddly
shy, which made him irritated with himself. Even though
Sarah had smiled, he could see that her main attention was
gone from him. She smiled as one might smile at the mailman.
They had been pretty good lovers, energetic and dirty. In her
khaki skirt and green-and-white-striped polo shirt, she looked
all set for her tennis lesson. Tucker believed he still loved
her and this made him angry. He wanted to force himself
upon her, touch her breasts, bite her neck, but her smile
lacked intimacy. They had become strangers again, as much
as when they had first met.

Tucker opened the screen door and kissed Sarah somewhat
clumsily on the cheek. "Is Jason around?"

She was looking out at his truck. Even parked at the curb
it looked hostile. Rooster was leaning out the window, snapping
at mosquitoes and wagging his tail. Sarah had never much
liked Rooster, saying he was too pushy.

"He's still taking his nap," she said. "Come into the living
room."

He followed her through the hall. The house was full of
loot: expensive antiques, pictures, Oriental rugs, lots of brass
and polished wood. Old things that had been stroked and
polished by hundreds of hands and now were in the possession

of Sarah's father, who prided himself on his collector's eye and ability to get good things cheap. Tucker imagined backing a truck up to the house, swiping this stuff and redistributing it amongst the people of Brooks. They'd probably wreck it. Anyway, he didn't particularly believe in redistributing the wealth. What do I believe? thought Tucker. He watched his wife's ass move under her khaki skirt. It made the question seem irrelevant.

Tucker put the toy for Jason down on a chair in the living room. "How long's he been asleep?"

"About an hour."

There was a note in Sarah's voice which Tucker didn't like. It wasn't coolness. Maybe it was that fact of separation again. He looked at her breasts and did it long enough so she could see where he was looking. Did he desire her? He thought he did. Again he wondered what he believed, and thought how he never asked himself such questions.

"Can't you wake him? Just say his daddy's here."

Sarah didn't answer and Tucker walked to the window. The small sloop had a dark red sail. Tucker had taken it out once. He'd even liked it. It occurred to him that this could be his life: living in Camden, having nice things. For a second he yearned for it, then he made himself hard again, clenching his heart like a fist.

"I been thinking," he said, with his back still to her. "I want you to move back to Brooks. I miss you and Rooster misses you too. I miss my little boy. I'll fix the place up, put in a lawn, get wallpaper. It'll be a real house."

"No, Tucker."

Tucker turned around. "Why not?"

"My hippy days are over. I don't like not having hot water or a regular toilet." She was standing by the door to the hall, leaning against the doorjamb with her arms crossed. He couldn't get over how separate from him she seemed.

"We'll fix those things."

"It's not enough."

He walked toward her quickly, trying to threaten her or at least jar her from her coolness. Sarah stepped back slghtly.

"So you don't want to be with me?"

"You come here. You get a job, a place to live and then we'll talk about it." She pushed her hands through her blond hair, pushing both hands up over her forehead and letting the hair fall back. This was one of her common gestures, even a sexual gesture. At one time, Tucker had been attracted by it.

"What kind of job?"

"There're lots of jobs. My father said he could help you get a job at *National Fisherman* or even *Down East*. You used to talk about writing."

"I don't want his help."

"Or there's teaching."

"I don't want to teach."

"Or you could work in a restaurant or do carpentry."

Again Tucker thought of how comfortable it would be. Even in winter Camden was tolerable. And he could forget about his house. Its unfinished state, its bare walls and hanging wires, those things dug at him constantly, even though he couldn't make himself fix them. Part of him wanted Camden, wanted to be here, but as he began to reach for it in his mind, he pulled his hand back.

"I don't want to live in Camden. It's full of twerps in pastel sweaters."

Sarah's face tightened. "Oh, Tucker, why don't you grow up."

They stared at each other. Tucker wanted to reach out and touch her, to tell her that he loved her, but the distance was too great. "Go get Jason."

She turned and Tucker watched her go. Her deck shoes and blue canvas belt with leather trim—all she needed was a circle pin to complete her Camden uniform. She was correctly dressed for her world, but then, thought Tucker, so am I. He felt suddenly angry and began to prowl around the room, opening drawers and cupboards. He wanted to steal something. Going to the liquor cabinet, he discovered an unopened bottle of Johnnie Walker Black Label. Tucker bent his knees and hopped up and down, making a happy chimpanzee noise. He took off his Levi's jacket, wrapped the bottle in it and placed the jacket on the chair by the toy. Then he began looking for something else. On the wall by the fireplace was a gun rack with three rifles. Tucker went to it quickly, walking almost on tiptoe. He grabbed one of the rifles and tried to lift it from the rack. It was locked in place. He yanked at it but it wouldn't budge. He tried the others and they were locked as well. Studying the rack, he saw it was screwed to the wall. He removed his Swiss army knife from the leather holder on his belt and opened the screwdriver blade. Just then he heard Sarah returning. He closed the blade and turned around with a big welcoming smile.

Sarah was holding Jason to her chest and his legs dangled down in front of her. His head rested on her shoulder. Jason wore khaki shorts and a yellow T-shirt. His blond hair was all sweaty from his nap. She set him down on the floor, kneeling before him and smoothing out his hair as he rubbed his eyes and began looking around the room.

"He's still pretty sleepy," said Sarah.

Jason saw Tucker and at first his face remained blank. Then he started to smile as Tucker made his own grin as big and foolish as possible. Taking the present from the chair, Tucker tossed it up and caught it. The purple paper made a crinkling noise.

"Hey, Mr. Man," said Tucker, "look what your daddy's brought you."

Jason looked at the package uncertainly, unsure whether his father really meant to give it to him. He had celebrated his second birthday at the beginning of the summer and he liked presents. He reached out his hands toward his father.

Fifteen minutes later, Tucker was sitting outside on the grass with Jason, who was pushing a yellow toy tractor back and forth on a small patch of dirt while making a *grrr*ing noise. Tucker watched his son play as he tried to work a couple of burrs out of Rooster's ears. Rooster too made an occasional *grrr*ing noise. Tucker pushed the dog away, then took a spotted brown cow from the farm set and began tossing it lightly from one hand to the other. Sarah sat on the front steps about twenty feet away, not saying anything but watching just the same.

Tucker couldn't tell if Jason liked the present. Basically, he thought, little kids weren't too quick in the head no matter how much you loved them. Jason had discarded the tractor for a plastic sheep and was fiddling with it in much the same way that Tucker was fiddling with the spotted brown cow, except that when he tossed it up, he dropped it. Tucker realized that his son was trying to imitate him and he felt touched. He brushed a mosquito away from Jason's forehead.

"Mr. Man, you come back and live with me and I'll give you a real cow and a real tractor," said Tucker. "You like sheep, little sheepies? I'll give you a sheep. Rooster talks about you all the time. He can't sleep at night, he picks at his food. Tell your mommy that you gotta live in Brooks. Bring her too. I'll learn some new jokes and keep everybody happy. Come back to the action, Mr. Man. I'll get you a gun. We'll hunt Martians and the blue Heebie-Jeebies."

Jason looked up from the plastic sheep. "What's Heebie-Jeebies?" he asked.

But Tucker was glancing around the yard. Then he turned back and stroked Jason's head several times. Jason dropped the sheep and picked up a little plastic man. Tucker glanced at his watch. Shortly he had to meet Phillip Sutton. He again thought of Talbot's proposition. If he could make twenty thousand dollars, he could hire a bunch of guys to finish his house and clear the land. Turn it into a real place that Sarah might consider coming back to.

Bending over, Tucker picked up Jason and got to his feet, holding his son like a chubby package, tickling him a little so he wriggled. Then he lifted him so their heads were about the same level, letting Jason face away from him. He began walking slowly toward his truck. Rooster ran ahead of them.

"You remember the old bomb," said Tucker into Jason's ear. "Just waiting for your orders, Mr. Man. We could get in that truck and go anywhere."

The whole idea of blessed escape began to form in Tucker's mind. He wished he could step through a door and find himself in another world. He wouldn't care if it was raining, snowing, even hurricaning so long as it was Other.

"Let's get the hell outta here," he told Jason. "We'll join a circus. You can be a clown and I'll be your red rubber ball. We'll meet the dancing bear and ride motorcycles through hoops of fire. *Vroom, vroom.*" Glancing toward the house, he saw Sarah walking toward them. She looked suspicious and alert.

"What's a dancing bear?" asked Jason. He liked bears. Not only that but he knew grown-ups liked him to like bears.

Tucker considered telling Jason about bears, especially the dancing kind, the ones that danced no matter what else they were told to do, that danced and danced and said to hell with the rest. But now Sarah was here.

"What are you doing?" asked Sarah.

Her voice was so calm that Tucker knew she was making it calm. "I miss my son," he said.

"He has to go in now. It's time for his snack."

"I want to take him for a ride."

Sarah reached out for Jason and he stretched his arms toward her. "No, Tucker, you don't have a car seat or seat belts or anything."

Regulations, thought Tucker, too many regulations. He looked at Sarah's lips and considered their softness. She wore a pale pink lipstick. Tucker had a sudden memory of the garlic kisses of Vietnamese women. Sarah never tasted of garlic. He reached out his hand and touched her lips with his thumb. Then he handed Jason to her.

"Be nice to him," said Tucker. "He likes sweet things."

Khaki pants, blue alligator shirt, Phillip Sutton was as correct in his appearance as Sarah, but in Phillip's case Tucker knew it was a fraud, that he dressed and acted so proper in order to lure the little fishies into his net. There was nothing Phillip wouldn't do for money, or almost nothing, since he liked his comforts too much to take major chances. So he dealt drugs, pills, lent money and involved himself in various schemes.

At the moment, he was sighting down the shaft of a green plastic dart toward the twenty on a dart board hanging to the left of the phone in the Garage, a Camden bar that had once been just that. Pipes and air ducts crisscrossed the ceiling. The Garage was dark and cool and at this time of the day nearly empty. At night it was jammed with tourists dancing to the various bands that the owner, a Frenchman, brought up from Boston. Tucker came with Phillip now and then to pick up girls, although Tucker could hardly stand himself for doing it, not because of the infidelity but because of the quality of female—young secretaries on a summer cruise wearing perfumes he didn't like. Tucker was never certain if it was the girls he didn't like or himself he didn't like for going after them.

Phillip threw the dart and it lodged neatly in the single-score ring of the twenty. They were playing tournament darts, working their way down from a starting total of 1001. Sometimes they played Around the Clock or Shanghai or Darts Baseball or Football or Scram or even Killer if they got more guys. Phillip would pick the game, always looking for the one in which he could beat Tucker, for although he was a good player, Tucker was better. At the moment, Phillip had thirty-eight points to dump in order to win and his last dart had to be in a double-score ring bringing his count exactly to zero. Tucker wrote the number on the blackboard.

"The problem is," said Phillip, "that they can't take the stuff into Searsport. Somebody's been talking. The last boat from South America had Customs agents all over it. Those dogs, you know, they're geniuses."

"They find anything?" asked Tucker. Noticing Phillip's watch, it occurred to Tucker that it must have cost a thousand dollars—lots of gold and as thin as a credit card. He guessed you could pick up girls just by showing them a watch like that.

Phillip aimed his second dart. "Wasn't anything to be found, although I gather some stuff got thrown away." Phillip threw the dart and it lodged in the eighteen. He turned to sip his white wine. He was dark-haired and tan and handsome, with a long straight nose as thin as the spine of a book of poems. In Vietnam, he had had all the American nurses he wanted despite not being an officer.

"So what are you going to do?" asked Tucker, writing the number twenty on the blackboard. He still wasn't sure what Phillip was proposing.

"We need to find another way to bring it in. That's why I gave you a call. It could mean a lot of money if you didn't mind the risk."

"What kind of risk?"

"Jail." Phillip threw his third dart at the double-score ring of the ten and the dart sunk into the single-score ring of the next sector, the six.

"Not a happy place," said Tucker, writing fourteen on the board. He knew that Phillip was angry at missing the ten but he showed no sign of it. Back in the kitchen two voices were raised in laughter, then grew silent again.

Phillip walked to the board to retrieve his darts. "But what have you got to lose?" he asked.

It seemed to Tucker that he had a lot to lose by going to jail. And even if he had absolutely nothing to lose, that nothing was still preferable to being locked up. His own score was seventy-six. He'd been teasing Phillip a little, letting him think he was winning. He aimed his first dart and sunk it in the single-score ring of the nineteen.

"You still living out in that wreck?" asked Phillip, writing fifty-seven on the blackboard. "Shit, I don't see how you can stand that life."

"It's mine, man. Nobody can interfere with it."

"Who else would want it?"

Phillip had once visited Tucker in Brooks and said he wouldn't do it again. Too much dirt, too much wildlife. "It's like you're making your own hootch," he had said, "your own Vietnamese slum."

Tucker drank some beer, then began aiming his second dart. "What about giving me some of the stuff to sell?" he said.

"Like how much?" Phillip had sat down and was leaning back in his chair. It always seemed that when he was asking, he leaned forward; when he was being asked, he leaned back.

"I don't know, maybe a pound." Tucker threw his second dart, placing it in the single-score ring of the seventeen. He had to dump forty more points in order to win.

Phillip raised his eyebrows, then walked to the blackboard to write down forty. "Are you nuts? We don't want that kind of attention around here. Besides that, what do you know about it and who'd trust you? No, this stuff goes right down south. Hey, I'm doing you a big enough favor by asking you to do the pickup." Phillip glanced at the blackboard as if realizing that Tucker had been fooling with him. "Let's go outside," he said.

"Wait," said Tucker. He threw his last dart and sank it

in the double-score ring of the twenty. But Phillip had already turned away, as if losing wouldn't be so bad if he didn't see it.

They walked out toward the dock. The schooners were gone from the wharf, ferrying tourists around Penobscot Bay, but there were still plenty of other boats in the harbor and plenty of tourists to take their pictures. The harbor opened toward the south but not much of the bay could be seen past Eaton Point and Curtis Island. To the north Mount Battie rose above the town and Tucker could just make out the round stone tower of the observatory. Across the harbor a power boat was moored; Tucker guessed it was over sixty feet long. He wondered what it would be like to have money, then told himself he didn't care about it. Did he want to redistribute the wealth out of fairness or so he could have more himself? He wished he had a little two-man sub so he could sink some of these fat cats.

"If you can get a boat," Phillip was saying, "then it's simple. The transfer can be made in the bay. They can just throw the stuff overboard. We wouldn't need Searsport at all."

"I don't know," said Tucker. He knew drugs were brought in by boat all the time but mostly it was by a fast boat going out to a mother ship and usually it was large amounts of marijuana. It had been the same during Prohibition and some of the older lobstermen still talked about how they or their dads had paid off their boats by bringing in European whiskey.

"Depends what you want, man. You want to stay out there in animal land, freezing your ass off come January? Man, you should put together a bundle and get outta here. You're not living, you're hiding out."

Phillip had put on dark glasses and Tucker couldn't see his eyes. "What the fuck do you know about it?" he asked. He decided that Phillip was still mad about being beaten at darts.

An elderly couple dressed in bright colors heard Tucker and moved away. Tucker picked up a stone and tossed it toward the water. It was low tide and there was a smell of fish. He was surprised the Camden Tourist Board didn't perfume the rocks during low tide. Tucker asked himself if he was afraid of being caught or breaking the law or changing his life. He was angered by Phillip's words, yet agreed with what he said. He was sick of Brooks but didn't know how to get away from it. He didn't think he was lazy. He just didn't know what to do. Could he live here in Camden and work in a store or teach school or get some kind of landscaping job?

"I've known you for years, right?" Phillip continued. "Now your wife's split, your kid's gone. Even if you don't do this, you should get out. What were you thinking of, moving out to Brooks and building a house? Are you Daniel Boone or something? Man, this is the 1980s."

Tucker turned away. "You sound like my old lady."

"I'm not saying you should teach school," said Phillip. "You like it back there in the woods? I bet you hate it."

Tucker looked again at the power yacht. It had lots of dark polished wood. A man and woman were standing in the stern. He couldn't see their faces but imagined they were young. They were probably also drinking champagne and laughing at the assholes who had to work and lead regular lives.

"I got an old high school buddy in Belfast who's got a boat," said Tucker. "He's a lobsterman."

"Does he need money?"

"Doesn't everyone?" Tucker didn't want to say any more. I could wind up in jail, he told himself.

"Can you trust him?"

Tucker didn't answer. The sun on his head, the warmth and smell of the water, the ringing-slapping noise of ropes against masts—it was all like something he wasn't experiencing but was looking in at, like looking through a window at people in a restaurant.

"Sure," said Tucker after a moment. "Back in school he used to be my shadow."

"So snap your fingers and make him jump."

"I like him, though. I don't want to get him in trouble. He's got a family."

Phillip started walking along the wharf toward the parking lot. Tucker followed about a step behind. People were sitting on benches eating ice cream. A Pekingese barked at Phillip's ankles and an elderly woman tugged at its leash.

"It's safe, man," said Phillip.

"You said there was a risk."

"Not if you don't fuck up. You just make the transfer out in the bay. It's these salt boats from Brazil. They been coming up every three weeks or so. Someone on the boat has about ten keys of pure cocaine. You wait out in the bay, make a signal and the guy tosses it overboard attached to a life jacket. Then you bring it to me. That's ten grand for being an errand boy."

As Tucker listened, he thought it seemed possible. No danger, no problems, everything as smooth as a summer afternoon. "When would this be?" he asked, making his voice sound serious and adult.

Phillip took off his dark glasses, his eyes following a young woman in red shorts and a halter top. "Very soon. Can you get the guy with the boat?"

"I've got to see him this afternoon anyway." That wasn't quite true, but Tucker had been meaning to ask Brian about the paintball game on Saturday. He had thought of telephoning. Now he'd pay a visit, get him right at work.

Phillip was pointing up the hill on the other side of the parking lot. "Look at that, see those guys?"

Tucker saw two men in uniform. One was scanning the harbor with binoculars. They looked liked police but Tucker didn't recognize their uniforms.

"Are they cops?"

Phillip shook his head. "They're Customs agents. They go up and down the coast looking for anything out of the ordinary.

What could be more ordinary than a lobster boat out on the bay?"

"Won't they be waiting for the freighter in Searsport?"

Phillip laughed, then took Tucker's arm and began to walk him in the direction of the girl with the red shorts and halter top who was bending over to scold a little dog. "Sure," he said, "but you'll pick up the stuff a couple of hours before. That ten thousand, it'll be like free money."

six

The chicken plant formed a ramshackle green corrugated metal sprawl about a block from the water and three blocks from the only stoplight in Waldo County. Several years earlier Belfast had had two chicken processing plants and the city had advertised itself as the Broiler Capital of the World. But now one had gone bankrupt and the other was barely holding its own against southern competition, while Broiler Capital was a name that the real estate developers and Chamber of Commerce were hoping to transcend.

Driving directly back to Belfast from Camden, Tucker had parked across the street from the plant, then hurried up the front steps and through the front door, walking with definite purpose in hopes that he wouldn't be stopped. Rooster remained in the truck. Who could guess what kind of wreckage the dog might cause in a chicken plant? Tucker had never been in the plant before but he knew that Brian worked downstairs. Although he didn't know what that meant, he intended to find out.

The main office was directly in front of the door and no one looked up as Tucker walked briskly past the window. The air smelled of chicken soup which grew stronger the farther he went into the building. From somewhere came a low metallic rumbling. A chalkboard around the corner informed him that 86,743 fryers were being processed that day and for a moment the air felt crowded with the released souls of anxious chickens. The distant rumbling grew louder and the aroma of chicken soup began to smell rancid. About a dozen people were in the hall. All wore knee-length white coats, rubber boots and either white paper hats or yellow plastic helmets. At the end of the hall, Tucker turned right and descended a flight of stairs. The rumbling began to divide itself into various rattlings and clankings. People looked up but no one stopped him. Many of the people Tucker recognized, having seen them in Rollie's or Clara's. They were people he had grown up with, played baseball with, fought, made love to, gotten drunk with.

At the bottom of the stairs Tucker came to an abrupt halt. He felt he had entered a kind of poultry hell. It was a large room, perhaps 10,000 square feet, and crammed with machinery, spraying water and men and women in white coats who all seemed to turn and look at him. Winding through the room at shoulder height was a conveyor belt which hung from the ceiling. Every two feet or so dangled chickens in various states of disrepair. The main clanking noise came from the belt, but workers were also shouting, hammering and rolling metal carts. Near the bottom of the stairs a man with a hose was washing down the concrete floor. Tucker walked over to him.

"Where's Brian, the foreman?" he shouted. To his left under a large metal vat, Tucker saw a white chicken—dirty, bedraggled but definitely alive and exhibiting no evidence of anxiety, while swinging in the air above its head passed hundreds of its comrades. Tucker could almost feel the steamy smell of sour chicken broth soaking into his clothes and skin.

The man started to point, but then Tucker saw Brian walking

quickly toward him, ducking every now and then under the conveyor belt. Like the others, he wore a white coat, boots and a plastic helmet. He shouted something but Tucker couldn't make out the words. He had a sense of efficiency that surprised Tucker, who'd always seen Brian as someone who was not quite certain of what he was doing. Tucker realized his sneakers were getting wet and he stepped back.

"What did you say?" he shouted, as he shook Brian's hand.

"I said, you're supposed to be wearing a helmet!" Brian looked exasperated, yet pleased to see him.

"Chickens are pretty soft!" He was surprised at how fast the conveyor belt moved and wondered how long it would take to process 86,000 chickens. That was about 10,000 an hour. He knew that each worker had a specific task. They stood up and the whole business looked exhausting. There was a wing man, a leg man, a craw man. One fellow armed with a kind of pneumatic pistol did nothing but shoot out chicken assholes all day long. Tucker imagined putting that on his résumé.

"It keeps the gunk out of your hair!" shouted Brian.

"What!"

"A helmet keeps the gunk outta your hair!"

Tucker raised his hand to his head. He saw people grinning at him. Turning away, Brian took a white coat from a hook on the wall. A man who was going upstairs tossed Brian a helmet. The coat was several sizes too small and Tucker felt foolish as he pulled it over his Levi's jacket. Brian motioned to him to follow as he continued along the production line.

"They weren't supposed to let you in here," said Brian.

"I told them it was an emergency."

"What kind of emergency?" It seemed that for every job of cutting or slicing, there was also an inspector who made sure the chicken was fit for consumption. He or she would nick a questionable part and a worker would cut it off, toss it into a bucket or into the gutter at his feet.

Tucker had to shout. "I wanted to see if you could play in this paintball game on Saturday. I need someone to guard my back."

"Game?"

It was impossible to talk with this racket. On the other side of the conveyor belt were great vats to scald the chickens before they were sent through the plucker, then to chill the chickens to keep them from cooking. Tucker had had the process described to him, but this was the first time he'd seen it. For a second, he saw the chickens as the corpses of naked Viet Cong all dangling by their feet. Then he shook his head to clear it of nutsy images. On the far side of the room, he noticed the chickens emerging from the blood room, their feathers still on and their throats cut, hanging by their feet from metal hooks. After being hung up by their feet, the chickens went through the stunner, the slitter, the scalder, the plucker, the chiller before they reached the actual assembly line, or perhaps disassembly line, thought Tucker.

"Is there any place more quiet?" Tucker shouted.

"Follow me!"

Brian turned and led the way across the floor, sticking close to the wall and away from the conveyor belt. Tucker's feet were sodden and his ears ringing with the noise. He thought of his students in Skowhegan and how eager they had been to quit school early. A couple of visits to a poultry plant might have cured them of that desire.

"What do they do with the cut-off parts?" shouted Tucker.

Brian paused and leaned toward Tucker's ear. "They're turned into pellets and fed to the chickens out in the barns. Nothing's wasted."

Tucker pointed toward a huge vat back by the blood room which had steam spouting from the top. "Is that what makes the smell?"

Brian winked. "What smell?"

They reached a small office over in the corner and Brian opened the door, then stood back to let Tucker enter. A plate-glass window looked out on the processing floor but with the door shut the room was relatively quiet. Tucker moved his toes within his wet sneakers. They felt squishy.

"Now what's this game?" asked Brian, leaning back against a desk and glancing out at the processing floor.

"You remember playing Capture the Flag as a kid?" said Tucker. "It's like that except everyone's got these pistols, these paint pistols, and if you get hit with a paint pellet, then you're dead." He stopped. Brian was looking at him as if he had lost his mind. The paintball game sounded too peculiar, even childish, but Tucker told himself it was because he was saying it wrong. He pushed on. "But the thing is, I need you. Some guys are out to get me and I need someone to cover my back. It'd be like being a team again." Tucker found that part hard to say. He disliked expressing any emotional need even more than he disliked manipulating Brian.

Brian took off his helmet and wiped his forehead. "And these are squirt guns?"

"No, man, they're compressed gas pistols that shoot pellets of yellow or red gelatin paint. But don't worry, it washes right out." Through the window, Tucker watched the workers in their white coats, the bald chickens and the conveyor belt continue their intricate choreography. Once when tending bar at the Belfast Cafe, Tucker had learned from a local doctor that the most common ailment at the plant was tendonitis of the wrist which came from making the same slashing or cutting gesture with a knife every couple of seconds all day, all week, all year, all life.

"I was supposed to take Margaret into the mall in Bangor."

"Can't you get out of it?"

"Maybe. Cindy could watch the kids okay. Is it dangerous?"

Tucker rubbed his hands together and tried to look fun-loving. "Nah, a lot of guys running around the woods and shit. It'll do you a world of good. But we need more people. You know anyone? They should be in pretty good shape."

Tucker knew one fellow who had broken a leg and another who had been hit in the ear with a paintball and still couldn't hear. Other than that there had been sprains, bruises, minor cuts. Also the paintballs could hurt. Get hit in the crotch or head or just the bare skin and it raised a hefty bruise.

"I guess I know some guys. There's that fellow Lowell Perry I told you about. Maybe some others."

"Why don't you round them up? Just tell 'em there's free beer. You out doing your lobsters this morning?"

Brian glanced at his watch, then looked out at the floor. "I do them every morning, seven days a week. How do you win in this game?"

Tucker pointed out through the window to another escaped chicken standing beneath the conveyor belt. He had now seen about three of them. How calm they looked in the midst of depredation. How full of confidence. "Just like that chicken over there, man. You survive."

Brian looked out at the chicken, then tugged at his small beard. "The clean-up guys kill those," he said. "They say they're the sweetest."

Lowell Perry had himself a little apartment in Belfast, four rooms fully carpeted. On the walls were promotion gimmicks given out by a dozen breweries. They made his rooms seem lively. He had gotten the idea from Rollie's Cafe, which specialized in such promotion gimmicks. On the walls of the bar or hanging from the ceiling were various clocks, flashing signs, fake waterfalls, teams of horses with moving legs, blinking lights, shimmering rainbows, glistening mountain streams, bubbling copper cauldrons—a small riot of light that existed in metaphoric relation to the shouting, drinking, pool-playing, flirting, joking, television-watching crowd that filled the long smoky room. Lowell Perry liked Rollie's. It too was lively. And if he went more often to Clara's, that was only to meet girls.

Tuesday evening Brian and Lowell Perry were seated in a booth near the front window of Rollie's with a pitcher of beer and a half-eaten pepperoni-and-onion pizza. Lowell Perry also liked the food at Rollie's and especially the pizza, although it meant he'd have to get up for a drink of water about five times during the night. He guessed the salt made people drink more beer, as if the pizza too was a kind of promotion gimmick. Of the thirty other people in the bar about half worked at the chicken plant and he and Brian knew them all.

Perry wore a grease-stained green shirt and green workpants. Overhauling the shivs on the trolley had taken longer than expected and he'd come straight from the docks. As he glanced around the room, he kept jiggling his car keys which were attached to a lucky rabbit foot. He had the look of someone who was not so much listening as overhearing. Perry had just told Brian that he had seen Tucker almost two years ago and Brian was surprised.

"So you knew Tucker was back here? Why didn't you tell me?" They had met in the bar about eight as they did nearly every Tuesday evening when Margaret had her church group at the house.

"Didn't seem important." Perry lifted a slice of pizza, then held it over his head, dangling the point toward his open mouth. He took a bite and chewed it slowly. This was almost the first thing he'd eaten all day and he still wasn't hungry.

"But we'd been good friends."

"Guess I forgot. Anyway, he was no friend of mine. Tell you the truth, there been stories about him out in Brooks."

Brian filled his glass from the pitcher, then filled Perry's glass as well. "What kind of stories?"

"Drugs and stuff," said Perry, lowering his voice. "I know a fellow out at the docks who scored coke off him." It amazed

Perry that Brian was still yammering about that asshole. Tucker had no sense of the rules, no sense of how to behave.

"I can't believe that," said Brian. "Tucker's broke."

"This fellow wasn't lyin'. He works on the hoist right next to me. He said Tucker was into a lotta stuff." Perry leaned across the table and the front of his workshirt just brushed the aluminum pizza tray. "Like a spoiled kid, doing whatever he wants and not caring about the consequences. I'm surprised he came back. Drugs mean trouble."

"You didn't mind selling that grass I dragged out of the bay," said Brian, lowering his voice as well.

"Grass is different," said Perry. "The more money involved, the meaner people get. Remember that guy that got killed in Searsport? That Colombian? I watched him come off that freighter and walk toward town. An hour later he's dead."

As a matter of fact, Perry knew more about that dead Colombian than he cared to tell. Not that he had killed him but he knew the Colombian had had money. Enrique, his name had been. The whores had known about him too so it wasn't like the money was a secret. When he'd been found in the vacant lot at the end of Navy Street, his pockets were empty. As for the marijuana, Perry had no trouble getting rid of it. He thought of himself as a middle man. He knew people with things to sell and people with things they wanted to buy. Information was Perry's business.

Brian reached out and gave the pizza tray a spin so that it rattled on the table. "So you won't come out on Saturday?"

Perry leaned back in the booth, took a cigarette from the pack of Camels in his breast pocket, lit it and tossed the match onto one of the remaining pizza slices. "I didn't say that," he answered, exhaling a puff of smoke. "Some foolish though, a bunch of grown men running all over Mt. Waldo with toy guns. Should be good for laughs. Anyway, I wouldn't want to see you get hurt."

It would be good to find out who the men were and what

friendships they had. As for Brian, Perry had several different reasons for wanting to keep him happy, and, if possible, he'd like to drive a wedge between him and Tucker. Perry and Brian had known each other almost forever, mostly because their mothers were close friends. Brian's mother was a licensed practical nurse at the hospital and Lowell Perry's mother was a nurse's aide, although usually she worked away from the hospital with terminal patients, sitting with them until they passed. Anyway, he and Brian had spent time together ever since they were a few weeks old, sharing bottles, diapers and pacifiers. It made the kind of bond you didn't want to see fucked with, thought Perry.

Brian reached out and plucked the dead match off the pizza slice, then he moved the tray over to the left under the little jukebox monitor. "Tucker says it's fun."

"Wouldn't believe anything he says. He's been an asshole since high school, hotshot athlete and lady's man. I saw him fighting in the street the other night. Jesus." Perry took another drag of his cigarette and glanced around the room. There was no point in telling Brian that he had followed Tucker down to Camden that afternoon. It occurred to Perry that Brian might be taking the rest of the pizza back to Cindy. He liked Cindy. He had liked the way she looked in her yellow dress. "How's your sister-in-law doing?" he asked.

"She's fine. Been working at the drugstore."

"She going back to school?"

"Sure, she'll be a senior. It'd be foolish to quit."

Perry had started to pay more attention to Cindy when he came over for dinner at the start of the summer. Of course he'd known her all her life, but now she was grown up and he couldn't get her out of his mind. "Say hello to her for me, will you?"

"Sure thing." Brian began wrapping the remaining pizza slices in about a dozen napkins. "I still don't see why you didn't tell me about Tucker. We were buddies."

Perry ground out his cigarette and poured some more beer. On the TV, the Red Sox were being beaten by Detroit and a couple of guys at the bar were shouting about it. He personally would have bought Cindy a whole pizza, fully loaded, all for herself if she wanted. It seemed cheap to take her the leftover pieces.

"I seen him at the Cafe tending bar," said Perry. "All these tourists and shit. He fit right in. Telling jokes and talking about the world. Guess I just didn't think to tell you."

seven

Tucker was running fast up a hill through the woods, running on the balls of his feet. In his left hand he held a can of Budweiser with his thumb over the hole. Branches slapped at him and he kept his left arm hooked in front of his face. The goggles too protected him, even though they were hot and kept steaming over. In his right hand he carried a .68 caliber black metal paint pistol which looked like a large automatic. It felt good in his hand. Besides that, it was his. He had rounded up twenty people for this silly game and Talbot had given it to him. All told, they had about ninety people charging around through the trees including some girls. The sun was hot and Tucker was sweating in his Levi's jacket and Red Sox cap. The woods were mottled in a hundred shades of green and shafts of two o'clock sunlight, poking down through the treetops, made the dust motes seem palpable and alive.

Talbot was only a few yards behind him—beer in one hand, pistol in the other. Both he and Tucker were running quietly, watching their feet, watching for hostiles. Ten yards back Brian was plowing through the underbrush like a scared bear. He had already almost taken a hit and seen another guy get it in the face during a fire fight. Tucker knew that Brian regretted coming. He knew he was afraid of getting popped. It made Tucker grin. This was good for Brian. It would give him backbone.

All three men wore yellow armbands. The opposing team wore red. So far today they had already played one game which Tucker's team had won after three hours. Some days they'd play on a twenty-acre field and the games would last about thirty minutes, but this Saturday they were using the whole mountain, maybe four hundred acres, which allowed for more complicated strategies. Poor old Rooster was back in the truck. Too many of these guys would think nothing of popping him in the face. Tucker had split his team into three groups of nine, plus another nine for defense, then three fast-moving hit squads of three men each. Tucker liked playing the hit squads best. "You bog down, you're dead": that was the motto and during the first game they'd done a lot of damage.

Twenty minutes into this second game, they were barely getting started but Tucker had just seen three or four of the red team ducking over the hill and he was running to cut them off. First wipe them out, then grab their flag. That's how he liked to do it. In the ammunition pouch hanging from his pistol belt, he carried twelve tubes of paint with ten paint pellets in each tube. A thirteenth tube stuck out of the rear of the top barrel of his pistol. He liked starting with thirteen tubes. It made him feel lucky.

Tucker spurted ahead, putting more distance between himself and Brian, who was making too much commotion. Then, as he crested the hill, he saw four of the enemy seated on the ground near a tree. One of them was that asshole Lowell Perry. Tucker flung himself forward and shot at the same time. The paint gun made a popping noise and the tree trunk above Perry's face went bright yellow.

"There they are!" he shouted. He had landed on his stomach

and he rolled over to reload and cock his pistol. Mostly it took about three seconds. Tucker could do it in two. There was a loud pop behind him as Talbot fired. The red players scrambled for cover. Tucker fired again, as did Talbot.

"Watch out!" shouted one, some guy who worked for St. Regis. He had yellow paint on his arm.

"You're hit," shouted Tucker. "Talbot got you."

"It splattered off the tree!"

There were several more loud pops as Brian fired into the trees and the enemy shot back. Tucker noticed that Brian squinched his eyes shot when he fired. Crawling forward on his belly, Tucker sighted along the top barrel, then squeezed the trigger. Another pop and a yellow stain appeared high up on the St. Regis guy's chest.

"Well, you're dead now," said Tucker. "Take off your armband and fall down like you're supposed to."

Lowell Perry and the other two men ran off. Talbot tossed the St. Regis guy a can of beer. "Careful when you open it," he said. "It's pretty shook up."

The man popped the beer and it sprayed him. He was wearing camouflage and he wiped his face with his sleeve. Then he looked over at Tucker. He seemed pretty angry. "You shoot to hurt, Tucker. Someone's going to get you."

"I shoot to win," said Tucker, turning his back to the man. Talbot was sitting on the ground trying to catch his breath. "Let's go," said Tucker and ran back over the hill. He glanced at Brian, who was trying to keep up. Brian was running flat-footed and stiff-kneed. Drops of sweat rolled down the sides of his face, mixing with the dirt and general mess.

"Let's get moving," said Tucker. "I got a plan."

Ten minutes later Tucker was balancing on his belly on the branch of a red oak. Talbot was up in a maple about twenty feet away. His eyes were shut and he appeared to be sleeping. Brian was down on the ground massaging his calf and slapping at bugs. At least he's not complaining, thought Tucker. On the other hand, he didn't seem to like it. Tucker loved playing paintball, loved setting up ambushes and zapping somebody. At the moment they were about to try the wounded pigeon trick, make the enemy think they were scoring a point, then blow them away. He could hear people shouting from other parts of the woods.

"Hey," Tucker called to Brian, "get ready. Go up the hill a little."

Brian got to his feet and walked slowly up the hill, rubbing his back and dangling his pistol from his right hand. He wore a dark red windbreaker, khaki pants, and looked pretty obvious. Many of the guys wore complete sets of camouflage, boots, one-piece suits, neck and face guards, hats, and then smeared camo paint over any bit of skin that still showed, but not Tucker. Even though his jeans and Levi's jacket made him more visible, they still couldn't get him.

"Hey," shouted Brian, "hey!" He began limping back through the trees toward Tucker and Talbot, dragging one leg and hobbling along.

"He makes a pretty good cripple," said Talbot.

"Be quiet."

Three of the red team came charging over the hill after Brian, who was now directly beneath Tucker's tree. He hobbled away, hopping on one foot. The red players didn't look up, didn't look left or right; all they wanted was to cover Brian with red paint. Tucker and Talbot shot two of them from about fifteen feet, a double pop which made all three yowl in surprise. Brian turned and fired at the third one, but missed. The man started to run back up the hill. Tucker reloaded and recocked his pistol, dropped to the ground and shot the fellow in the neck.

"Yow, that hurts."

The three dead players sat down in the dirt, yanked off their red armbands and looked depressed. Tucker reloaded. In Vietnam, he'd never done any ambushing from a tree. It was too dangerous when the enemy had automatic weapons. They'd spray you right through the leaves.

"You guys are three dead soldiers," said Talbot, climbing down from his tree. "Go back to base and get yourselves a beer." Tucker was already jogging down the hill with Brian a little behind him. Talbot reloaded and ran after them.

"Aren't there any rest periods in this game?" asked Brian.

"What d'you mean?" said Talbot, catching up with him. They were running through a grove of white pine and the ground was spongy with pine needles.

"You know, breaks."

"Sure, man," said Talbot. "You can break an arm, break a leg; there's all the breaks you want."

Tucker stopped at the top of a narrow ravine and waited for Brian and Talbot to catch up. Then he slid down the side on his butt, crossed over a dry creek bed and climbed the farther side, pulling himself up by grabbing the roots which stuck out of the dirt. Brian made a sighing noise, then followed. The woods were silent and Tucker could hear some birds twittering among the leaves. Way off to the left he heard a whole bunch of crows, like they were having a war of their own.

Keeping the ravine at his back, Tucker crawled to the top of the rise and looked over through the maples and white birch. Nobody in sight. "We'll rest up here," he said to Brian. "You go up farther by that big pine and watch for anyone coming over the hill."

Talbot crawled up next to Tucker, then rolled over on his back and put his hands under his head. He shut his eyes. "We need leeches, man. Leeches and elephant grass and swamp and those punji sticks. That's what we need, fuckin' punji sticks to fuck up their feet."

Tucker didn't answer. This wasn't anything like Vietnam. Here there was actual winning and losing and when it was over everyone went home more or less intact. He sat with his back against a poplar, took off his baseball cap and wiped his forehead with it. The bugs started in on him immediately.

Talbot rolled over and sat up, leaning back against the other side of the same tree so he could see if anyone was coming. They sat quietly for a moment, listening. In the distance they heard shouting but none of it was getting closer. After a moment Talbot said, "What'd you find out down in Camden?"

Tucker didn't want to talk about it, mostly because it took his attention off the game, which was dangerous. "There's some stuff coming in like I said."

"And can you get some?"

Even though Phillip had said no, Tucker thought there might be a way. Or maybe he could get Phillip to change his mind. "I'm not sure but maybe I can. Though not half a key." Tucker had four paint pellets left in his pistol. Taking another tube from his ammunition pouch, he discarded the first tube and inserted the second, giving him thirteen pellets in the top barrel and one in the chamber.

"How much can you get?" Talbot was writing his initials in the dirt with the barrel of his paint pistol.

"Maybe a quarter. But it'd be pure. It's never been cut. Are you positive you could sell it in a couple of days?" Tucker listened, almost pointing his ears into the woods. He felt someone was sneaking up on him. It was an itchy kind of feeling like dead leaves under his shirt. He considered changing his CO_2 capsule but decided to wait. Usually a capsule was good for at least two tubes of paint.

Talbot wiped his pistol on his pants leg. He wore camouflage that he used for bow hunting in the fall. Since he owned the game, he should have been referee. But he liked playing too much to stand back and watch, so they played without referees, which often led to sharp words and sometimes fights. "Four days at the most, and if it's pure like you say, then we're talking about forty thousand easy."

That was more than Tucker had supposed. Five, ten or

fifteen thousand for delivering the stuff was one thing, but twenty, forty, sixty thousand meant something else. It meant getting the hell out of here. It was like being given wings. He could make a new life with Sarah or he could just grab Jason and go. Then he froze. He heard the braking of twigs and jumped to his feet.

"Watch out," called Brian, running back toward them. "Here they come."

Tucker looked to see five men with red armbands spread out in a line at the top of the hill. He heard a crashing noise to his left and saw five more men down in the ravine. He fired at the nearest man and missed. "Split up," he shouted.

Talbot took aim from behind a tree and fired as well. He also missed. "They want your ass, Tucker."

But Tucker already knew that. Somebody had planned a little pincer movement, a little ambush just to trap him. Farther ahead where everything was quiet he knew that several more red players were waiting to gun him down. He bounded over the edge of the hill, then into the ravine, leaving Talbot and Brian to escape toward the ridge. One red player started after him. They wouldn't expect him to come this way, right where they seemed strongest. Tucker dodged around a beech tree, then ran back at the red player, distracting him and forcing him to shoot. The pellet struck the side of the ravine. The man frantically tried to reload, but jammed the pellet so it broke within the barrel. Red paint oozed out over his hand.

Tucker trotted up to him. "Where do you want it?" he asked. The man looked angry and scared at the same time. He too wore camouflage. It hadn't helped much.

"In my back, asshole."

Tucker shot the man in the chest, high up so paint splattered onto his face. The man shouted and stumbled back. Tucker then scrambled out the farther side of the ravine. This was the part he liked, the part when the enemy thought they had him and once again he got away.

Brian lay on his stomach in a field trying to make himself invisible. His feet hurt, his legs hurt, his hands and face were scratched. He had grass under his shirt and a bug was crawling up his leg, a big bug, maybe a grasshopper. Talbot was lying nearby. He had just told Brian, "Don't think about them. Think you're a log. If you think it hard enough, then you'll be one."

Brian thought that was crazy. Whoever heard of a log wearing a dark red windbreaker. He was glad his wife couldn't see him. He'd never hear the end of it. And rightly too. He thought he was behaving like a fool. About twenty yards away a whole bunch of red players were strung out in a line and were coming toward them. Brian had already seen them shoot half a dozen yellow players and he was afraid he'd be next. He was hot. He was thirsty. He wanted to give up. Last night he'd worked a pickup crew, loading twenty-two thousand pullets, and he hadn't gotten home until four. Then he'd gone out to haul traps. He wanted to stand up and surrender and maybe they'd let him go home so he could sleep. But he didn't want Tucker mad at him. God knows where Tucker had gone. He'd run off by himself. Ditched him, just like he used to whenever he had a girl or a chance at a six-pack or anything which he thought too exciting or outlawish for Brian to take part in. And now all these damn red players were going to get him.

It was the fact that it was a game that Brian didn't like. If these guys were after him, then why was he messing around with a toy gun? Why not just stand up, take off his goggles and beat the shit out of them? Brian was good at fighting. He had no doubt that he could half cripple three or four of these guys before they took him down. But Tucker had said he couldn't hit anybody. What was the point of having a war if you couldn't fight? All these rules were a nuisance, they kept it from being real. Football was the only game Brian liked, maybe baseball too. But this paintball stuff, it wasn't anything. It was just fooling around.

Talbot jumped to his feet, fired, then took off toward the woods. "Run," he shouted. He was bent over and ran in a zigzag pattern.

Brian ran after him. He didn't bother shooting and he didn't bother bending over. Not only that but he ran straight as an arrow. He figured he hadn't done this much running for fifteen years, maybe more. He could hear shouting behind him and recognized Lowell Perry's voice. Too bad Lowell was on the other team. Maybe he could surrender to him.

Ahead was a line of birches. They were on an open part of Mt. Waldo and off to the south Brian caught a glimpse of the bay. To his left was the Penobscot River heading up toward Winterport. Brian ran after Talbot's back. When they were about fifteen feet from the trees, Talbot shouted. Brian looked and saw about five red players running toward them. He thought of shooting, then decided why bother?

"Oh, shit, I'm hit," said Talbot, dropping to the ground.

Brian fell and lay still, pretending he'd been hit as well. He lay on his stomach, breathing heavily. The muscles in his thighs felt beaten and stretched. Maybe he could shoot someone when they got close, but his pellets kept breaking when he tried to reload and now his whole pistol was gummy and blotched with yellow paint. Maybe they'd be good guys and leave him alone. Or maybe they'd shoot him someplace simple like on the heel of his shoe, then he could go back to base like going to heaven.

Talbot took off his goggles and rubbed his forehead. "What a bummer. My own goddamn game and I get blown away." There was a splash of red paint in his black beard.

"Capture the other one," someone shouted. "Don't shoot him."

Just as Brian was wondering what this meant, two guys jumped on him and yanked his pistol from his hand.

"Hey," he shouted. This was playing too rough. One of the guys pushed his face into the grass so he got dirt in his mouth. Then his arm was twisted behind him and he was pulled to his feet. Surrounding him, the red players looked like a private army with their camouflage suits and camo paint on their faces.

"Hey, what are you doing?" said Brian. "That hurts." He tried to pull free and the man wrapped an arm around his neck, yanking him back so he choked. He started to reach back so he could flip the guy over his head. He figured it would take two seconds to break his arm. But again Brian stopped himself. It was against the rules to hurt anyone. This was supposed to be fun. About fifteen red players walked toward them from several directions. Brian recognized some, but most were strangers. He knew their leader, however, Frankie Bottoms, who was a carpenter out in Brooks and who used to date Brian's younger sister before she moved down to Bath.

Frankie walked up and jabbed his paint pistol in Brian's stomach. "Where's Tucker?" he demanded.

Two men started tying Brian's hands, pulling the ropes tight. He saw Lowell perry watching him from a few yards away.

"I don't know," said Brian. "Cut it out. Those ropes hurt." Since none of this was serious, he didn't like getting angry, but he felt irritated with Tucker for getting him involved with these crazy people.

"Tough shit," said Frankie. A couple of men were grinning. They looked pleased with themselves.

"He's probably watching us from the tree line," said Perry. Several men turned to look. Brian looked too but he couldn't see anything.

"Lowell," he said, "tell 'em these ropes hurt." There was

sweat running into Brian's eyes. He tried to wipe his face on his shoulder but it wouldn't reach. He felt depressed that he couldn't kick Frankie Bottoms in the balls.

Perry raised his hands to indicate helplessness. "I can't, Brian, I'm on the other side."

"You're lucky we didn't kill you," said Frankie, giving him another poke. He was a thick man with a thick neck and the solid rectangular shape of a brick. He too wore camouflage which covered everything except a large handlebar mustache that must have taken a lot of special attention.

"Come on you guys," said Talbot, getting to his feet. "You can't just drag him off. It's against the rules."

"Shut up," said Frankie. "You're dead."

Several men laughed and pointed their pistols at Talbot, who raised a hand to shield his face. "Yeah, but it's still my game," he said.

"Hey," said Frankie, "you're the one who said we don't need referees."

"What are you going to do with him?" asked Perry, lighting a cigarette. Off in the woods Brian heard the squawk of a pheasant. He looked from Perry to Frankie Bottoms. A mosquito landed on Brian's cheek. He tried unsuccessfully to blow at it.

Frankie stuck his paint pistol in its canvas holster. "He's bait, man. We're going to catch ourselves a Tucker."

He took Brian's left arm and another man took his right. Then they led him toward the woods. The other red players trailed after them, followed by Talbot, whose camouflage suit had a big red paint stain on the chest. A couple of the men were drinking beer. They were joking and acted like they had already won. There was no breeze anywhere and the sun baked the sweat on Brian's face.

They led Brian to a clearing a couple of hundred yards into the trees. There was an old cellar hole and even a couple of gravestones. By the cellar hole was a gnarled oak. From it flew the red team's flag which was also red and had a picture of a black cat. Two men were on guard nearby, one of them sitting on three stone steps that led nowhere. Between them was a blue Coleman cooler filled with beer.

"String him up," said Frankie.

Brian's right hand was freed, then the rope was thrown over the branch of the oak. At first he thought they were really going to hang him. Everyone was behaving crazily, even his friends, even Tucker and Lowell Perry. Brian imagined the police going to his house to tell Margaret he'd been killed. She'd been angry that he had broken their date to the Bangor Mall to go off with Tucker. If he got hurt, she'd say he deserved it.

But they didn't mean to hang Brian by his neck but by his hands, and shortly he was dangling from the limb with his feet just touching the ground. He could barely support himself on tiptoe. His wrists hurt and his arms felt stretched. He was surprised at how angry they seemed and couldn't believe they were doing this just because he was Tucker's friend. Even though he had spent his life in Belfast, Brian didn't know many of these men. They weren't local, they hadn't been born here. Some had come over from Bucksport and apparently worked for the paper company, St. Regis, but others were like Talbot—guys who'd built their own houses somewhere in the woods. There were so many houses for sale throughout the county that Brian couldn't see the point in building one. He slipped and fell against the ropes, then got his toes back on the ground again.

"Let me go," he said. "You're hurting me." Six men sat on the ground around him drinking beer and smoking. Several had taken off their goggles, which was against the rules. A few players were hiding either in the cellar hole or by the trees. Others had gone off to find the yellow team's flag.

Frankie lay on his back in the grass, supporting himself on

his elbows. He wore tinted skiing goggles and looked sinister. At the moment, he looked pleased with himself. "Call for Tucker," he said. "Just shout his name."

"No," said Brian. He saw Talbot sitting on a broken wagon axle trying to comb the red paint from his beard. He was frowning and seemed angry.

"Shout his name," said Frankie, sitting up cross-legged.

"No. Let me down!" He was mad that they believed he'd betray Tucker so easily. It made the pain go away a little just thinking about it.

"It's going to get worse, man," said Frankie. He raised his pistol and pointed it at Brian, then he lowered it, pointing it at Brian's gym shoes. There was a popping noise and a paint pellet hit Brian's foot. It stung a little, but not much. He jumped up, swinging on the branch and yanking his arms.

"Hey, you're messing up my shoes."

"Call for Tucker," said Frankie.

"No! Lowell, tell 'em to let me go."

Perry sat down and began scratching his neck. "Why don't you shout for Tucker? He won't come anyway."

"Come on, fellas, let me go." Brian didn't like how serious this was getting. He again looked at Talbot. Why didn't he stop it? Brian hardly ever got angry. He was barely angry now, but he stared at the men's faces and tried to make sure he'd remember them. Frankie Bottoms, for instance. The next time Brian saw him, he'd give him a belt in the mouth.

Another guy aimed at Brian's feet and fired. He missed but a third man fired and hit him. Then a fourth hit him and laughed. It didn't hurt much but he could feel his socks wet from the paint. Then a fifth shot hit him as Brian hopped and danced. Now several men were laughing. Another fired and missed. Brian's feet, even his shins were covered with red paint.

"Call for Tucker and we'll stop," said Frankie.

"No," said Brian, "you can't make me."

"Then you're in for a little pain," said Frankie. Removing the tube of paint from his pistol, he rummaged around in the grass until he found an acorn which he slipped into the barrel. He aimed at Brian's feet and fired.

"Yow!" cried Brian. It felt like somebody had kicked him. Men were looking at him as if wondering how he'd react. Then another red player removed his paint tube and replaced it with an acorn.

"Hey," shouted Talbot, "you could hurt him."

"Then why doesn't he call for Tucker?" said Frankie.

A red player fired an acorn at Brian and missed. Then another fired and hit him. It hurt a lot, like being hit with a hammer. Brian kept jumping and swinging his feet as several other players removed their paint tubes and began looking for acorns. Another acorn hit him and Brian yelped. He was sure they were breaking the skin. Again he felt deserted by Tucker. In high school Brian had sometimes imagined great roles for Tucker, for example that he was an exiled prince and Brian was helping him to regain his rightful kingdom. But here in this fool game Brian was forced to play the victim while Tucker was seemingly indifferent to his sufferings.

"He's not going to show up," said Lowell Perry. "He's going to let you hang there. Say where we can find him."

But suddenly Tucker was there, running among them. From the woods, from the cellar hole, Brian hadn't seen him and neither had the others. Suddenly he was there. He had his paint pistol in one hand and a branch in the other. One of the red players turned toward him, meaning to shoot, and Tucker clubbed the pistol out of his hand. Men were jumping to their feet. Quite a few had unloaded their pistols to look for acorns and now they were hurriedly trying to put their paint tubes back again. Some had also taken off their goggles. Tucker shot one of the players in the face. The man shouted and began rubbing at his eyes. Tucker was running fast, zigzagging and silent. He was right there, swinging that stick, making people duck, loading and firing again as the red players struggled with their pistols, tried to shield their faces or just hide. Some other player was trying to shoot and Talbot knocked him down, then pretended to apologize. It was all happening fast. Lowell Perry was trying to get a shot and Tucker backhanded him with the branch, smacking Perry across the head so he cried out. People were yelling. Several players fired and missed. One red player accidentally shot another red player in the leg and the man fired back at him.

Tucker was running around the tree toward Frankie, who was trying to get the paint tube back into his pistol. Cocking his pistol, Frankie aimed at Tucker, who abruptly threw the branch at his head, making him duck. And before Frankie could turn again, Tucker had tackled him, knocking him down. It was hard for Brian to see, half dancing and dangling from his branch. Tucker had shoved the barrel of his paint pistol into Frankie's mouth while pinning him in the grass with his elbow across his throat. Another player aimed his paint pistol at Tucker and Pete Talbot grabbed his arm.

"Cut him loose," shouted Tucker, "or this man's dead. I mean really dead. I'll shoot a gob of paint into his fuckin' lungs."

"Tucker, it's a game," shouted someone. The red players looked mad but no one did anything. Brian tried to keep his toes touching the ground so he wouldn't swing back and forth. Some yellow players were coming out of the woods.

Tucker shoved the pistol farther into Frankie's mouth. He was making awful choking noises and wriggling as Tucker crawled around to sit on his chest. "Cut him down or you'll carry this fucker down the mountainside so full of paint he'll never breathe again."

"Let him go, Tucker, you're hurting him."

Lowell Perry was sitting up rubbing his head. Nobody knew what to do. They had lowered their pistols and were looking at one another. It seemed they all thought Tucker was crazy and were scared what would happen next. Back in the woods dozens of crows were cawing wildly.

Tucker was crouched on Frankie's chest with his knees under Frankie's armpits. One hand was on Frankie's throat and the other was shoving the pistol. Frankie was flapping his arms against the grass, afraid to touch Tucker, afraid he might shoot.

"You want this asshole dead? Now! Now! Do as I say!"

Jimmy Peters tossed his pistol on the ground by one of the gravestones and a second man did the same. Then more. Talbot started to gather them up, wiping them off on his camouflage suit. Perry was still rubbing his head. Several other players, both yellow and red, had come out of the trees and were standing around, not knowing what to make of it. One of the St. Regis workers took a buck knife from his belt and cut the ropes tying Brian's wrists. Brian dropped to his knees. There were red welts around his wrists and he rubbed at them. His ankles were a mess of red paint and bruises. He looked around for someone to hit, but it seemed too late for that.

Tucker pulled the pistol a little way out of Frankie's mouth. "You surrender?"

Frankie tried to struggle free but couldn't. Tucker still had one hand on his throat. "This is against the rules, Tucker."

"Fuck your rules. You surrender or you want a gob of paint in your gut?" He grabbed Frankie's chin with one hand and shoved the double barrel of the pistol back into his mouth. Brian heard it click against Frankie's teeth. "You shouldn't of strung him up like that," said Tucker.

Frankie was garbling something, arching his back and trying to twist away. Tucker pulled the pistol out of his mouth. "Surrender, surrender!" shouted Frankie.

Tucker scrambled to his feet, giving Frankie a little kick in the ribs. The red players looked furious but nobody had the nerve to do anything. Anyway the game was over. Talbot kept grinning, as he walked from player to player, taking their pistols.

Tucker went to the oak tree and yanked down the red flag. He threw it at Frankie. "Well all right then, asshole. You lost!"

eight

Stiff breeze, a few whitecaps, no clouds, it was the sort of
Sunday afternoon in August that people come to Maine for,
temperature in the mid-seventies, endless blue sky. From the
deck of the _Margaret_ more than a hundred sailboats could be
counted between Isleboro and Castine, Sears Island and Temple Heights. To the east lay the turtle's hump of Blue Hill
and, closer, the oil storage tanks in Searsport and the three
hoists at Sprague Docks; to the west was Belfast Bay and the
clutter of boats in the harbor, work boats mostly, as well as
two tugs and a half dozen powerboats. South was the channel
to the open ocean between Saturday Cove and Isleboro, with
Ram and Seal islands. Gulls swooped and dove, while over by
Bayside a flock of ducks flapped westward in a ragged V.

Tucker saw none of this. He was standing by the wheel of
the _Margaret_ kicking the bulkhead with his sneaker.

"Dumb machine, dumb machine," he kept saying. The
Margaret had stalled and was gently rocking back and forth.

Behind him, sitting on a lobster pot in the stern, Cindy
made a _tsk-tsk_ noise. "I thought you told me you could run
this," she said. She wore dark blue shorts, a blue halter top

121

and looked very pretty, like something spread upon a cracker, Tucker had thought earlier. The breeze was scattering her blond hair around her face. Rooster was sitting at her feet. He had a clean red bandanna around his neck and looked pleased with himself.

At the moment, Tucker hardly thought of Cindy as he pushed the starter button, shoved the throttle back and forth and fiddled with the hand choke. He glanced at her, making an exaggerated grimace, then went back to jamming his thumb at the starter. Even when he'd had it going, he'd been unable to steer the boat in a straight line. The whole thing was nothing but trouble. Twice he'd been badly goosed by the revolving drum on the pot hauler. There seemed no way to turn the damn thing off.

"Brian says it's easy to run," said Cindy mockingly. "He's even let me do it. You just have to be patient."

Tucker didn't look at her. The choke was all the way out and he pushed it in again. The starter continued its mechanical growl. "I don't like machines and machines don't like me. It's a racial thing." He hadn't meant for Cindy to come along but she had asked. Although he had little sexual interest in her, she was cute and the more he saw of her the cuter she got.

"Brian says it's like a woman. You have to be gentle."

"I spank my women." The engine sputtered, then died. He kept pushing the starter. "Shit," said Tucker. Over toward Northport a Starcraft powerboat was pulling a water skier in a wetsuit.

"Now you flooded it," said Cindy. She was half stern, half teasing. Although she was flirting, Tucker knew it didn't mean much, that for adolescents it was a form of practice, like puppies pretending to quarrel. On the other hand, she was seventeen and when Tucker was seventeen he'd had several girls.

"If you're so smart, then fix it," said Tucker. He turned to face her. With her head tilted to one side, she was gently tugging at Rooster's ears as the dog tried to lick her hand. Her belly between her shorts and the bottom of her halter top was bronze and soft looking. Tucker went back to poking the starter. A large herring gull perched on the boom of the pot hauler said, *"Kee-ow, kee-ow."*

"Nobody can do anything now," said Cindy "We've got to wait."

Tucker gave the bulkhead another kick for good measure. The paint pistol he'd gotten from Pete Talbot was stuck in his belt. He yanked it out, cocked it and sighted down the barrel at the herring gull which chose that moment to depart. Tucker fired and missed. *"Pow, pow, pow,"* he said.

"You like guns?" asked Cindy.

"This is my pistol. My gun is for fun." Tucker reloaded the pistol and stuck it back in his belt.

"Brian said you saved his life yesterday."

"Only metaphorically." Tucker glanced at the starter but decided to let it sit for a bit.

"How come you talk so funny?" asked Cindy. It seemed a serious question. She raised her arms and linked her fingers behind her head, lifting her breasts and flattening her stomach.

"Because I used to be a schoolteacher. How come you look so cute?"

Cindy smiled and recrossed her arms. "What do you call a deer with no eyes?"

"Is this a joke?"

"No idea?"

A can of Budweiser rested on the console and Tucker took a drink. "Beats me," he said.

"That's the answer," said Cindy, clapping her hands.

"What, a 'beats me' ?"

"No, a 'no-eyed deer.' Get it? *No idea.*" She looked pleased with herself and started out across the water toward Belfast, which from this distance was a blur of red brick buildings and white spires.

"Jesus," said Tucker, finishing the beer. She's a child, he told himself, a nice child, a tasty looking child, but still a child. He guessed she'd been about one year old when he was graduating from high school. Tucker liked that. It meant she didn't know shit.

Tucker's tone had irritated Cindy. "You know, if you want to get that engine started, you can take out the spark plugs and dry them off."

Tucker opened the cabin door and looked in at the engine. It smelled of gasoline. Except for the mainfold, it seemed pretty much like a regular engine. He had never been good with cars, never liked mucking with them. He made out three spark-plug boots down by the valve cover. It seemed complicated.

"Maybe if I just leave the door open, the breeze will dry 'em off," he said.

Cindy made a serious face, then grinned. "Maybe. But if you plan to sit here long, then you better drop the forward anchor so we don't wind up on the ledges."

"What's the forward anchor?" Tucker asked, looking around. He knew there'd been a good reason why he'd never spent any time on boats.

"It's that anchor on the bow. You want me to do it?"

"I guess I can do it all right." He came out of the shelter and climbed up on the gunwales on the port side, holding tightly to the shelter roof. Then he walked along the side of the cabin to the foredeck. He considered what it would be like falling into Penobscot Bay. Cold. Reaching the anchor, he freed it from the cleat, pushed it over and felt a slight sense of accomplishment as it splashed into the water. Then he made his way back. Rooster jumped up on him, placing his paws on his chest as if welcoming his safe return.

"I don't know why Brian does all this shit," said Tucker, half joking.

"He needs the money," said Cindy.

"How come he's broke? Does he have a mistress or something?"

Cindy laughed, then looked embarrassed. "Things just cost a lot, that's all. We always need money."

"Why doesn't he get another job?"

"There aren't any. Besides, he's already got a good job. It just doesn't pay much."

Tucker took another beer from the Styrofoam cooler on the deck of the cockpit. He offered it to Cindy. "You want a beer?"

"Just a sip."

Tucker cracked the tab and handed it to her. She took a drink and started to cough. Then she handed him the can. There was lipstick on the rim. He looked at it, then took a drink. He loved beer. He could drink it forever.

"Brian said you were in Vietnam," said Cindy. "What'd you do over there?"

"The usual stuff."

"You kill anyone?"

Tucker took another drink. He didn't like talking about Vietnam with people who knew nothing about it. "If I did, they didn't tell me." Another seagull flew slowly across the bow and over the cabin. Tucker pulled the paint pistol from his belt, cocked it, aimed and fired. Again he missed.

"Fuck, I almost got him."

"What was it like over there?" persisted Cindy. She had moved forward and stood with her hand on the yellow davit of the pot hauler. The sun was hot and there were drops of perspiration on her belly. Tucker imagined touching his tongue to them.

"It was odd," he said. He realized he should have brought some soda for her.

"I mean what was it really like?"

"Really odd." Tucker reloaded the paint pistol.

Cindy walked to the Styrofoam cooler, took out the remaining four cans of the six-pack and held them over the side of the boat. "You want to see these disappear?" she said.

Tucker felt pleased with her. He liked how she tried to get her own way. "What're you doing, writing a term paper or something? It was like sailing."

Cindy continued to hold the cans of beer over the water. "Is that another joke?"

"Not particularly. I got a friend in Camden who hates sailing. He says he's bored most of the time and scared shitless the rest. Vietnam was like that."

Cindy hesitated, then put the beer back in the cooler and squinted up at Tucker, who stood between her and the sun. "Lowell Perry says it was easy. He spent his time learning how to surf."

"Lowell Perry's a twerp," said Tucker. That wasn't the right word. Thinking of Perry, whom he'd disliked nearly all his life, it seemed he was someone who never did anything without first thinking what he would gain from it, as if each action had its price. Tucker glanced around for more seagulls but there were none within range. He found himself thinking about Vietnam. It felt both close and far away at the same time. "I don't know," he said, returning to Cindy's question. "We flew around in helicopters and went out on patrol and frightened a lot of people and got bit by bugs and sometimes we got shot at and sometimes we shot back, though you hardly saw anyone."

"But what did it feel like?" Cindy sat up on the washboard with one hand on the davit. The breeze kept blowing her hair around her face so that the ends flicked at her eyes and mouth. She brushed her hair away and looked at Tucker.

"Feel like?" said Tucker. As he spoke he had the physical memory of standing up to his chest in warm muddy water supporting his rifle, keeping it dry, standing for hour after hour, trying to peer through the darkness, feeling the bugs bite him, the leeches attaching themselves to his flesh, him and half a dozen other guys all dressed in black pajamas, waiting for Charlie to come by on a little path, finally giving it up after the whole night had passed.

Tucker drank some more beer, then folded the can into a metallic wedge. "You just found yourself doing stuff you never thought you'd do," he said. "I mean, you grow up and play pretty fair and think you're a pretty good kid and you hate the bullies and the cheats. Then you go someplace and suddenly you're the bully and the cheat. You know, I once shot a water buffalo, just out of meanness and spite. Cut its face off with my M-16. I told myself it was fixing to charge but it was just chomping grass. This woman ran out and she cried and cried. She was about four feet tall. I was just a piece of bad luck that had fallen into her life." He saw the woman for a moment—a brown leathery face that reminded him of those pictures of old Germans or Danes who had been dug up in some bog in Europe. Bog people, they were called. That's what the old woman had looked like, a bog person.

"Are you sorry you went?" asked Cindy. She held a hand to her forehead and peered under it to keep from looking into the sun. He thought she seemed concerned, not quite sympathetic but ready to be sympathetic.

"It just happened," said Tucker. "I even wanted to go because I figured it would tell me about myself, tell me whether I was tough or a coward or incompetent." He took another beer from the cooler. "Man, I thought that was the adult world. Well, going over there was just a piece of bad luck, like my shooting the gook's water buffalo. I was back here in the States doing nothing and I wanted to fly helicopters, so I signed up for three years and then washed out of preflight school. After that I was just a grunt."

"You sound like you feel sorry for yourself," said Cindy.

The breeze was still whipping her hair across her face. Was she teasing him? He didn't particularly care. Her halter top was like a blue bandanna, exactly matching the red bandanna around Rooster's neck. She had said it made them cousins. Staring at the blue bandanna, Tucker wanted to take it off, just yank it away. He stopped thinking about it. Did he feel sorry for himself? He didn't know.

"Maybe I am, maybe not. I can never tell. I think about what went on over there and the stuff I saw and did and it amazes me. I mean, it was horrible and horrible things happened. And I look around me now, you know, at the bay and everything, and I think how beautiful it is but it doesn't seem real." He paused and squinted his eyes at the water so that it shimmered back at him. "Sometimes I think the real world was over there and this is the dream," he continued. "You ever have those dreams where you like the dream but you know it's a dream and you're afraid you'll wake up? Well, I'm afraid I'll wake up."

"You mean because it was so violent?"

Apart from wanting her body, it occurred to Tucker that he liked Cindy. She was brand new. He wished he could take her into himself, absorb her freshness.

"Not just violent," he said, "although the violence was part of it. But it was strange and humiliating and frightening. Sometimes it was even fun. I mean, it can be fun running around with rifles and shooting at people. Then you catch yourself later and say, 'I was out there trying to kill people. How can that be fun?' So you lie to yourself and say the fucking gooks deserved it and talk about the terrible stuff they've done which isn't the point. I mean, so what if they're scum? You're scum too. No, before I got there I had this whole idea what it would be like. Like a whole big story. Well, it wasn't like that. It was something bigger and much different. But it's as if there's a space between what I thought it'd be like and what it was really like. And right now it feels as if

I'm stuck in that space, that's where I'm living, where I'm spending all my time."

Tucker became aware of the boat rocking beneath his feet as it drifted around its anchor. He drank some beer, letting the beer wash around in his mouth before he swallowed. He had a sense of fragility and it frightened him.

Cindy looked out at the water. "That's too complicated for me," she said. A tugboat was steaming out of Belfast harbor toward Searsport.

"Yeah, me too."

"What about girls?" said Cindy more brightly.

"What d'you mean?"

"Did you have girlfriends over there?"

Tucker thought of the bargirls, the hookers, the girls that little kids tried to sell you. "Well, you know, whores."

Cindy looked shocked, but not really. She opened her eyes wide. They were blue with little flecks of gold. "You really went to whores?"

Tucker laughed. He decided to startle her a little. "Sure. You'd go into a bar in Saigon or someplace for a beer and a hand job. I even caught the clap."

Cindy made a squealing noise, but she was still playing. "That's disgusting. Weren't there any glamorous women, you know, mysterious ones?"

Tucker noticed the red tugboat approaching them. Then he looked at Cindy again. Like something on a cracker, he repeated to himself.

"No, there were no glamorous girls for us grunts. Though I once met a whore who didn't have any nipples." He paused and looked at Cindy's breasts. He could just make out the outline of her nipples under the blue fabric of the halter top. She was staring at him. "She'd cheated on her pimp," continued Tucker, "and had her nipples removed. And they weren't cut off either. They were bitten off."

All that was a lie, although Tucker knew worse stories. It

struck him that no matter how bad a story he could imagine, he could remember a more terrible one which had taken place.

Cindy put a hand over her mouth. "How awful," she said.

Tucker took a step toward her, but slowly, giving her the chance to move back if she wanted. She didn't move.

"Terrible," said Tucker. "How'd you like that to happen to you?"

Lifting his left hand, he touched his fingers to the side of her breast. She knew what he was doing, she could have stopped him if she didn't like it. She kept her hands at her sides and stared into his face, still slightly open-mouthed but now from a kind of breathlessness and surprise. He continued to touch her breast, moving forward so that his whole hand covered it, touching it with more firmness, then harder.

Lowell Perry stood in the pilot house of the *Douglas F.*, one of the two tugboats usually docked in Belfast. He held a pair of binoculars to his eyes and was fiddling with the central focusing drive, getting a sharp image of the *Margaret*.

Behind him at the wheel, Jimmy Hoblock watched him curiously. "What's so interesting out there?"

Perry could see Cindy's back and Tucker standing directly in front of her, almost on top of her it seemed. That damn black dog was with them too. "I'm watching a rat trying to eat a little bird," he said.

Jimmy didn't know what in the hell he was talking about. "What's a rat doing out on the water?"

Perry felt knotted inside. He wished he could see better, see what Tucker was doing to Cindy. He wished he had a rifle, a thirty-ought-six. He'd shoot the top of that fucker's head off. "That's what I'd like to know," he said.

With a small fork, Phillip jabbed the mussel, extricated it from its black shell and dipped it in the wine and garlic broth.

Then he looked at it—orange and vaginal. How female it seemed. The word was from the Latin: little mouse. He slipped it into his mouth, letting it brush across his lips.

Across the table, Tucker was watching him with disgust as he chewed a piece of steak. The trouble with Tucker, thought Phillip, was that he wouldn't try anything new. He turned his whole life into a fortress and anything outside became the enemy. One had to grow. Living as he did, Tucker seemed to be paring down his life to what he could easily defend. But you can't live by saying no, thought Phillip. You had to go out and engage the world. You had to take chances.

He sipped his wine (Tucker was drinking beer), then tried to catch the eye of the waitress to get more bread for Tucker. They were having dinner at the Waterfront Restaurant in Camden. It was Sunday evening and they were surrounded by well-dressed men and women eating expensive meals. Tucker was wearing what Phillip thought of as his lumberjack outfit— jeans and a plaid shirt. He hadn't shaved and had even wanted to bring his dog into the restaurant. Most likely he'd have been just as glad to eat at McDonald's. Also Phillip wasn't pleased with how Tucker kept eyeing the female help, as if he wanted to add them to his meal. It showed a predatory nature. Not that Phillip objected to the predatory but it seemed counterproductive to display one's desires so openly. For that matter, much of Tucker was display: the way he dressed and spoke and moved his arms and heaved himself around in his chair, as if he was constantly saying fuck you and didn't care who knew it. Phillip guessed this particular display was far more important to Tucker than love or money or good times. Once again, he wondered if it was smart to include Tucker in his plans. But who else could he use? Besides, he wanted to help Tucker, help him out of the mess he was in.

Phillip leaned across the table. "The trouble is, you can't run the boat. I mean, you might be able to doodle around the bay, but you can't take a boat out to a specific place at a specific time. You'll have to find someone else to run the boat and you'll have to find him fast. We've got two ships coming up the coast and we've only got a few days to get this arranged."

Tucker glanced around, seemingly uncomfortable that someone might overhear, but at the nearest table, six feet away, two young men were analyzing a tennis game, while their wives or female companions were discussing suntan oils. "What if I can't find anyone?" asked Tucker.

Phillip speared another mussel, being careful not to splash the broth on his cream-colored linen jacket. "I guess it depends on how much you want the money. What about this friend with the lobster boat? Wouldn't he do it?"

"I don't know if I want to get him involved."

Phillip felt impatient. It seemed he'd been helping Tucker for years and now that Tucker had a chance to make real money, he was dragging his feet. Tucker wasn't realistic enough. He wasn't pragmatic. Phillip asked himself what in fact he liked about his friend. At first he thought it was Tucker's sincerity, but it wasn't that. After all, Tucker was a happy liar. Yet there was a way that the world sat uncomfortably on Tucker's shoulders. Phillip had a mental image of a boa constrictor that had eaten a small pig, a snake with a great swelling in the middle. That was Tucker's relationship to the world but he could neither digest it nor puke it back up. It was Tucker's vulnerability that Phillip liked, the fact that he was vulnerable without realizing it. Indeed, Tucker imagined he was just the opposite—tough and ready to do battle with his little toy sword.

"What's there to worry about?" asked Phillip soothingly. "As long as you keep your mouth shut and don't attract attention, who's to know anything? All you have to do is follow directions and not do anything stupid."

Tucker wiped his mouth with his napkin, took another chunk of bread, started to bite into it, then didn't. "Who are you working for?"

"What do you mean?"

"Who's running the operation?" Tucker lowered his voice and leaned across the table. "I mean, are they gangsters or locals or college boys? How much do they know?"

"They're businessmen, although I doubt they have college degrees. I thought we agreed not to discuss that."

The freighter would arrive in a week, maybe less. If Tucker refused to do the pickup, then Phillip would have to paddle out to the freighter in a canoe, even though he couldn't swim and hated the water. But if he didn't then Marston would beat the shit out of him.

Tucker again attacked his food. Steak, baked potato, an ear of corn—the American specials. "I was just curious," he said.

Phillip tried to appear genial and comforting. "I've been working for them for a couple of years. But just on the selling end, you understand."

"So this is a kind of promotion?"

"I guess you could call it that." Especially since Searsport was no longer available, Phillip told himself. Again he thought of Marston's ruthlessness. Although perhaps that was the wrong word. Perhaps Marston was just the ultimate pragmatist. "But look, Tucker," added Phillip, "these guys have lots of operations and this is just one of them, a small one. They're not pushovers. They play strictly hardball."

"Me too," said Tucker, who was concentrating on cutting his steak.

Phillip reached out his fork and tapped Tucker's hand. It didn't seem that Tucker fully comprehended the seriousness of his message.

"It's not the Customs people you got to watch," said Phillip. "It's the guys we work for. It's like they own us. They say, 'Jump through hoops' and we jump. That's why they give us money. You just got to play it straight, that's all."

———

The islands seen from Mt. Battie looked like the backs of surfacing whales, while the dozens of sailboats resembled white moths against a blue window. Tucker liked how manageable it seemed, as if he could take one island and put it here, put another over there. To the east was the ragged line of Isleboro and beyond it was the more even line of Castine—these horizons defined his world, as if what lay beyond were stories, bad stories. One could deal with this. If you always saw your world from this perspective, thought Tucker, then the bits and pieces wouldn't keep slipping away.

Tucker glanced over at his wife sitting on a rock nearby. She looked bored and was poking at her tennis shoe with a twig. He wished he could make her move back to Brooks, make her be happy and tolerate his—what were they? Idiosyncrasies, eccentricities, foibles? He hated wondering about the big questions—the whys and the whithers. In the same way that he wished he could make his wife do things, he wished he could make himself do things. Be happy, he'd say. Straighten yourself out.

Tucker sat on the ground with his legs outstretched and his hands resting on a red rubber ball. He gave the ball a push, rolling it to Jason who was sitting in a similar fashion about five feet away, looking at his father expectantly. Rooster was sitting near Jason, hoping to be included. He liked all games.

"But what if we go to some third place?" asked Tucker, trying to make a joke out of it. "You don't come to Brooks and I don't come to Camden, but we all go someplace else."

Sarah glanced up. Tucker thought she wanted to believe him but didn't quite have the energy to pull it off. She managed a smile. "What sort of place?"

Jason pushed the ball back and Tucker tossed it up, then rolled it again to his son. "You know, California or Key West or Montana or the Dominican Republic, even Europe—just someplace else."

Sarah stopped smiling and returned to poking her shoe with the twig. Her back was to the ocean. She doesn't care how beautiful it is, thought Tucker.

"But what would we do there?"

Tucker tried to sound enthusiastic. "Just get started again. I'd get a job. You'd see, it'd be great."

"But what could you do?"

Tucker hated her questions. He hated to have doubts thrown up even before they'd even discussed it. What one needed was the attitude, the positive attitude that whatever they did would be all right, that everything would work out just fine.

"I don't know, there's all sorts of stuff. Or I could try something in the Foreign Service. I've always been good at languages."

Sarah broke the twig in half and tossed the pieces into the grass. She wore a yellow polo shirt and green skirt. Around her neck was a thin gold chain that her father had given her for her thirtieth birthday in April. "But we'd need money to get started," she said.

Tucker found himself growing angry. It wasn't a matter of being reasonable; she just didn't trust him. If Jason hadn't been there, he might have tried to get close to her physically, even take her for a walk in the woods. He got to his feet, throwing the ball back at Jason so it bounced over his head and into the weeds. Rooster galloped after it.

"Why'n the hell are you always sticking in these objections? Don't you want to be with me?"

Sarah didn't look up. "I'm not sure. But apart from that none of your ideas are practical."

She raised her head and Tucker was surprised at the intensity of her expression, as if she were trying to lift something very heavy. He wanted to say, hey, it's not that serious, I was only joking, but he didn't know how to talk to her like that.

Sarah crossed her legs Indian fashion and put her hands on her knees. "I mean, I agreed to leave Skowhegan and move to Brooks because I thought you'd know how to build a house and do all those things. But you didn't know it and you didn't like it and you didn't want to learn it. Brooks and Freedom and those places are full of guys with unfinished houses. The voluntary poor. I liked you better as a schoolteacher."

"I'm trying to fix things," said Tucker. "I want us to get back together."

"You just want to take off someplace else. You're like some crazy rocket shooting off any which way. I want a regular home, a regular job. I want Jason to have a regular life."

It seemed to Tucker that her words were accurate and wrong at the same time. He knew there were arguments for his position, he just couldn't think of any. Although unhappy, he was afraid to show it. She'd just take advantage of him. Rooster brought back the ball and dropped it at Tucker's feet. Then he stood back, wagging his tail. Tucker ignored him.

"Maybe I should just take Jason and we'll go off on our own," he said angrily.

"You know I couldn't permit that."

"I could, you know. I could just grab Jason and make a run for it."

Sarah stood up and turned half away from him, looking down at Camden spread out like a toy village. The harbor was curved like a horse's head, while the moored sailboats were like spots of sweat or froth. She turned back to Tucker. The wind was mussing her hair and she smoothed it back with one hand. Jason sat in the grass watching Rooster, who had nosed the ball a few inches closer to Tucker's feet.

"I thought you were going to be serious," she said. "Either you should take some responsibility and get a regular job or we should get divorced. I'm tired of living with my parents and I want to get out of here. I want to go to Boston or New York, go someplace where I can get a job and do things like normal people, like go to concerts and nightclubs and museums."

"And you'd take Jason down there too?"

"Of course. I've already written to friends about it."

She turned away again and Tucker thought she was trying to spot her father's house on the eastern side of the harbor, as if seeing it would make her stronger against him. "Written to them about what?" he asked.

"About finding an apartment and places to work."

She's afraid to look at me, thought Tucker. Jesus, she's just going to pull out. "Fat chance, lady. Jason's my kid. I don't want him disappearing on me."

"I'm his mother. I'd have custody."

She turned back and Tucker was surprised to see that she was on the verge of tears. He couldn't tell if this was a good sign or a bad sign.

"I mean, if you're not going to make up your mind about what you want to do," she continued, "then I'll have to make the decisions myself."

She made a movement toward Jason, and Tucker had the impression that she was going to take him right then, just pack him down to New York in the next few minutes. He jumped forward and scooped Jason up, grabbing him by his arm and startling him. Then he started trotting backward.

"Hey, hey," said Tucker, "maybe I'll make a run for it right now. Catch the baby and his bad daddy."

Sarah took a few steps after him. "Tucker, stop this. We were going to have a serious talk."

She was angry and that pleased him. He wanted to make her as mad as he could. He tickled Jason a little so his mommy could see he was having a good time. Rooster ran after them barking, thinking it was a game.

"I'm done talking," said Tucker. "You're not taking this kid down to some city. No way. We're gonna disappear." He kept backing toward the parking lot, holding Jason to his chest.

"Tucker, I don't want any of your jokes. You're frightening Jason." Sarah carefully enunciated each word.

She thinks I'm nuts, thought Tucker. The realization made him feel lonely and isolated. Okay, let's pretend that we're nuts. Tucker dug his finger into Jason't ribs so that he wriggled and laughed. Rooster kept barking and running around them in circles.

"*Ooo*, the bad daddy's going to get away. The bad daddy's going to take his little boy and we're going to join a circus."

Sarah tried to grab him and Tucker dodged into the parking lot and around a car. A busload of tourists was just filing down the steps of a Greyhound and the lead tourist, an elderly woman, stopped to look at Tucker in surprise. Sarah ran around the car after him as Tucker jogged backward up the sidewalk. He had a sense of defeating her.

"Tucker, let me have him. I'm getting angry."

"We goin' to be the clown's best friends," he said in an exaggerated southern accent. "We goin' to be best buddies to the dancing bear." Tucker dodged around a tree.

"Who's the dancing bear?" said Jason, pressing his face into Tucker's neck.

"He's our pal," answered Tucker, again tickling him so Sarah could see him laugh. "He's the guy that makes it work out all right."

Sarah was still hurrying after them, but she had slowed down and her arms were crossed. "Tucker, give him back. I'm not going to let you see him again."

Tucker was aware of people watching from the parking lot. Not only the people off the bus or standing around the parking cars, but picnickers and hikers who had climbed up the trail from Megunticook Lake.

"Uh, oh, the rube princess is getting angry, baby," said Tucker. "She don't like circus folk. She gonna stick to the tennis set, the Volvo and quiche crowd."

"Dammit, Tucker, I want him right now. You think you can just do what you want anytime you want? I'm tired of being bullied by you."

She ran at him again and he ran around a tree, keeping it between them as she circled it. Rooster kept barking, a cheerful barking. Then Tucker ran up onto a large boulder. Glancing at the parking lot, he considered waving to all the people, but then he saw Lowell Perry watching him from the curb, just watching with no smile, no frown, no sign of emotion. It bothered Tucker to see him. He couldn't understand what he was doing there. Tucker turned and ran toward the monument, a round stone tower about twenty feet high that overlooked Camden and Penobscot Bay.

"Watch out, little boy, the princess is pulling out her power. We better be acrobats and fly into the sky."

Tucker jumped up the three stone steps and through the archway leading to the circular stone staircase. He wished he could actually fly, maybe have one of those little planes built out of plastic bags and bicycle parts. He'd do almost anything to get out of this place where he found himself stuck. How could she threaten to take Jason down to New York? Didn't she know that he loved him? Tucker ran up the staircase. He stepped out on the top of the flagpole and stood back away from the wall, which rose to about waist level. Jason was still laughing. Rooster stood at Tucker's feet, looking up and wagging his tail. Nobody else was up there and for a moment Tucker tried to think he was alone, that he and Jason were the only human beings on Mt. Battie. Then he heard her voice calling from below.

"I want him, Tucker, I'm sick of this stupid behavior!"

Just the tone of her voice cut into him. He thought of the times they'd made love. How could you be that intimate with a person and have it all fall apart?

"Tucker, give him back!"

He looked out toward the bay. The trees going down the mountain looked soft and feathery, while the water looked like blue paper, that blue tissue paper that people wrap presents in.

"Tucker, you'll never see Jason again!"

He'd frighten her. He'd throw a real scare into her. It was like the paintball game: the only way to win was to push the whole mess to the limit. Stepping to the wall, Tucker climbed onto it, still holding Jason. Slowly he lifted his son. He looked down at Sarah thirty feet beneath him, staring up, not believing.

"You want him, lady, then why don't you catch him!"

Sarah screamed, then Jason screamed. Tucker pulled Jason back into his arms. He was aware of about twenty people staring up to where he stood balancing on the wall. He looked out again at the ocean, at all that space. He imagined the blue tissue paper ripping open, making a great dark place that he could fly into. Dumb thoughts, dumb thoughts. He jumped back onto the floor of the tower, then sat down by the flagpole, holding his son tight and rocking back and forth, trying to get him to stop crying. He'd been joking. He wouldn't have dropped him. He kept rocking Jason, then he began to sing a little.

"Hush little baby, don't you cry. Papa's going to buy you a pizza pie. . . ." Rooster pushed between them, licking both their faces.

I've got to get busy, Tucker told himself, I've got to start taking control before the whole business goes bananas.

nine

What Lowell Perry liked about his Camaro was that when he drove fast the car's red hood stretched ahead like a red shovel, as if he could push everything else to the side of the road. With a Corvette, on the other hand, the hood was nearly invisible, being lower down and more sexual. It was like driving your body, like having sex with the highway. Lowell Perry appreciated both effects. If he got that Corvette, he wasn't sure he wanted to sell the Camaro. Some people had lots of cars. Look at Elvis Presley.

Monday afternoon, Lowell Perry analyzed the two cars as he drove back to Belfast from Camden. By the time he passed Clara's Place, however, it seemed that the big difference was that the Corvette amounted to fifteen thousand dollars more automobile and that meant a whole lot of extras. Better get one, he thought, as he turned left at the light. Better get cooking.

Lowell Perry began looking for a place to park. That Tucker Morgan was so crazy that he'd be doing the world a favor to squash him like a bug. In fact, he couldn't see how Tucker had managed to stay alive so long. But it was no punishment just to kill a person. You had to make them hurt first, you had to make them really want to die.

Lowell Perry parked in front of Weaver's Bakery. He had a hankering for something sweet so he strolled inside and bought an eclair. He liked the girls there. He liked to tease them about eating too much of their own stuff and getting fat. As he walked out, eating the eclair, he saw Chuckie Evans drive by on his Kawasaki Eliminator and he waved. He'd kill himself one day on that thing. It seemed madness to drive anything that left you so exposed and Perry imagined saying this to people at Chuckie Evans's funeral. But he liked Chuckie. They'd been as close as two sticks in a Popsicle ever since first grade.

As Lowell Perry waited for the traffic to clear, he wiped a little whipped cream from his bottom lip. Then he crossed the street. There were a lot of tourists around—flatlanders who were so bored with the dumb places they lived that they had to come to Belfast for a good time. Up at the Belfast Plaza, the "L" had fallen off the old sign so it said BE FAST PLAZA, and the other day Lowell Perry had seen some flatlanders getting their picture taken under it, smiling and waving like they were as fast as spit.

Shoving the rest of the eclair into his mouth, Perry turned right up the street toward Kirk's Drugstore. He liked these hot summer days when you could drive around with your windows down listening to the radio. But he also liked it in the fall, once the leaves were gone and the tourists had driven back down south. He liked it when all these people weren't here buying stupid shit and cluttering the streets.

Perry wiped his mouth on his sleeve and entered the drugstore. Cindy was standing by the cosmetics counter. She had just put some purple nail polish on her fingernails and was holding them up to see how they looked. When she saw Lowell, she blushed slightly, then smiled.

Lowell Perry tossed a twenty-dollar bill on the counter in

front of her. "Give me a pack of Camels, will you, Cindy?" Although she had smiled, he knew it wasn't a special smile and that she was doing it just because he was Brian's friend.

She took the pack from the display behind her, put it on the counter, then took Lowell's twenty-dollar bill. "How you been, Lowell?"

"Can't complain." He opened the pack with his teeth and tapped out a cigarette which he offered to Cindy. She shook her head and he stuck the cigarette between his lips, then put the pack in his breast pocket. Taking a Zippo lighter, he brushed it against his designer jeans so it lit, then he held it to the cigarette. He exhaled a little smoke and drew it up through his nose. "Want to go riding later?" he asked.

Cindy handed him his change. "What do you mean?"

Lowell Perry wasn't fooled. He knew she knew what he was talking about. "You know, riding around. I'll buy you an ice cream."

"I'm afraid I'm busy."

Lowell Perry took another drag and tapped some ash onto the floor. "Maybe some other time," he said, looking away.

"Don't you know any girls your own age?"

Glancing back, he realized she was irritated and that surprised him. "Come again?"

"Don't you know any older girls?"

He didn't see that she had any call to be angry. After all, lots of girls would jump at the chance to go riding with him. He leaned across the counter, lowering his voice. "What about Tucker Morgan?" he said. "Is he your age?"

He could see that had gotten to her. He gave her a little smile just to show that he knew what was what, then he turned and strolled out of the drugstore.

Brian stared at Lowell Perry's back, which was enveloped in a black jacket made out of some material that made it look wet. Down each sleeve ran a long red stripe. Brian was standing beneath Perry on the short stairway leading to the control cab of the center hoist on Sprague dock, watching Perry manipulate the long levers sticking up from the floor at his feet. The cab was about five feet by five feet with open windows on three sides so the wind came rushing through it. Perry stood looking down thirty feet at a coal barge that was moored in the slip. The bucket was poised above the hold of the barge, then, as Perry pushed a lever forward and stepped on the left pedal, the bucket descended. The cables slapped and banged against the pulleys. Brian was surprised at how fast it all was. Perry could make five trips a minute from the barge to the hopper just to the right of the cab. It was past nine and dark, and out toward the water Brian could see the red lights of several buoys and the red light at the top of the radio tower at the end of Sears Island. Over toward Isleboro another barge was waiting its turn at the dock. Lowell Perry had called half an hour before, saying he had something important to talk about and Brian had driven right out thinking that he might be in some trouble, but so far it seemed he only wanted to talk about Tucker.

"He was out in your boat, just sitting there," said Perry over his shoulder. "He was there for over an hour."

"Is that why you wanted me to come out here?" Monday night was one of the few nights when neither he nor Margaret was busy and he had been hoping to spend the evening with his wife. Tomorrow night he'd have to work a pickup crew again. "He already told me about it. He flooded the engine. He's lucky he ever got it started." Brian had to raise his voice to speak over the noise.

"What's he want to use your boat for?" asked Perry.

"He just said he wanted to go for a ride."

"He pay the gas?" Perry pulled the lever and the bucket began to rise, carrying a load of coal. Behind Brian the huge wheels began spinning on the old steam engine and the cables rattled as they were wound up on their drums. There was a whoosh of released steam as the bucket paused above the hopper.

"What's it matter?" Brian couldn't see why Lowell was bothering about his. He guessed that he bore a grudge from the paintball game when Tucker had clubbed him. In the window he could barely make out Lowell's reflection, but just the cheekbones and forehead. The eyes seemed gone.

"He ever ask to use it at night?"

"Why would he want to use it at night?"

Perry released the gate on the bucket and the coal tumbled through the hopper and onto the conveyor belt with a roaring clatter. The belt itself made a rumbling whining noise. There was another whoosh of steam. "He might want to pick up something from a ship," said Perry, dropping the bucket back toward the barge. "I told you he was into drugs."

"I can't believe that." But even as Brian said it, he wondered about Tucker's interest in his boat. "Anyway, would it bother you? You been into drugs yourself."

Perry turned around. The interior of the hoist was lit by a weak yellow bulb above Perry's head and it made his thin face look sallow. "It's just that there's two ways to make money from drugs—one's by selling them and the other's by making a deal. I know a guy who made sixty thousand that way, pulled in money four different times. You get twenty-five percent of what they confiscate—their cars, boats, the money they're carrying—and on top of that you can get a reward." As Perry spoke, he tapped his middle finger into the open palm of his left hand.

"You mean a deal with the police?"

Perry turned back and pushed the left lever forward to bring the trolley toward him along the boom as he raised the bucket. "Customs Patrol," he said.

"What makes you think Tucker wants to pick up something

from a ship?'' It occurred to Brian that maybe it was his boat that had interested Tucker all along, not their past friendship or getting to know each other again.

'' 'Cause some people've been smuggling coke in through the docks,'' said Perry. ''They been bringing it up on these Brazilian salt boats. Last time they almost got caught. Coast Guard and Customs went all over the ship with their dogs.''

Brian shifted his weight from one leg to the other. There was no place to sit and nothing to lean against that wouldn't get oil or grease or coal dust on his chinos. ''How d'you know there was anything to be found?'' he asked.

''I know all right.'' Perry released the coal into the hopper, then waited a moment for the noise to subside. ''The thing is, they're still sending up the cocaine. Maybe they know Customs will be waiting and maybe they don't. But if they know, then they gotta offload it someplace out in the water. That means a guy with a boat.''

''But why Tucker?''

''Because I been watching him and he's into it and right now he seems pretty interested in boats.''

''He's my friend.'' For Brian that answer seemed sufficient.

Lowell Perry turned again. Brian's head was about level with Perry's belt buckle. ''This guy I know who made the sixty thousand, the Customs people don't even know his name. He's got a number, that's all, and nobody knows a thing. They been bringing coke in here for over a year. Salt boat comes in. Customs and Immigration do the paperwork. Then at night a couple of whores arrive, you know? They work their way through the crew, servicing these Brazilians. When they leave, one of the whores is carryin' a suitcase.''

''You know a lot about it,'' said Brian.

''I make it my business to know what's going on. The thing is, Customs is wise to the setup. That's why the people who been doin' the smuggling need Tucker.''

"He's still my friend," said Brian. He began to wonder why Perry was telling him this. To protect him? To hurt Tucker? Perry was also his friend, although he didn't feel close like Tucker did. Perry was too hard, he didn't need anyone. Brian and Perry would go fishing or hunting or work on Perry's car but there was always some purpose to what they were doing, some purpose other than spending time together. He asked himself if he trusted Perry and he guessed he did as long as he didn't get between him and something that Lowell Perry wanted.

"You know," said Perry, "when Tucker was out on your boat, he wasn't by himself."

"What d'you mean?"

"Cindy was with him."

It struck Brian that he must mean some other Cindy. "You mean Margaret's sister?"

"Sure. Didn't Tucker tell you?"

Brian stared at Perry's reflection in the glass as Perry pulled one of the levers to raise the bucket of coal. "What's the harm of her going with him?" he asked.

Perry released the gate, then turned again as the coal crashed and rattled down upon the conveyor belt. "Depends what they do," he said. He was trying to smile but it was more of a leer. "Seemed to me like he was feeling her up."

When Tucker danced, he looked like a wooden puppet hanging from a dozen strings—both animated and awkward, as if part of him were standing outside watching him making a monkey of himself. That was why Brian didn't dance, although sometimes he'd slow dance with Margaret. But this rock-and-roll dancing made you look cracked in the head, although certainly Tucker didn't look any more foolish than anyone else jumping up and down and waving their arms at Clara's on this Wednesday night.

Several of the people were men and women who worked under Brian at the plant and he was interested to see this new side of them. It was like seeing them fresh and he realized he'd been wrong not to imagine their lives beyond being tied down to that line—cutting out the craw, pulling the lungs. Dancing in the corner by herself was one woman whose job was to back up the slicer in the blood room, cutting the throats of the chickens that didn't look dead. Usually she wore boots, yellow oilskins and a plastic bonnet and every inch of her was covered with blood, including her face. Brian had done that job once and he couldn't think of any worse, especially since you were stuck in a little passageway at the bottom of the U of the conveyor belt as the chickens screamed and flapped and sent their warm blood flying all over. It was hard to breathe and the smell was terrible. And here was this woman dancing like there was real joy in her life. It made Brian glad to see it.

The song ended and Tucker walked back toward the bar with his arm around the waist of Betty Frazer, a recent divorcee who worked out at the rope factory. She left Tucker, heading for her own table and Tucker gave her a little pat. When he had nearly reached Brian, Clara stuck out an arm to stop him. She was an attractive blond woman in her fifties.

"You behave yourself, Tucker."

Tucker gave her an innocent grin. "I be good as gold, Clara."

"That's what you said last time."

Tucker sat down on the edge of a stool next to Brian and retrieved his beer bottle from the bar. "How come you're not dancing?" he asked.

Brian nodded to some guys who worked under him, then looked back at Tucker, who was trying to balance his beer bottle on his index finger. "I'm not much of a dancer," he said. Brian had agreed to join Tucker at Clara's Place only after Tucker had called him about five times, including once at the plant. Margaret hadn't wanted him to go. Really Brian had at last agreed only because he had something to tell Tucker, but now that they were together he wasn't sure how to begin.

"You dance in the privacy of your home?" asked Tucker. "You and Margaret with your shades drawn?"

Brian didn't find that funny. The band had begun another rock-and-roll song. Brian looked down at his feet, then turned back to Tucker, who was glancing around for another dance partner. "Why didn't you tell me that Cindy was with you out on the boat?"

Tucker glanced back at him. The corners of his mouth were twitching as if he were trying to keep himself looking serious. "Is that what's worrying you? You been quiet as a mouse."

"I want you to stay away from her. She's only seventeen."

Tucker rocked back on his stool, then lifted his beer bottle to his lips. "That's what's nice about her. She's got no past. Everyone else around here is walking wounded."

"She's only a kid," said Brian. "She's in high school." He had to practically shout because the music was so loud.

"She looks pretty grown up," said Tucker.

"That's just play acting. She doesn't know anything." Brian leaned forward, almost touching Tucker's arm. Out on the dance floor, people were carrying on like they'd never have to work again.

"I like her," said Tucker. "I like her a lot."

He seemed to mean it, which surprised Brian, but it didn't make any difference. "Leave her alone," he said.

"Okay, okay."

They were silent for a bit. Tucker was watching the dancers and drinking his beer. Brian didn't like people to see him in Clara's and he knew he'd be teased about it at work. It almost amused him to consider the change in himself. Before his kids had been born, he'd gotten in bar fights about once a month. It was what he did instead of watching the TV. Glancing around, Brian saw Lowell Perry sitting alone over against the wall.

"There's Lowell," said Brian. "Hey, Lowell!"

Lowell Perry gave a little salute. Tucker glanced over but didn't wave. "He's a fuckin' pogue," he said. "He gives me the creeps."

Brian had wanted to suggest that they sit down with him. "He says you hit him pretty hard up there on Mt. Waldo."

"I should have hit him harder."

"You want another beer?"

"Let's get out of here," said Tucker. "I want to talk to you about something."

The knowledge seemed to come to Brian through his stomach: here it comes, he's going to ask about the boat.

Half an hour later Brian and Tucker were leaning against Tucker's truck which was parked down by the shore in City Park. Both were drinking beer and Brian thought he'd had more beer that night than he'd drunk in three months. He hoped he wouldn't have a sore head in the morning. Maybe he'd had six beers all told. The air felt very soft and the breeze off the water smelled slightly of fried food, probably from the lobster pound across the harbor. From where they stood they could just hear the bell on the buoy out by Steel's Ledge. Rooster had run down to the water for a swim. In the dark, he was no more than a black shadow. The dog ran back up to them to shake himself off and Brian wiped several drops of water from his face.

Brian was talking about football and he was joking, but actually he wasn't happy. He could tell that Tucker wanted to talk about something serious and Brian worried that whatever it turned out to be, it was that and not friendship which had caused Tucker to call him during these past two weeks.

"You know, the kids playing now just aren't tough," Brian was saying. "I mean they don't care about the game. When we were playing it was the biggest thing in the world. These kids don't give a shit. They lose, you know, they just can't win."

Tucker had a Frisbee which he had found in the grass. He kept tossing it up and catching it. Sometimes he'd catch it on the mouth of his bottle. A streetlight stood at the entrance to the parking lot and the light flickered on the Frisbee each time Tucker tossed it in the air. Rooster kept jumping at it, wanting Tucker to throw it to him. "I want to talk to you about making money," said Tucker.

"I remember we'd even practice on weekends," said Brian. "And you and me, we were always throwing a ball around."

"Money, Brian, let's talk money."

"Remember that trick where I'd run out, then pretend to stumble over my feet? I'd fall on my face and the linebacker would go right over me. Then I'd jump up and catch the ball. You threw that fucker straight as an arrow." As he spoke, he could almost feel the air of those autumn afternoons as well as his own exhilaration. How long ago that seemed. He guessed the teams now weren't that bad, but he couldn't believe they felt as he had felt. For one thing it had seemed so crazy, as if football was the only thing anywhere.

Tucker stepped away from the truck. Then he threw the Frisbee at Brian's stomach, making him jump and forcing him to catch it. "Money, money, money," he said.

Brian held the Frisbee away from Rooster, who kept barking and whining, then he tossed it back. "You got a plan for my boat, don't you." It wasn't a question.

Tucker stopped. He had been in the process of returning the Frisbee but he paused on one leg and now looked like a statue called something like the Frisbee Thrower or maybe the Sportsman. "How'd you guess that?" he asked.

Brian almost smiled. "I'm not stupid, you know."

"We go out, not far. Maybe a few miles. Someone throws a package over the side of a boat, a big freighter. We pick it up and come back in. I deliver it. We get ten thousand dollars. We split it fifty-fifty. Simple."

"Like the paintball game was simple?"

Tucker walked around to the truck and took something from the glovebox. Brian saw that it was a couple of palm-sized camping flashlights. Tucker handed him one. "Simpler than that," he said.

"Why you doing it?"

"To get outta here, man. The fact is I was talking to Sarah, she's planning to take Jason to Boston or New York. There's no way I can let that happen. We do this a coupla times and me and Jason, we're gone."

Brian considered how he'd feel if Margaret took their kids and moved to Portland where she had an aunt. "Why doesn't Sarah want to be with you?"

Tucker threw the Frisbee, very slow and high. Brian aimed the flashlight at it so the white plastic shone and the gold letters sparkled. Then he caught it. Rooster tried to jump up on him and Brian pushed him away. The dog was sopping wet.

"I'm not clean enough for her," Tucker said. "She wants to scrub me, cut my horns, dress me in tweed and stick me in a classroom. That's not my life, I just want to grab Jason and get out. Maybe we'll go out west. You know, there are ghost towns out there with perfectly good houses just waiting for someone to move into them?"

"What would you want to live in a ghost town for?" It seemed like a crazy idea.

"It'd be a start. I mean, you've got to live someplace and it'd be cheap."

It didn't seem that Tucker was lazy or good for nothing. If Tucker could fix his life by moving to Camden, then Brian couldn't imagine why he didn't do it.

"Smuggling cocaine is illegal," said Brian. He threw back the Frisbee. Tucker spotted it with his flashlight so the Frisbee seemed balanced on the beam of light. Then he caught it.

"Lots of things are illegal."

"It's dangerous."

"Where's the danger? The slightest sign of anybody and we drop it overboard."

Tucker threw the Frisbee. Brian caught it but didn't throw it back. He wondered if it would help Tucker to get this money. Would he be any better for getting his kid and going to a ghost town? Then he began to think of the five thousand that would be his own share. "Tucker, what do you want?" asked Brian. "What's important to you?"

"My kid, man." He said it angrily as if to show there was nothing else and no point about asking about anything else.

"Then why don't you patch things up with Sarah?"

Tucker went to the truck and took two more beers from the Styrofoam cooler in the front seat. He offered one to Brian but he'd had enough. He couldn't drink and talk seriously at the same time. Tucker opened the beer, then walked to Brian and lightly slapped his face. He started to slap him again and Brian blocked his arm.

"Don't fuck with me, Tucker. We aren't kids anymore." In high school they sometimes had pretend fights where Brian would let Tucker win. This had amused them both since Brian was probably the best fighter in the county. Rooster tried to yank the Frisbee out of Brian's hand and Brian pulled it back.

Tucker turned and stared out at the water. It looked big out there. "Because patching it up isn't so simple. I just can't live the kind of life that Sarah wants. It doesn't take the world into account. That world, man, it's out to get you, but the only way it can do it is when you want something. You want a house or a wife or a kid, then the world's got you by the balls, because once you have it, the world can always take it away. Well, I'm going to grab Jason and run. The world's not going to catch me."

Brian thought that sounded ridiculous and when Tucker

turned around, Brian threw the Frisbee at him. Tucker made a diving catch, landing on his belly with his beer in one hand and his Frisbee in the other. It occurred to Brian that Tucker lived for dramatic catches like that, as if he hadn't changed in fifteen years.

"How come you think it won't get you?" asked Brian. He felt irritated and tried to keep the emotion out of his voice.

Tucker got to his feet, slapping at his legs with the Frisbee. Rooster kept leaping at it. "Because I move fast and watch my back."

From up on High Street, Brian could hear a car peeling rubber. He realized he was wrong, that Tucker had changed after all. "You're not the same as you were," he said.

"How do you mean?"

"You remember that time you shinnied up and put that flag with the skull and crossbones on the pole over the police station, then cut the rope? It hung there a week before the cops got it down."

Tucker threw the Frisbee back hard, aiming at Brian's head. "What's that got to do with anything?"

Brian dodged to one side and the Frisbee banged against the truck. He stooped to pick it up. "You're more serious now. Like saying the world's out to get you and not believing in anything. You didn't used to be so desperate."

Tucker had backed up until he was just a shadow. "Not desperate, man, I'm just careful."

Brian threw the Frisbee at the shadow. The flashlight clicked on and spotted the Frisbee spinning through the air. "Is that what you're doing in Brooks?" asked Brian.

Tucker caught the Frisbee and flicked out the light, becoming a shadow again. "I'm running my own life."

"Running or ruining?"

Tucker was silent a moment. "I don't need that." He spoke so quietly that Brian felt sorry for him, even while feeling exasperated.

"Okay, okay," said Brian, "but over the years I'd wonder what you were doing and I figured you were a big success somewhere like the president of some computer company. So I was amazed, you know. I mean, there you were in Brooks." He guessed that was true. Since he'd seen Tucker as heroic, he had always assumed that someplace or other Tucker was still being heroic.

"What's wrong with Brooks?" asked Tucker defensively.

"Nothing, probably," said Brian, not wanting to hurt his feelings. "It's just not where I thought I'd find you."

"I like it. It's my life."

"Then why d'you seem so unhappy with it?"

Tucker made a sudden motion and Brian realized he was throwing the Frisbee. He flicked on his light, swung it in a circle until he found the Frisbee, then let the plastic disk glide toward him like a flying saucer riding its energy ray. Catching it, he said, "Just stay away from Cindy, all right? You're twice her age and you're married."

Brian was aware of copping out. Instead of pursuing Tucker about Brooks and his unhappiness, he had switched to something else—partly because he wasn't sure how to talk about it, partly because he didn't want to make him even more unhappy.

"What about the boat?" asked Tucker.

Brian threw back the Frisbee. "Tucker, I'm foreman at the chicken plant. I've got a place in the community. This is my home." Rooster reappeared with a stick and dropped it at Brian's feet. Brian threw it toward the water and the dog bounded after it. This is nuts, thought Brian.

"But do you like it?" asked Tucker.

"I like my kids."

"Hey, Brian, I'm trying to help you just as much as I want you to help me. You're working lobsters in the morning, chicken barns at night and then you're at the plant all day. What the fuck's that get you? I bet you hardly see your kids."

"There's weekends." Not that Tucker was wrong. Sometimes it seemed to Brian that he was slipping behind in everything.

"If you do this," said Tucker, "that money will be like a wall between you and all those fuckers who want something from you."

"If I do this," said Brian angrily, "it sure won't be for the money."

"What do you mean?"

"I'd be doing it to help you out."

"Forget that stuff," said Tucker harshly. "If you do it, then do it for the cash. The rest is just words."

Five thousand would put them ahead. It would be a big step toward having a down payment for a house. It would mean he wouldn't have to be constantly counting and adding up and calculating little savings and expenditures until his whole life resembled one great debit book.

"Say it," said Tucker, "Say, 'I need the money.' "

"I need the money."

"Say it louder."

Brian began to laugh. "I need the money!" And he did need the money, he always needed it. Rooster banged the stick against his leg. Brian took it and threw it toward the trees.

"We'll go out," said Tucker, "we'll pick up the stuff and nobody will know shit. Say it again, really shout it this time."

"I need the money!"

Brian imagined that the dark was full of policemen who were perking up their ears. He wondered what he was letting himself in for. But he wanted to help Tucker. And the money would make things easier. He'd have more time. He wouldn't always be worrying. Then he saw Tucker make a throwing motion and saw his light flick on. The Frisbee was floating out over the little hill toward the beach. Brian aimed his light at it so both lights illuminated the Frisbee which glided down toward the water. It settled onto the ripples, rode there for a moment, then went under.

Ten minutes later Tucker drew his truck to a stop in front of Brian's house. The brakes squealed and the whole contraption rattled. Tucker sometimes called his truck the Depredator, sometimes the Wreckage. He imagined people hearing it and sitting up in their beds, wondering fearfully what was approaching. It was nearly midnight. I'm coming to take you from your comfort, he thought. I'm coming to be bad.

Brian opened the door and got out. "I'm counting on you," said Tucker. He thought he had Brian about ninety percent convinced. Again he asked himself if he was putting Brian in danger, but where was the danger? They could always drop the stuff overboard. Anyway, set against the danger was Brian's share of the bucks—five thousand smackers.

"I'll talk to you tomorrow," said Brian. He shut the door quietly.

Tucker sat for a moment, watching Brian walk up his front steps. The house was dark. In the best of all possible worlds, he wouldn't be picking up the cocaine. He'd live in a little gingerbread house with his happy wife and happy kids and they'd laugh all day long. Tucker started the truck and drove slowly down the street. He could feel his heart pumping hard. When he had got about fifty yards past Brian's house, he stopped again and stared back into a dark area among the trees. After a moment, he saw Cindy running toward him with her blue jacket open and her hair fluttering about her face. How pretty she looked—the girl without a past. It seemed to Tucker that an electrical current was passing through him, making him feel about sixteen. Cindy opened the door and climbed into the truck. Tucker reached for her, fastening his hand behind her neck and pulling her toward him, reaching a hand up under her sweater, kissing her and feeling the strands of her blond hair caught between their mouths as she unbuttoned his shirt, dug her fingers into his flat belly. Tucker popped the clutch and the old Depredator, the old Wreckage squealed its tires down the street.

Lowell Perry quietly walked back up the hill along Mack Point away from the Searsport docks where he had parked his Camaro. He was going to be Mr. Stealth himself and one fault of his Camaro was that it wasn't stealthy. On his left lay the water and on his right was the air force tank farm—the seven huge tanks connected to the pipeline which carried jet fuel up to Loring Air Force Base in Limestone. Lowell Perry guessed the Ruskies had Searsport on a little map and when the big bang came they'd blow it to smithereens just to get the tank farm. If Lowell Perry was working that day, he'd be a disgruntled Sprague Oil employee one moment and bits of air the next. And if he wasn't working, well, fuck it, he didn't much like Searsport anyway. He'd seen bombers like that in Vietnam. He'd no doubt it was coming.

Right across from the main gate of the tank farm was the entrance to the lobster shack run by Superior Shellfish, a big corrugated tin building down by the water which used to be a fertilizer plant and now sold lobsters to tourists throughout the summer, although why anyone would want to eat in such an ugly place, Perry couldn't imagine. Beyond it was a small mountain of salt from those Brazilian boats and beyond that was a little dirt track leading to a slight hill over the water which was where Lowell Perry was heading. He'd seen them turn there and had no doubt what they were up to.

The truck was parked at the crest of the hill. Lowell Perry stayed over by the cattails and skunk cabbage growing in a creek bed. The only light came from the docks where a freighter bound for England was taking on a load of lumber. He could hear the rumbling of the derricks, the whining motors of the forklifts. Then, looking up over the truck through the rear window, he saw the yellow lights at the dock. Super-imposed against the lights were Tucker and Cindy, or at least he saw Tucker reared up and without a shirt. The doors were open and Lowell Perry saw Cindy's head hanging out on the passenger's side, her blond hair hanging down toward the ground. She pulled herself up, grabbing at Tucker, then fell back again, her head tilted so far back as to be upside down. Perry could tell she was naked, and briefly he saw her bare shoulder. She reared up again as Tucker leaned back. Perry saw her catching at Tucker's neck and pulling herself up to kiss him, saw their two naked bodies wrapped together, framed in the rectangular rear window of the pickup truck.

Lowell Perry lit a cigarette. He'd investigated that truck before. The seats were cracked vinyl and there was a spring poking out in the center. The whole floor was filthy with beer cans and food wrappers and white Styrofoam cups. He thought of his Camaro with its thick plush burgundy seats and thick rug which he kept spotless. Lowell Perry simply couldn't understand it. It was like she was crazy or maybe Tucker had given her some drug, something to make her act like that. But he'd get her in his Camaro someday, he had no doubt about it. Maybe he'd even get her in his Corvette. As for Tucker, his time was coming. Doing this, doing that, he had no sense of the big heavy thing that was about to fall on his head.

Cindy took a drag on the cigarette, then coughed. Maybe she wouldn't start smoking after all. There seemed a lot of good reasons not to. She looked at Tucker standing by the water about ten feet away, skipping stones toward the lights over the docks. His dog kept dashing into the water after the stones. She felt tender toward Tucker and wished she could wrap him up in her arms. At the same time she was frightened of him, not that he would hurt her of course, but that he wasn't entirely in control, like taking a bike down the hill with no brakes. You knew it was going to crash but you just didn't know where. But she liked being with him, liked the way he touched her. He was different from the boys at school. Bo Mitchell, the only other boy she'd had sex with, hadn't known what in the world he was doing and left a big stain on her skirt. She'd told her sister it was ice cream. Even when Bo had gotten better, he was still clumsy and had no sense of what she wanted. But Tucker wasn't like that. He was careful of her and she wished she could help him.

"What do you want?" asked Cindy, not even quite sure what she was talking about. She stood up and took several steps toward him over the stones. "I mean, what do you want more than anything else in the world?"

Tucker skimmed another rock across the water. "I want to get my kid and get out of here."

His voice was hard and she wondered what he had been thinking. "And will you?"

"Sure. I got it all planned out."

She didn't like it when he tried to sound tough. "I guess I just want to be happy," she said, regretting the words as soon as she said them.

Tucker laughed and sat down on a rock near her feet. He wasn't wearing a shirt under his Levi's jacket and the skin on his chest seemed to shine. "What an answer. How old are you?"

She had a sudden wish to kick him, not hard but hard enough for him to understand that he shouldn't fool with her. "You know damn well how old I am."

"You can't trust happiness," said Tucker. "It's one of the things the world holds out to tempt you and trick you and trap you inside its great big machine."

She didn't like how he was talking to her like a teacher and she didn't like being caught vulnerable. He should be softer with her, considering they'd just made love. "Why do you always act so cynical?" she asked angrily. "What are you going to do, go get your little boy and be miserable? Sounds like a great life, doesn't it? Where would you take him?"

Tucker stood up and took a few steps toward the water. His dog stood beside him, as if they were both looking out at the same place in the darkness. "Just away," said Tucker. "You ever felt like living in a ghost town?"

His voice had a wistful quality that made him seem like a kid. Cindy was moved by it but her few minutes of tenderness had gone by. He shouldn't have made fun of her. "I already live in a ghost town," she said. "I want to go someplace where there's more than one movie theater and music and dancing and lots of bright lights."

Tucker threw a bigger rock into the water, then jumped back as it splashed him. "Just like my fucking wife," he said.

ten

The bay was choppy and the lobster boat heaved. It was just dark enough and foggy enough for Isleboro to be a blur across the water, while on the opposite shore in the old spiritualist community of Temple Heights a few lights were visible. Ghost talkers, thought Tucker. He should pay a call to those old folks, see if they could rouse anyone he'd known in Vietnam, like Frankie Liebowitz, see how he felt about getting castrated by a Bouncing Betty, then cutting his own throat in a hospital in Japan. Or Jack McClatchy standing at parade rest during orientation in Bien Hoa a scant half hour after landing in Vietnam and getting turned to confetti in a rocket attack, ask him if he had any word of consolation for his chums on the plane. Or some of those gooks that got pushed out of Hueys, give them one more chance, were they really VC? Could spiritualists talk to foreigners? Man, there must be some angry chattering over there in Temple Heights. How could you get through to your Aunt Sally with all those righteous dead jamming the ghostways with complaint and indignation?

Tucker raised the binoculars and looked forward over the

bow of the *Margaret*. He didn't want to think about the war but it keep coming back to him. Maybe it was because of how they'd been sneaking around all evening, getting the boat, sneaking out into the bay, as if that's what Vietnam was all about: radical sneaking. You lose that war in Vietnam? No, sir, we got out-snuck.

"Crabs crawl out into the channel in the summer," said Brian. "They like the deep water. If we get stopped, I'll say I'm setting out crab traps."

"We won't get stopped," said Tucker. It had taken more arguing to convince Brian to come with him, and Tucker still worried that he might change his mind. It seemed to Tucker that Brian's motives were much like his own: he needed the money and this was an easy way to get it. But beyond the money Tucker realized that Brian was helping him because he felt sorry for him because of his trouble with his wife, but this exasperated Tucker, making him think Brian was a sentimental fool. Why did Brian have to complicate everything? Money meant freedom; they could both change their lives. Maybe Brian could come out to his ghost town with him, maybe Pete Talbot as well, and Tucker imagined a ghost town populated entirely by his friends. But that was nutty thinking again. Beyond the money and sentimentality, there was still another reason, meaning that this was the nature of their relationship. In high school Tucker had called the shots and Brian followed, even though he was stronger and had more common sense. Tucker knew that in the past few weeks he had again forced this relationship on Brian, who had pretty much accepted it despite his own changes and greater maturity. Thinking about it, Tucker felt slightly ashamed and instead he tried to concentrate on Cindy, but he couldn't make her picture take shape before his eyes.

"You know," said Brian, "the whole bottom of the channel is probably covered with pots whose lines got cut. They get wrapped up in the props of the big ships. Don't hurt the ships none. After a year or so the pots fall apart and the lobsters crawl right out."

Gradually, even before he realized he was hearing anything, Tucker became aware of a noise like the low bass note used to frighten the audience in that movie *Earthquake* a few years back. At first he didn't recognize it. Then he knew. "I hear it," he said.

"What?"

"The ship, man. I hear it coming!"

Brian steered the lobster boat farther into the channel. By now the sun must have gone down, although there was still light, a gray shimmering through the fog. The noise of the freighter got louder. Then Tucker saw it, a great gray shape looming up over to his left. He imagined it running them down, casting them into the water. Brian bore off a little.

"It picked up a pilot in Monhegan or Matinicus," said Brian. All merchant ships navigating the bay were under the guidance of a pilot. "We can't let him suspect anything."

Tucker watched the freighter slide by. It had lights forward and aft and lights up on the wheelhouse and radar mast. He thought it made a noise like a very big washing machine. Tucker didn't like how close they were and how the water kept splashing over the gunwales. Just as the bridge was even with the lobster boat, Tucker began flicking his flashlight off and on. They hit the freighter's wake and the lobster boat reared up, then sank down into the trough so the propeller was exposed and whined loudly. The *Margaret* tilted dangerously to the starboard side. Grabbing onto the edge of the shelter, Tucker barely held on as water sloshed onto the deck. He was up to his ankles in it. Brian worked furiously to turn the boat and it came up level again. Tucker aimed the light across the foredeck and kept flicking the switch. The lobster boat fell behind the freighter, violently rocking up and down in its wash. Nothing's going to happen, thought Tucker, except us getting drowned.

Then a light blinked once from the stern of the freighter and a green light tumbled over the side.

"There it is!" he shouted.

Brian pushed the throttle forward and the roar of the *Margaret* drowned out the sound of the freighter as it drew away, its red stern lights getting smaller. The green light came from several Cyalume lightsticks which were bobbing in the water off to starboard. Brian eased back on the throttle. Tucker aimed his flashlight at the lightsticks and picked out a bundle of orange life jackets. Reaching over with the gaff hook, he tried to pull them up but they were too heavy.

"Here," said Brian, handing him a rope which he fed over the davit of the pot hauler.

Tucker fastened the rope to one of the life jackets. "Okay," he said.

The orange life jackets rose out of the water and Tucker swung them onto the washboard. Then he undid the O-rings that held the green lightsticks to the jackets and threw the sticks over the side. As they sank, he caught a glimpse of their green light. He wondered how long they would stay bright and shiny down on the floor of the bay. Tied between the two life jackets was a package about the size of a medium TV wrapped in black plastic. Tucker untied the life jackets and carried the package into the cabin and placed it on the table. Opening it by the light of his flashlight, he saw it contained ten smaller packages. He guessed that each contained a kilo of cocaine. Tucker's hands were trembling from the rush of adrenaline. He liked that. He liked how excitement took him away from himself. Going into the stern of the boat, he got two lobster pots and dragged them back into the cabin. "Let's go home," he told Brian.

The ten packages made everything seem easy. He put five in each of the lobster pots, wrapping them first in the black plastic. Then he carried them to the stern of the boat, lifting them up onto several other traps so he could push them over the side if necessary. He kept pausing to take a deep breath and quiet his breathing. He moved quietly, like he was out in the jungle doing his LURP work. Briefly, he imagined him and Brian in black pajamas, sneaking back onto the Belfast wharf and being stopped by the cops. Why you guys dressed so funny? Extravagant thinking, said Tucker to himself, better calm down the old brain. Then he looked back at the two lobster pots. There was a whole shitload of money in there, enough for lots of people.

Lowell Perry had brought back a lot of merchandise from Vietnam. It had been a real business for a while—stereos, cassette recorders, cameras, which he had sold around town, a slide projector, a microwave oven, and also this sniperscope which he'd held onto, thinking it might come in handy, even though Nicky Beaumont had offered him a hundred bucks for it. Over the years Perry had kicked himself for not selling it but right now he was glad he hadn't. Parked on a hill near Saturday Cove, Perry looked out the window of his Camaro. Through the sniperscope he saw three Brazilians several miles away laughing and smoking cigarettes on the fantail of the salt boat as it headed toward Searsport.

He kept the sniperscope to his eye and after another few minutes, he spotted Brian's lobster boat. He knew it would be coming since he'd seen it go out an hour earlier. Lowell Perry was a patient man and through the sniperscope he could plainly see Tucker standing by some traps on the aftdeck, standing smack in the center of the cross hairs. That Tucker was about to get himself into a heap of trouble. It made Lowell Perry smile to think of it. It was like having a sweet taste in your mouth. As for Brian, Perry hadn't decided about him yet. It had to do with lots of things. It even had to do with Cindy.

Tucker's pickup needed rear shocks. He'd once bought a pair on sale from Monty Wards but they were somewhere out in his yard covered with a sheet of plastic. Pete Talbot said he'd help put them in but they hadn't gotten around to it yet. Whenever Tucker hit a pothole, which was about every ten feet, the back of the truck hopped up and down like a pogo stick.

Partly that was because Tucker was driving very fast, heading out to his house in Brooks, hitting about seventy on Oak Hill Road which was empty even though it wasn't yet ten. Partly it was because he was trying to fish another beer out of the Styrofoam cooler on the floor and was having to steer with his knees while Rooster licked his face and looked worried. Partly it was because his mind wasn't on the road but on a discovery he'd made about Vietnam. But every time he hit a bump, he saw the two lobster pots leap up in the bed of his truck and he imagined one of the pots bouncing over the side and into the yard of one of the many Harvey families who lived in this particular area, covering their muddy acreage with five keys of blow. Then he thought of how they'd look, three or four generations of Harveys, down on their knees, sniff-sniffing along, like a cross between a bloodhound and a lawn mower.

His new thought about Vietnam concerned the Vietnamese cooks, waiters, busboys, dishwashers, kitchen help, janitors, hootch girls, laundry women, barbers—all those Vietnamese who worked on the American bases. What he was thinking was why hadn't they poisoned the food? It would have been no trouble for the Viet Cong to get into the kitchens. They could have planned to do it all at once, dump a shitload of cyanide into the soup, the gravy, the mashed potatoes for the evening meal on every American base in Vietnam. They could have wiped out a hundred thousand soldiers, no sweat. It wasn't as if they lacked the chance. It almost made Tucker think well of them. The Viet Cong had killed the Americans in every way they could, but they had never fucked with the food. Like it was nice of them, almost sweet. Who would have thought it?

Ten minutes later, Tucker made the turn down the dirt track toward his house. The driveway was like a shotgun barrel between the trees. The truck roared through it, then jounced into the open area near the woodpile. Greased lightning, a speeding bullet, he had to be that fast. Throwing open the door, he jumped out, grabbed the lobster pots and ran with them toward the steps while his dog galloped ahead. The chickens were napping in their pen. Tucker pushed open the front door with his boot, crossed the bare floor and heaved the pots onto the table. Then he flicked on the light. Nobody home. That was just the way he liked it. Rooster ran to his food dish to see if anything new had been put in it since he'd been gone.

Quickly, Tucker removed the two packages of cocaine from the lobster pots, opened them up, then took the ten smaller packages and put them in a row. They were sealed with plastic and tape. He rubbed his hands together, took a drink of beer and carefully removed the tape from each of the packages. Then he folded back the plastic. Each package contained one kilo of cocaine which had been broken into large shiny white chunks. At the end of the table was a Cuisinart Precision Portion Scale and a package of lactose, which Tucker had bought that morning. The scale had been a wedding present. From each package Tucker removed twenty-five grams of cocaine, putting it in the bowl on the scale. Then he replaced the missing cocaine with an equal amount of lactose. After mixing the lactose thoroughly with the cocaine, he began rewrapping the packages, using new tape. Every now and then he had to turn away and take a deep breath in order to steady his hands.

"Goin' to get my ticket outta here," he sang to himself. "Say good-bye to the tarpaper shack. Good-bye Belfast, good-bye Brooks. Good-bye Sheetrock, good-bye pulp wood, good-bye chain saw, good-bye winter, good-bye chickens, good-bye trouble, good-bye." Rooster sat at his feet wagging his tail.

When he had sealed the ten packages, he combined them again into the two larger packages. He knew he was taking a chance at making somebody very angry but when he considered it and thought about it and tried to look at all the angles, he didn't see why he couldn't get away with it.

Picking up the packages, he stuck one under each arm and hurried back out to his truck. Rooster ran after him. Tucker had been in his house about twenty minutes. Fast, he thought, but it should have been faster. He put the packages in the cab and started the truck. Then, giving it the gas, he popped the clutch, spraying dirt and gravel back toward the chicken pen, fishtailing wildly down the dirt track to the road. Rooster began barking excitedly as he slipped off the seat onto the floor. Tucker realized he was sweating, that his heart was pumping. He liked that. He'd been living too soft a life.

"Boom, boom, boom," he sang, "we gonna buy Grant's tomb."

As he headed toward Camden, Tucker realized that the reason the Viet Cong hadn't poisoned the food was they knew they'd get nuked. Just like General Curtis LeMay had said, they'd get bombed back to the Stone Age. It wasn't kind feelings or delicacy or a sense of sportsmanship. They were scared. Damn right, he thought, we would have popped them back ten thousand years.

When Phillip Sutton heard the bell, he knew it was Tucker. Even so he took his time walking to the door. Phillip's apartment in Camden was decorated with the fruits of his labor—a Taba-Tabriz Persian rug, a leather Chesterfield sofa, expensive prints including a Picasso and a Rauschenberg, a Neal Welliver drawing of a waterfall and lots of poster-sized photographs of local scenes done by the photographic workshop right here in town—schooners at full sail, Mt. Battie in the snow, the harbor at night. Phillip liked brass and some of the pictures, including the Welliver, had brass frames. There were also several brass lamps, as well as a floor lamp with a green glass shade.

Opening the door, Phillip looked suspiciously at Tucker, who stood in the hall with a package under each arm. Tucker's cheeks were red and Phillip realized he'd been drinking. Rooster nosed past Phillip into the apartment. "What took you so long? The freighter went two hours ago."

Phillip knew that Tucker would lie, but he was curious what sort of lie he would choose. Actually, Phillip felt scared. He didn't want to fuck with this stuff. He didn't want to make anybody mad. But then he saw Rooster gobbling down the crackers and cheese that Phillip had set aside for a snack. He shooed the dog away. He didn't like dogs in the house, didn't much like them out of the house either.

"Cops stopped me for drunken driving," said Tucker, talking jive talk as he entered the apartment.

He thinks it's a game, thought Phillip. Tucker's black T-shirt under his Levi's jacket had a red tongue and mouth—the rude logo of the Rolling Stones—printed on the chest. Phillip was struck by how much Tucker and his dog resembled each other—those pointy irreverent faces. He again pushed Rooster away from the crackers and cheese, then put the plate on top of a chest of drawers. How ridiculous the dog looked with that red bandanna around his neck. He didn't see why Tucker didn't buy him a regular collar.

"Can you believe it?" continued Tucker, going into the kitchenette to see what was in the refrigerator. "Didn't even have a beer. Had to walk a straight line, puff into a little balloon. Then they followed me halfway down. Man, all this blow in the front seat. I told 'em it was my laundry."

Phillip took the packages and carried them to a flat-topped wooden trunk in front of the Chesterfield which he used as a coffee table. He considered opening them to see if they had been tampered with, but Rooster was right at his feet and Phillip was afraid the dog might get into the packages as well. Let Marston take care of it. Phillip lifted the lid of the trunk and put the packages inside. "Be careful, Tucker. These guys we work for are very mean. They think you're playing with them and they'll swat you. Just like a fly."

And me too, thought Phillip, they'll swat me too. He hoped Tucker hadn't done anything stupid. But then why was he lying? There was no way he could have passed a Breathalyzer test. Phillip took pride in the fact that he was not a person to panic, but as he thought about Tucker and why he might have been late, he felt his stomach go jittery.

"Who are these guys?" asked Tucker more seriously. He had a bottle of St. Pauli Girl in one hand and his Swiss Army knife in the other.

"Businessmen, just like I said." At least the outside of the packages looked okay, although that didn't mean anything.

"They live around here?"

"What do you care?"

Tucker shrugged and popped the cap on the St. Pauli Girl with the opener on his knife. "You got my ten grand?"

Shortly past eleven that same night, Tucker coasted his truck to a stop in front of his father-in-law's house, being careful not to touch his squeaky brakes. The house was dark. Tucker sat looking up at the upstairs windows and imagined everyone asleep in their beds—Sarah, her parents, her younger brother, Ralph, who worked at the country club, and Jason, his own little kid, curled up in his pajamas with bears on them. He smelled sweet when he slept. Jason liked to pull the covers up over his head and often when Tucker was going to bed he would pull back Jason's covers and a little cloud, a little whiff of sweetness would rise up from the boy. Tucker could almost smell it right now mixed in with the smell of the sea.

He took a Budweiser from the cooler and got out of his truck, leaving the door open. Rooster jumped out and started peeing against the trees. Leaning against the hood, Tucker cracked the beer and took a drink. He shouldn't have told Phillip he hadn't been drinking. That was an obvious lie and Phillip had seen through it at once. Tucker asked himself why he was trying to fuck himself up. If he was careful and sold the cocaine through Pete Talbot and kept his head down, then he might clear thirty to forty thousand. One could live in a ghost town for maybe ten years on money like that. Jason was two. If Sarah took him away, then Jason would forget him immediately. But if Tucker could snatch him, then Jason would be his. It would serve Sarah right. What was he planning to do that she wasn't planning herself? Jason would be a lot better off out west with his daddy than down in New York or Boston with all those crazy people buying yuppie gear as fast as they could get the money out of their pockets.

Tucker took another drink. What evidence did he have that he could pull off any of this stuff? For a moment, he wondered if he was thinking realistically. All these folks—Brian, Pete Talbot, Phillip—if he didn't watch it, he'd mess them up. He glanced at his watch. In half an hour he'd meet Cindy. He felt his skin tingle at the thought of it. He wished he could take her too, both her and Jason, take them to this ghost town and tell them about the world. He wouldn't tell them about war and desperation. He'd tell them about nice things, about green fields and the goodness of animals. He wouldn't tell them about anything that could do them harm. But maybe it was too late. Cindy might be a kid but she'd already gotten a taste of the world. That taste, that's what tricked you. It was sweet at first. Only later did it become bitter. It was like a drink, like Campari, and Cindy had already begun to sip at it. He'd been teaching her himself.

Lowell Perry's Corvette felt closer. He couldn't smell it yet, couldn't feel himself getting situated in the driver's seat, but he could sort of see it, a red shape through the fog. "A subtle brutality" is how the advertising brochure described it. He liked that. It was a little how he saw himself.

Perry was standing by his Camaro parked near the radio tower off Mortland Road in Searsport. It was Sunday morning and he was telling Harry Nixon what he wanted, like giving him a shopping list. Nixon was looking down the hill toward the bay. From this distance, the sailboats looked like little flecks of white. Lowell Perry wanted Nixon to pay better attention. He wanted Nixon to look him in the eye and nod his head and say yes, sir, Mr. Perry, I'll see that you get just what you want. You want that young girl? I'll see that you get her too.

"The boat's worth twenty-five thousand in auction," said Perry, "so I want six thousand of that. Then I want six thousand more." He figured that twelve thousand would almost pay the trade-in difference for a new car. The morning was bright and sunny and Perry considered fishing his dark glasses out of the glove box.

Harry Nixon was leaning back against the side of his dirty brown Ford which was parked nose to nose with the Camaro. "Twelve thousand's a lot for a tip," he said.

"You'll be pulling in over a million in drugs, what's the trouble?"

Nixon kicked at a stone in the road. Lowell Perry couldn't see driving such an ugly car as that Ford. It looked like a schoolteacher's car, but maybe it came with the job.

"Who's he deliver it to?" asked Nixon.

Perry had been afraid of this question. The Corvette drifted away a little. "Someone in Camden. I followed him once, but he was just visiting his kid."

"Is he dangerous?"

"He's got a mean temper." If Nixon didn't give him all the money, then he'd have to get the rest someplace else. Maybe he shouldn't have called the Customs man before he'd gotten it sorted out in his head. On the other hand, he knew Nixon was angry. He knew he'd spent hours searching that salt boat in Searsport last night and had come up empty-handed.

"Is he armed?" asked Nixon.

Perry thought how Tucker had been waving that paint pistol around. "I expect so," he said.

Nixon nodded slowly. He was still looking out at the water. "What about the guy who owns the boat?"

Why doesn't he look at me? thought Lowell Perry. Why does he keep staring at that stupid bay? "He doesn't know anything. He's just doing a dumb favor for a dumb friend." Perry couldn't decide about involving Brian. It partly depended on whether he could get the entire twelve thousand. Sure, he could buy a cheaper Corvette, the economy model, but what was the point of getting a Corvette with cloth seats and without the high-performance package?

"Can you make him stay out of it?" asked Nixon.

"I'm not sure yet," said Perry.

Pete Talbot dropped a smidge of cocaine into a glass of Clorox bleach and waited to see what would happen. The cocaine hit the surface and spread out at the top, then it began to descend through the bleach in streaky, milky lines that wavered slightly as they dissolved. Then it disappeared. Nothing. Talbot waited. Still nothing. Quinine fizzled. Procaine turned pink. The various sugars would sink to the bottom. Wherever Tucker had picked up this stuff, it was pure, untainted blow. It should be in a museum.

"Hey, man, this is top grade," said Talbot, unable to keep the glee out of his voice. "How much d'you say you have?"

Tucker was standing by the woodstove watching. It was Sunday morning and Tucker had arrived at Talbot's house half an hour earlier. He was quiet and Talbot thought maybe he was coming down with the flu or something. Either that or he was hung over. Talbot wished he'd take better care of himself.

"Maybe half a pound."

"And where'd you get it?"

"Can't tell you."

Talbot's house resembled Tucker's, but it was more finished and there was Sheetrock on the walls, although it hadn't been painted. However, he had a hardwood floor and some rugs and the ceiling fixtures were in place. But the molding and mop boards were missing and he still had to put up the window casings. He'd get to it soon enough and with the money from this blow, he could get the whole place finished before winter. His wife would like that. She was beginning to complain.

"How much can you sell it for?" asked Tucker.

Talbot poured the glass of Clorox back into its plastic bottle and put the bottle in the cabinet under the sink. He was barechested and wore yellow running shorts. The black hair on his chest and back was so thick that it was like a black shirt. He scratched his ribs and looked down at the floor.

"This stuff's never been stepped on," he said. "I can cut it and we'll have three fifty, four hundred grams. That's maybe forty thousand."

"When can you have the money?"

"Under a week. You want a beer? Take one." Talbot watched Tucker walk to the refrigerator. Maybe he's just scared, Talbot thought. Maybe he's worried about the cops. Tucker took out two cans of Rolling Rock and tossed one to his friend.

"You been out in the woods?" asked Tucker, opening his beer.

Talbot began putting away the cocaine, taking care not to spill any. Then he cracked open his beer, took a drink and wiped his mouth on his bare arm. Little drops glistened on the black hairs. Out in the yard he could hear his two boys shouting and the dogs barking, both Rooster and Spike, his golden retriever.

"Not for a coupla days," he said. "I was going to take that paintball money and invest it in some grass. Maybe make enough money to see me through the winter. Other than that I been feeling a little restless." Talbot walked to the window. His boys were six and seven. At the moment, they were kicking a soccer ball after the dogs, trying to bounce it off them. Talbot's wife was at the store getting some stuff for a barbecue that afternoon. It was a good day to go to the lake. Talbot turned back to Tucker. "You still have dreams?" he asked.

"What d'you mean?" asked Tucker.

"Vietnam dreams, man." Talbot put the cocaine on a shelf over the refrigerator. What still impressed him about Vietnam was what he called the big contradiction: that it was boring and exciting at the same time, that no matter how bored you were, you could always get killed, which at least kept you alert. Nowadays things were mostly boring. Talbot walked back to the table. "I have this same dream about getting wasted," he continued, "you know, blown away. We're doin' a platoon sweep through a rice paddy toward a village and I'm running fast but looking for trip wires and shit like that." Talbot took another drink. The beer was cold with bits of ice which felt good on his tongue. "Suddenly there's Charlie standing in the doorway of a hootch, standing right in front of me. And he's a great big guy, like a gook basketball player. He's just standing there with his AK. I swing up my rifle but he beats me to it. Smoke and noise and this awful burning in my chest. I have this dream over and over."

Tucker got off the table to toss his beer can in the bag of trash by the sink. "I don't remember my dreams," he said.

Talbot waited for him to say more but he didn't. What did Tucker care about? Why did he try to seem so hard? Talbot kept remembering the dream. He could almost see the bamboo thickets and a small grove of banyan trees. Tucker had taken another beer. Talbot looked at his back and wondered what he felt, what scared him. That Tucker felt miserable about Jason, Talbot had no doubt. Once in the woods Tucker had listed for Talbot his five loves: his son, his dog, his wife, his truck and his chain saw. Talbot felt that if Sarah had come before Rooster, she might still be around.

"You still planning to get outta here?" Talbot asked.

"Damn right, I should probably split when you pay me."

Again Talbot thought Tucker was going to say more but he didn't. Where had he gotten the cocaine? That guy in Camden? "Is there any danger?" asked Talbot.

"Not that I can see."

"Where'd you get the stuff?"

Tucker walked to the window and looked out at Talbot's two sons who were fishing the soccer ball out of the vegetable garden. "You're better off not knowing," said Tucker. "Anyway, when I collect the money from that next shipment, then I'm gone. Anything you want from my place, you can have it."

That surprised Talbot. Tucker could have a lawn sale and make a thousand bucks. His wife, Janet, loved lawn sales. She'd even do it for him if he asked. "I'll pay for it," said Talbot.

"Forget it. It's all junk anyway."

."At least let me pay for your chain saw."

Tucker shrugged and turned back to the window.

Talbot felt guilty. He wanted to ask Tucker what was bothering him and instead he was thinking of the profit he could make from selling off Tucker's stuff. The chain saw alone was worth one fifty. "Where you goin' to go?" asked Talbot.

Tucker looked back over his shoulder and Talbot was surprised at the intensity of his expression, like he was carrying some big log or stone and wanted to give it up but was too stubborn to let go. "Far, far away," said Tucker. "Man, I don't even want to stay on the fuckin' planet."

———

Phillip Sutton had several different girlfriends and he liked to keep them separate. But there was one, the wife of a restaurant owner in Camden, who could be counted on to drop by unexpectedly any time of the day or night, depending on what her husband was doing at the restaurant. Not that she'd stay long—ten, fifteen minutes. Bang, bang and she'd be on her way. It made for a crazy sex life.

When the doorbell rang Monday night around eleven-thirty, Phillip assumed it was her, Gladys, and as he walked to the door he composed his face into an expression of bemused tolerance. He wore a bathrobe that was more of a smoking jacket, some shiny dark purple material with wide black velvet lapels and collar. He'd been reading a mystery novel about horse racing and drinking a little Martell, but he was slightly bored and the prospect of a tumble with Gladys was agreeable to him. The bell rang again.

"All right, all right, I'm coming."

As Phillip unlocked the door, it was immediately shoved open and two big men in beards and blue-jean overalls burst into the room. Before he could focus on them, one of the men hit him in the stomach. Phillip bent forward retching and the other man picked him up as if he were a package and threw him at the wall. There was a smashing of glass as he hit a photograph of Camden harbor. He fell and tried to cover his head. He caught a glimpse of a work boot swinging toward him, then felt a blow in the ribs. Then another. The pain of it kept him from thinking or wondering or even feeling fear. It was as if he was being ripped apart, like ripping a sheet of paper into little bits. One of the men grabbed him by his velvet collar, tearing it, then yanked him to his feet. The other man hit him in the face, knocking his head back against the wall. Again there was the breaking of glass. He was hit a second time, then a third. The blows knocked his teeth together and exploded in his head like slamming doors. Phillip shut his eyes and let his body go slack. In his mouth he could taste the mixture of bile, blood and good brandy.

He was shoved up against the wall again and held there. He kept his eyes shut. Then someone slapped his face. Phillip opened his eyes and saw Marston's face about two feet from his own. Marston slapped him again.

"Hey, what's going on?" said Phillip. "Marston, what the hell?"

Marston had short-cropped sandy hair and a face the color of raw steak. He wore a dark suit, white shirt and a dark blue tie with little sailboats on it. Marston spat at him. "You fucked with me, man."

"No, man, I don't know what you're talking about." Phillip's mouth felt swollen. It was hard to say the words.

Marston let him go and Phillip fell to the floor. "Hurt him, Seymour," said Marston.

The taller of the two bearded men stepped forward and kicked Phillip in the stomach. Then he kicked him in the ribs when Phillip turned and began to vomit onto the rug. Sticking out his foot, Seymour wiped his vomit-spotted work boot on Phillip's smoking jacket. When the boot was clean, he kicked him again. Phillip's head was knocked back against the coffee table.

"Someone tampered with the product, Phillip," said Marston.

"No, man, I don't . . . ."

"Hurt him again, Seymour."

The bearded man in the lumberjack shirt kicked him again, aiming for his stomach. It seemed to Phillip that he didn't so much feel pain as become pain. He *was* pain, and Phillip, the person, was off someplace else scared and running. The second bearded man dragged him to his feet and began slapping his face, while the first tried to kick him again. They let him go and Phillip fell forward onto the rug. The central square of the rug had a red and blue pattern on a white ground. Phillip saw that the white was stained with blood and for a second, he couldn't think whose it was.

"There was fucking sugar in it, Phillip," said Marston. "Lactose. You think I'm stupid? You think I won't test it? You fuckin' stomped on it. You fuckin' jumped up and down on it. Now Seymour's goin' to jump on you."

Phillip tried to crawl back toward the wall. There was glass everywhere and he was afraid of getting cut. "Marston, listen, Tucker was late getting here. It had to be him."

"You said we could trust him," said Marston.

"I thought we could."

"Break something, Seymour."

Seymour picked up the brass floor lamp and smashed its green glass shade against the Neil Welliver drawing on the wall. The shade broke and the picture fell to the floor. Using the rest of the lamp as a club, Seymour proceeded to smash the other pictures. The air was full of flying glass. When he had finished, he smashed the base of the lamp into the television screen. There was a small explosion and sparks and an acrid smell. Marston stood by the door smiling at Seymour as if he were showing off a clever trick.

"No, no," Phillip kept saying, "I'll get it back."

"He's already sold it, Phillip. You know what'll happen to him for this? He's one dead soldier. Sun come up tomorrow, he'll be already cold."

Phillip got to his feet. The room kept tilting like a boat in rough water. "Marston, you can still use him. There's another . . ."

"Make him be quiet, Seymour," said Marston, lighting a cigarette.

Seymour spun on one leg and kicked out at Phillip, hitting him in the chest and knocking him back against the wall. Phillip tried to fold his arms over himself. He felt he was breaking into many pieces and that he'd never be able to find them again. He slid down the wall to the floor. The glass beneath him made a tinkling, cracking noise.

"I'll talk for you, Phillip," said Marston, tossing the match on the rug. "I don't want to hear your voice. When the other ship gets here in a few days, we'll let the soldier do the pickup and get him when he comes in. Him and his buddy. Then they'll disappear. And you, Phillip, you make a noise and you do too."

Phillip nodded but kept his lips shut. They were swollen and with his tongue he could feel a broken tooth.

Seymour folded his hands together and cracked his knuckles. He seemed happy. "Can I hurt him again, boss?"

Marston shook his head. "Not today, Seymour. We've got to let him rest."

The Far Horizons Travel Bureau in Bangor specialized in European package tours, Caribbean weekends and Club Med adventures in thirty locations. But in a pinch they could also book a ticket, which was what Mrs. Bouvier was doing for this somewhat rustic looking young man, Mr. Tucker Morgan. He was cute, if you liked that unshaven look, which Mrs. Bouvier did.

"And how old is your little boy?" she asked.

"He's two," said Tucker.

"Can you hold him on your lap?"

Mr. Morgan didn't seem to understand. His face was brown from the sun. Perhaps he worked outside as a landscaper or on a road crew. Mrs. Bouvier didn't think he was from Bangor. Next to Mr. Morgan sat a big black dog with a red bandanna around his neck.

"Can't he have his own seat?" asked Tucker. "He'd like that better."

"It'd be half price," said Mrs. Bouvier. "Often there are extra seats. If you can hold him in the beginning, then they can find you another seat later on." There was something

about the young man's face that she couldn't identify, almost
a softness or gullibility. It gave him a faraway quality.

"I'd rather pay," said Tucker.

Mrs. Bouvier couldn't imagine why he wouldn't prefer to
hold his child for ten minutes in order to save a hundred
dollars. He seemed to think it a matter of pride to pay, as if
it somehow made him a better parent. "Will your wife be
flying with you?" she asked.

"She's coming later."

It occurred to Mrs. Bouvier that he was lying. The man had
a hard looking body, no excess, and his hands were rough.
Mrs. Bouvier was forty-five and still attractive. Not that she
wanted to start anything, far from it, but sometimes a person
just liked to be looked at and Tucker Morgan kept looking
out at the traffic. The dog, on the other hand, hadn't taken
his eyes off her.

"What about Rooster?" said Mr. Morgan, pulling at the dog's
ears. "Can he have a seat?"

"He'll have to go with the baggage. Salt Lake's very pretty
this time of year. Do you ski?"

Tucker continued to look out the window. "Not so you'd
notice. Couldn't I pretend he was a seeing-eye dog? I could
carry a white cane and wear dark glasses."

"I'm afraid they wouldn't believe you," said Mrs. Bouvier.
"And what's your little boy's name?"

The young man thought a moment and began to smile. It
made him seem about eight years old. He glanced at Mrs.
Bouvier, then looked at the rest of her in a way that was
startling, although not disagreeable. "Mr. Moon," said Tucker,
"my kid's called Mr. Moon."

eleven

It seemed to Brian that Tucker was happy for the first time since the fight outside of Clara's three weeks before. Or maybe he'd been happy in that paintball game. But even as he pronounced the word, Brian thought that "happy" might be wrong. It was more like he was running at a higher speed, like a long-playing record played at 78 rpms, so the voices become squeaky and manic. He was joking with Cindy in the stern of the lobster boat, something about blind deer and blind moose and blind rabbits. Brian couldn't make any sense of it. Margaret was in the cabin with the kids. She said it was too windy but Brian thought she hadn't liked Tucker's fooling. He had stopped trying to make her like his friend and only hoped they wouldn't quarrel. Sometimes it was hard to be married to a person who expressed her mind so strongly. This picnic today was a test. Tucker had suggested it and Brian thought it sounded like a good idea. He hadn't been on a picnic all summer and here it was the end of August. Looking ahead across the water at Isleboro, Brian could see some maples with flashes of orange and yellow in their upper leaves.

Brian was steering for Sprague's Beach in Turtle Head Cove.

He didn't see any other boats anchored in the area and hoped they'd have the place to themselves. Of course there were dozens of sailboats out on the bay even though the water was choppy and touched with white caps. The *Margaret* rose and fell in the successive waves. Looking over his shoulder Brian saw that Tucker was shooting at seagulls with his paint pistol, while making a *rat-tat-tat* noise.

Maybe it was just the money that was making Tucker exuberant. Brian didn't want Tucker to mention it. Maybe he should warn him. He hadn't told Margaret anything about the freighter, although he knew she suspected something. Even now, he was surprised how easy it had been, like being an illegal water taxi. He'd been wrong to worry about it. It had been simple, even exciting, even a little fun. As for his five thousand, he had hidden it in the house. He'd tell Margaret about it when the time came, long after Tucker had gone and their life settled back to normal. But the presence of that money made everything better. Tucker was right. The money was like oil on a rusty set of gears. It freed you up, it gave you the chance to live your life. In fact, he hadn't agreed to work a single pickup crew since that night they had met the freighter.

Fifteen minutes later Tucker was rowing Brian into the beach. Rooster was standing behind Tucker, sniffing and biting at the air. Brian couldn't tell if Tucker was just an inexperienced rower or was splashing him on purpose. He suspected both. Even Tucker's joking was aggressive. Tucker clipped the oar against the water, sending a substantial spray onto Brian's windbreaker and chinos.

"Hey, Tucker, quit it. I'm getting wet." It was hard not to laugh. Even the dog looked like he was laughing. Ahead of him, Brian saw Margaret waiting on the beach. The kids were running around. Cindy was already gathering firewood. A herring gull made its horn-like protest, as if saying, "Mine, mine, mine!" When the dinghy touched the sand, Margaret grabbed the painter and pulled it farther onto the beach. The kids splashed through the water chasing Rooster. Brian hoped they wouldn't catch cold. It was low tide and Brian helped Margaret pull the dinghy up past the high-water mark. Then they all walked up the beach carrying bags of food and the blue Coleman cooler. Brian's five-year-old son, Jimmy, kept running behind Tucker and trying to snatch the paint pistol from his belt. After several moments, his sister, Caroline, joined in, tiptoeing behind Tucker and giving his belt a yank. Tucker growled at them like a lion, getting down on all fours in the sand. Under his Levi's jacket he wore a bright yellow T-shirt which gave his thin face a kind of glow.

"How'd you little kids like me to throw you in the water?" he asked, making a face and showing his teeth.

Caroline bounced up and down in front of him. "We'd hate it," she said.

"You leave them alone, Tucker," said Margaret, walking last in line. Brian thought she was being too serious.

"Yup, yup, yup," said Tucker.

After putting down their stuff in several different places, then changing their minds, they settled on a spot near a large birch that afforded both sun and shade. It was too cold to swim but both Tucker and Cindy said they didn't care, they were going to swim anyway. Even in August the water was freezing. Brian guessed he hadn't tried it for fifteen years. Tucker and Cindy went off to gather firewood while Brian started the fire. Margaret was spreading peanut butter on crackers for the kids who, she said, were too hungry to wait for their hot dogs.

Through the trees, Brian could see Tucker and Cindy joking together. She wore a red bathing suit and they stood close to each other in a way that bothered Brian. They seemed too intimate. Tucker was acting even younger than Cindy. If Margaret had any idea that Tucker had designs on her sister, she'd go through the roof. But maybe I'm wrong, thought

Brian, maybe they're just being friendly. There, that time he actually saw Tucker touch Cindy, reach out and poke her in the ribs. But they were kids; she was, in any case, and Tucker was certainly acting like one.

They ate hot dogs, hamburgers, macaroni salad, potato salad, lots of cookies and corn on the cob. Jimmy and Caroline were finished almost immediately and ran off to play with a beach ball, seeing how close they could get it to the water and still get it back. About ten times Brian or Tucker had to fish it out, until Margaret said she'd take it away if they didn't stop.

Tucker sat cross-legged on a blue towel as he drank beer and finished yet another hot dog. He had taken off his T-shirt and Brian was struck by how white his body was compared to his face and neck. Rooster lay beside him gobbling down a hamburger that had fallen into the sand. Brian couldn't remember how many hot dogs Tucker had eaten but he himself had had four. As for corn, he'd had five ears and felt stuffed. The kids threw the corn cobs into the water. Tucker said the fish would eat them. Margaret said they'd litter the beach. The whole afternoon had been like that, although Tucker had kept up his cheerful, nearly electric mood. Cindy sat near him, burying Tucker's feet in the sand. Margaret sat on a log drinking Diet Coke. They were talking about Tucker's decision to leave Maine.

"No, man, I've had enough of Waldo County," Tucker was saying. The sun was in his eyes and he kept narrowing them. "I'm just going to pack my bags and tiptoe away. Maybe find some nice young woman to go with me. Someone cute like Cindy. We'll just disappear."

Cindy tossed a handful of sand onto Tucker's bare stomach. "I'll introduce you to my friends."

"Too young," said Tucker, wrinkling his nose. "I need a real woman."

"What about your kid?" said Brian. He sat on the sand in

front of Margaret. Although he couldn't see her, he could feel her displeasure.

"I'll take him too," said Tucker. "Me, the bimbo and Jason, we'll just fly away."

Cindy threw more sand on Tucker's belly. "No girl's going to go with you if you call her a bimbo."

"I don't see why you don't move down to Camden," said Margaret. She had a way of enunciating each word when she didn't like something. "Your boy's there. You could get a job, move back with your wife. You'd make more money teaching than cutting pulp wood."

Tucker sat up and dusted the sand from his belly. He squinted at Margaret. "You know, when I was in Skowhegan, the only way I could control the class was to be tougher than everyone else. I had this civics class where they put all the bad kids. The first week two kids jumped me when I came in the door. They were going to tie me to my chair or something. This kid grabbed me from behind and I threw him over my shoulder. All the time there was stuff like that. Then they slashed my tires."

"Camden would be a lot different," said Margaret, again enunciating each word.

Jimmy threw Tucker the beach ball and he punched it back over the boy's head, making him run down the beach to chase it. Rooster ran off after the kids. "I'm not going to be tied to that rat life," said Tucker. "I'll just get Jason and go."

"How could you do that?" asked Brian. Tucker seemed to be joking but there was little humor in it. Brian wished he'd talk about something else, even though he thought Tucker had a point. Maybe he shouldn't teach, maybe he should really seek out his ghost town if that would make him happy.

"Just take him, man."

"You'd be breaking the law," said Margaret.

Tucker scratched his head and grinned his dog-like grin.

"There are two kinds of laws. Those you make for yourself and those society makes for you." He paused and tossed some sand back at Cindy. "I only care about the first kind."

"What sort of girl would you take with you?" asked Cindy. "What would she look like?"

"Fat. I want a nice fat girl to keep me warm in winter."

"Don't you like thin girls?"

"Too bony. You can't get comfortable with them in bed."

"Aren't you afraid of getting in trouble?" asked Margaret.

Brian felt his wife's voice was getting into a dangerous area. He could imagine disliking Tucker, but Margaret's feelings seemed stronger than dislike. He knew himself that many of the laws governing lobster fishing were unfair. Look at the law that said all lobsters with carapaces over five inches had to go back in the water. What made it especially unfair was they could haul those big lobsters in Massachusetts and make a lot more money. Jimmy again threw the beach ball to Tucker, who hit it back over his head.

"They have to catch me first," said Tucker, looking at Cindy rather than Margaret.

"But what do you want to do?" asked Brian. "Don't you want some kind of job?"

Tucker finished his Narragansett and dug into the cooler for another. "I just want to be left alone."

"So you can drink beer and smoke dope?" asked Margaret.

"Yeah, lady, so I can let the wind whistle through my ears."

This was followed not so much by a pause as by a hole in the conversation. Brian could almost see it, as if all four of them were gathered above a deep well. He wanted to tell Margaret to lay off but he didn't want to speak sharply to her in front of Tucker and Cindy.

Cindy looked at her sister in surprise, then she turned back to Tucker. "Don't you believe in being with someone, you know, being in love?"

Tucker poked at the fire with a stick so it sparkled and

several of the smaller twigs caught and snapped. "I just believe in doing things, like having Jason and being someplace where I can live like I want. Words like love and the rest of it, they're what get you in trouble. They tie you to the world like miles of Scotch tape and keep you from being able to protect yourself. You get so you really love something and the whole world conspires to take it away. I want to take Jason someplace where that can't happen. And Rooster too, we're all going."

Margaret stood up and took a few steps toward the water, scattering the seagulls that were waiting for scraps. She wore a denim skirt and a white blouse she had made herself. When she turned around to look at Tucker, Brian experienced a sinking feeling. "The only thing I like in what you say is that you're leaving. The rest sounds like a spoiled child."

"Margaret, cut it out," said Brian standing up as well. "This is supposed to be a picnic." Even as he said it, he knew it sounded foolish. But it made him angry for people not to get along together.

Margaret turned away to face the water. In the distance, one of the Camden schooners was heading toward Castine, its great sails billowing in the wind. "Whoever promised him anything anyway?" Margaret asked. "He's got a wife, a little boy and a chance to make something of himself and all he wants to do is joke around."

"Hey, Margaret," said Tucker, "I just want to make my own life." He seemed surprised by her anger and Brian wondered if he ever noticed anything.

Margaret looked back at him, then shook her head so her hair swung back and forth. "You want to do what you want without having to do anything for anyone else. You know, for years I've listened to Brian talk about you: how great you were, what a hero you were. When you showed up the other night, I just felt sorry for him."

Brian glanced at Tucker to see if he was angry, but his face showed no expression. "Margaret, stop it. Tucker's been through a lot."

"You mean the war?" asked Margaret. She kicked her foot in the sand, sending a spray of it into the fire. "I'm sick of hearing about Vietnam. No matter what happened, at some point you've got to pick up your life and get going again."

Tucker jumped to his feet, tipping over his beer can. "That's what I'm doing, goddammit!"

"No, you're not," said Margaret, glaring back at him. "You're just looking for another place to hide. It's just too bad for your son, that's all."

As quickly as Tucker had gotten angry, so it disappeared. "I love him," he said. Tucker shook his head as if trying to clear it. Briefly he looked at each of them in a way that made Brian think he meant to ask for something, some favor. But he remained silent and after another moment he picked up his Levi's jacket, turned and began walking down the beach. Cindy stared after him, then looked at her sister, uncertain what was happening.

Margaret took a few steps after Tucker. "That's not enough," she called, "and according to you it doesn't matter."

Tucker paused very slightly, then continued walking. Rooster ran down the beach after him. Margaret began looking around for the kids.

"Jesus, Margaret," said Brian, "lay off."

Margaret spotted the kids playing in the dinghy and waved to them to come back. "I just wanted you to see what kind of person he is," she said.

"What do you mean?"

Margaret looked into his face. Despite her sharp tongue, Brian knew that she cared for him, even loved him. It kept him from getting too angry at her.

"He's no hero," said Margaret.

Sometimes the size of the ocean and the sky frightened Tucker, as if he might lose his balance and tumble into them. Like in the movie *2001* where the astronaut tumbles into all that black space after the computer goes crazy or whatever. That's what Tucker thought could happen to him, but in his case it wouldn't be black space, but bright light—the sea and the sun and the clear blue sky. When he felt like that, he'd dig his heels into the dirt and curl his toes as if trying to hold on. He was doing that now, curling his toes into the sand as Brian stood a few feet behind him trying to explain why Margaret had gotten mad. Why did Brian bother? It wasn't his fault that his wife was pissed off.

"That's okay," said Tucker, "I probably deserved it. I been getting wound up tighter and tighter." He picked up a stone and threw it toward the water. Make the water angry, he said to himself, make it rise up. Rooster splashed into the water after the stone, then brought back the wrong one. "You know," continued Tucker, "in one way everything she said was completely true and in another it's not true at all." He hadn't minded that Margaret had gotten angry. He wouldn't mind it if she slapped his face, although he might hit her back. Sometimes he felt like doing the same thing to himself, just hauling off and slapping his face. After all, she was right, but in some way, she was also wrong. Tucker couldn't understand it.

"You don't think you could patch things up with your wife?" asked Brian.

Tucker picked up a flat stone about the size of his palm, drew back his arm and skipped it across the water. Five, six, seven times, how perfect it was. You couldn't do it if there were any waves but now with the tide just turning, the water in the cove was flat and expectant. Just waiting for my stones, thought Tucker. He picked up another.

"I guess I could patch things up," said Tucker, not sure if it were true. "But every time I think of living in Camden my insides go cold. I mean, it's like death, man. So your old lady's right but I just can't do it. I'm not trying to explain myself or excuse myself but I can't do it. I keep thinking of these ghost towns and I say, 'That's a stupid idea to take a little kid to an empty town with nothin' but prairie dogs and coyotes.' But whenever I think of it, it makes me happy."

"There wouldn't be any people," said Brian.

Tucker skimmed another stone and watched it sink after four hops. Rooster spashed around after it. It occurred to Tucker that maybe he could teach the dog to hunt for lobsters: a lobster hound. He'd make a fortune. "Yeah, man, no people. Not only that but the houses are already built. They're empty and waiting to be moved into."

"That's not very sensible," said Brian.

Tucker turned to look at him. Brian's blue windbreaker was zipped up to his neck and his hands were in the pockets. He wondered why Brian chose to wear that little leprechaun beard and what he saw in the mirror when he looked there and what he thought about it. Tucker hated looking in mirrors and all those reminders of the passage of time. His wife once gave him a watch and he'd given it to Talbot. And calendars, he hated calendars. "Yeah, it seems eccentric to me too," he said, "but I gotta try it." He picked up three stones, then discarded one as too bulky.

"What's wrong with you anyway?" asked Brian.

Tucker was surprised at the concern on Brian's face. It again struck him that he was wrong to get Brian involved with the cocaine. On the other hand, it would only be a few more days. Then he'd be gone and Brian would be ten grand richer. Shit, he was doing the man a favor. The only trouble was that he hadn't told Brian about the second boat yet. As for what was wrong with him, Tucker had no idea.

"I just feel stuck," he told Brian. He repeated the word to himself, letting it sound in his head like a loud noise in an empty room. "You know that story about Winnie-the-Pooh where he's been at Rabbit's house and he's eaten too much and he gets stuck in the doorway and has to stay there a whole week until he gets thinner? Well, I keep thinking that's like me, that I'm stuck between two places waiting to get thinner or change in some way."

"You can't just wait for it to happen," said Brian. He'd sat down on a boulder and was picking at the barnacles with his fingernail.

"That's why I want to try out this ghost town idea." Tucker skipped another stone. It hit once, then went under. He was getting worse. Maybe once he was settled he'd try writing again. Even in high school, he'd wanted to be a writer. Once he'd even thought of doing a book about Vietnam, not a whole history, but what he saw there. The Night Stalker, some of the guys had called him. He could use that for the title, but it wouldn't be one of those gung-ho books. Or if not a writer, maybe he could try being a stuntman in the movies or maybe a land surveyor and walk all over the place.

"What about Cindy?" asked Brian. His voice was flat, as if he were trying to sound reasonable.

Tucker turned away. The late afternoon sun shone bright on the Belfast shore, making it all sparkly. "I don't mean to take her with me, if that's what you're afraid of." Farther up the beach Tucker saw Cindy tossing the beach ball with the kids. She'd put on a red sweatshirt that covered the bottom part of her bathing suit, making it seem that she had nothing else on.

Brian was still picking at the barnacles. "I'm worried about the kind of person you're turning into," he said.

"You going to start that again? Man, I'm not a football star anymore. My life is more complicated." Tucker had had a funny experience in the night. He'd woken up around three and he was crying. He didn't know why. He guessed he'd had some dream but he couldn't remember it. At first he'd laughed it off but now it bothered him. He started to tell Brian about it, then changed his mind.

Brian stood up and tossed a big stone into the water, not trying to skip it at all. It made a *ker-plunk*ing noise. Rooster splashed his way to the right stone but couldn't budge it. "You know," said Brian, "you remind me of these guys who believe in flying saucers and conspiracy theories and the devil sending messages through rock-and-roll lyrics."

"What d'you mean?" asked Tucker, suspicious.

"You hope something might be true so you decide it must be true. You believe it's true just because you want to believe it, not because you have any proof or evidence." Brian paused a moment, thinking about what he was saying. "It's like you mix up proof and desire. That kind of thinking has nothing to do with the real world."

"That's nonsense, man. I don't know what you're talking about." Tucker felt angry. What did it mean to mix up proof and desire? He bent over and held his stomach as if experiencing a little pain. Again he noticed Cindy. How pretty she was—a girl who was both proof and desire in one package, like a hundred proof, or that Slivovitz stuff that took the tongue right off you. Looking at Brian, Tucker felt pissed at his worrying, like he was his old lady or something. Tucker began to grin, faking it. "Anyway, I'm worried about you too. I mean, the way you've changed. You've become too tame. There's no action in you."

But Brian was in no mood for joking. "I'm thirty-four; I'm too old to hang out. Besides that I don't want to. I'm a grown-up."

Tucker decided to back off a little. "Look, we do one more trip. The next day, I promise, I'll be on a jet plane and I'll be gone." He put a lot of emphasis on "gone," making it several syllables.

"So you can go some new place and make new problems?"

"Not problems, man," said Tucker, angry despite himself. "Solutions."

twelve

Phillip looked scared and Tucker didn't like that. It was like the muscles in his face were tight. He looked scared and he looked as if he was lying. There was a bandage on his cheek which Phillip had attributed to a boating accident, getting hit by the boom, etcetera. But Phillip didn't like sailing, didn't like boats of any kind.

It was Monday afternoon and they were sitting at a table in the Garage in Camden. Tucker was drinking a Molsen's. Phillip was just sitting. He hadn't even wanted to play darts, even though Tucker had offered to spot him twenty points in a game of Fives.

"You know what Mainers call a blind deer?" asked Tucker.

"I don't give a fuck," said Phillip. "The ship's coming in tomorrow night, but it'll be late. You might have to sit out there for several hours." They were whispering even though the Garage was empty. The waitress at the bar was reading a magazine about quilt-making. From a radio in the back Bruce Springsteen was singing about cars.

"I'll take a book," said Tucker. Had he ever seen Phillip scared before? There'd been a time in Saigon when a Vietnamese cop, one of the white mice, had taken a shot at him when he and Tucker were doing the rounds of some particularly sleazy clubs. Maybe he'd been scared then.

"Where'd you dock last week?" asked Phillip. He wore a green alligator shirt under a green cotton cardigan sweater and looked as if he'd just come from the golf course. In fact, Phillip hated golf.

"Belfast. Right downtown."

Phillip looked at Tucker for a moment, then blinked. "You mean you walked a million bucks of cocaine right onto the town wharf?"

"We loaded some lobster pots onto my truck. It was in the pots. There weren't many people around." That time in Saigon Phillip said he'd made a pass at the cop's wife. Tucker knew he'd been lying then as well.

"And you'll do the same tomorrow?"

"Sure. What's bothering you anyway?" It occurred to Tucker that maybe he too should be scared. Then he dismissed the thought. He was going to be fast, like Mr. Jet Plane himself. Thirty-six hours and he'd be gone.

"I told you these guys are tough," said Phillip in an angry whisper. "This isn't fooling around, it's real life."

Tucker studied Phillip's face. Not only was there a bandage on his cheek, but his lip was bruised and discolored. "Is that what happened to your face?" he asked.

"I've known you a long time, Tucker," he said. "These guys don't like you. They're suspicious."

Tucker felt something like a cold finger brushing the back of his neck. He almost enjoyed it. "So what are you telling me?"

Phillip put his cigarettes back in his pocket, then stood up and tossed two bucks on the table for Tucker's beer. "I'm not telling you anything," he said.

As Tucker watched Phillip leave, he wondered if Phillip would betray him and guessed he would if the price was right.

Then, almost in surprise, he realized that he had already betrayed Phillip by stealing the cocaine. But it would only be real betrayal if they knew he had stolen it. Judging by Phillip's behavior, however, Tucker figured they knew. He felt bad about that, bad about getting Phillip in trouble. As for these other guys, they were just shadows. If they wanted him, they'd have to catch him and Tucker didn't intend to let that happen.

Tucker retrieved his truck from the parking lot by the wharf and drove over to Sarah's parents' house. It was a typical August day in Camden, meaning the sidewalks were jammed with people buying nautical souvenirs and the traffic was all fouled with Winnebagos. Tucker swung back by the YMCA, then took the road toward the golf club. He hadn't seen Jason since that day on Mt. Battie when he'd had his bad joke. He talked to him on the phone of course but only to say hi and that he loved him. Sarah had refused to speak with him. He hoped she had cooled down some. He had apologized and said he hadn't been serious about dropping Jason over the side of the monument but he knew she didn't believe him. It seemed crazy to think he would ever hurt Jason.

Tucker wanted to give her another chance to change her mind and come back to him. If she did change her mind, then he'd take the money from the cocaine and use it to go to school or invest in something like part of a restaurant, one of those fake French restaurants where they give half portions and charge you double. There was a cooking school in Montpelier; maybe he'd apply. And if she didn't change her mind, then to hell with her. He'd take Jason to that ghost town and it would be her own fault. When you came down to it, a lot of their trouble was her fault. She was too impatient. All right, so he'd been slow getting the house finished, but he'd other work to do like Sheetrocking and tending bar and cutting wood with Ezra. After a full day in the woods, he couldn't be expected to Sheetrock his own house at night.

But by the time Tucker pulled up before his in-laws' house,

he told himself he was lying. It had been a bad plan to move to Brooks and if his wife had turned against him, it was no fault but his own. But he couldn't face teaching and he couldn't face Camden. At least with a ghost town, the houses were already standing. Maybe windows would need replacing and of course you'd have to clean it up, but then it would be done. Tucker got out of the truck and told Rooster to stay. Then he slammed the door and slammed it again when it bounced back open. Maybe he was lying to himself again. Hell, he should ask Cindy if she'd like to take a trip. She'd never been out of Belfast. Probably she'd jump at the chance to go out west. But he'd ask Sarah first. He liked her. Shit, he even loved her. And he would have liked her more if she weren't so stubborn. He hoped she'd gotten over being mad at him. Maybe he should have brought her a present like one of those big bars of white chocolate. When they'd been together, she'd do anything for white chocolate.

As it turned out, Sarah wasn't at home, although when his mother-in-law told him this, Tucker didn't quite believe her.

"I don't know where she is," his mother-in-law said through the screen door. She was a stocky white-haired woman on the verge of getting fat. Although her real name was Hermione, everyone, including Tucker, called her Miner. He had never particularly liked or disliked her. She was just there.

"Is Jason around?" asked Tucker. At least he could see his son.

Miner stepped back from the door. She wore a blue polo shirt, khaki skirt and boat shoes. She's scared of me, thought Tucker, almost embarrassed. "I can't let you in the house," she said.

"Is Jason here?" He had a sudden memory of Miner at their wedding, half soused on champagne and dancing with him to the rock-and-roll band that Sarah's father had hired. Tucker had had to hold her up. She'd told him how happy she was and he told her the same.

"I'm sorry, Tucker," she said. "I can't let you in the house."

Tucker pulled at the screen door. It was locked. The idea of it being locked against him was like being hit in the stomach. Almost without thinking, he stepped back and kicked at the screen, making a big hole. Then he shoved his fist through the hole and reached up to unfasten the lock. Miner stared at him. She looks terrified, Tucker thought. He pulled open the door.

"He's my kid, lady," said Tucker.

Miner backed away, keeping her hands in front of her as if shielding herself. Tucker felt surprised that she would think he'd want to hurt her. Her eyes were open so wide that her face looked stretched. "I'm calling the police," she said.

Tucker ignored her and began searching for Jason. This will be a practice run, he thought, for the time when I really come get him. "Jason!" he called. He wasn't in the library, wasn't in the kitchen, wasn't in the solarium. He tried upstairs and shortly he discovered Jason in his own room sitting on the floor surrounded by about thirty stuffed animals. He didn't seem to be playing with them so much as sitting among them like someone caught in a crowd leaving a theater or a baseball game, just a kid surrounded by a bunch of strangers who happened to be furry and have bright colors and silly grins.

"Hey, Jason," said Tucker, entering the room. "Look who's here. Give me a hug and a kiss."

Jason looked up. At first his face was a blank, then he smiled.

"No presents today," said Tucker. "I thought I'd just see how you were doing." He bent down and picked up Jason, tossed him in the air, gave him a hug and a kiss, then sat down with him again on the floor, pushing aside a stuffed elephant and stuffed gorilla to give himself room.

"So what's new in your life?" said Tucker. "Mine's pretty much shot to hell." Jason was wearing a blue sailor suit which Tucker thought looked faggy. No wonder they hadn't wanted him to see his son if they were going to dress him like that.

Jason stared at his father to see what he would do next. When Tucker did nothing but keep smiling, Jason looked around, located a pink beagle and held it up for Tucker's inspection. "Dog," he said.

"You betcha," said Tucker. "The world's full of them." He reached out and ruffled Jason's hair. "Rooster's out in the truck right now. He sends you his best and a coupla big licks."

The walls were covered with posters of Walt Disney characters: Mickey, Donald, Goofy. They filled the room with artificial cheer. Tucker reached under him and found he was sitting on a book, an illustrated Mother Goose. He showed it to Jason. "Book," he said. "You dig this stuff?"

"Book," said Jason, putting down the pink beagle.

"If wishes were horses, beggars would ride," read Tucker. "If turnips were watches, I'd wear one by my side."

Jason crawled up beside his father. "Book," he repeated.

Tucker leafed through a couple of pages. He heard a car pull up out in front. "Tom, Tom, the piper's son, stole a pig, and away he run, the pig was eat, and Tom was beat, and Tom ran crying down the street." Tucker put down the book and Jason reached for it. "Man, that says it all," said Tucker, running his fingers like a miniature stampede up Jason's back. "The same stuff happening over and over. So what do you say, Jason, you want to take a trip with your daddy?"

Jason tried to balance the book on his head. It slipped down to the floor. He picked up an orange plastic squirt gun by the barrel and began chewing on it. "What's a trip?" he asked.

"It's a gas. It's where you turn your mind inside out," said Tucker, leaning back on his elbows and stretching his feet out in front of him. "But our trip will be simple. We'll just climb into a silver bird and disappear."

"Bird?"

"That's right, a silver bird, and it'll take us far away and then we'll buy ourselves a Jeep and head into the mountains, find a place where no one will think to look for us. We'll have a log cabin. It'll be a beautiful place with waterfalls and antelope and shit like that." And Tucker imagined exotic birds and deer and maybe elk grazing at the edge of his yard.

"Dancing bear be there?" asked Jason, crawling into Tucker's lap.

"Damn right, man. They'll all be there. We'll have the time of our lives."

"Mommy coming?" asked Jason.

Tucker heard feet on the stairs, several sets of feet. Big feet. He put his arms around Jason and nibbled his ear. How soft it was. "Maybe later," he said.

The door opened and two Camden policemen tried to shove through it at the same time, jouncing and jostling each other. They appeared to be expecting bloodshed. When they saw Tucker, they stopped. Their expressions changed to surprise. Miner entered the room behind them.

"Uh, oh," said Tucker, sitting up straight, "here's the law."

The larger of the two policemen pushed his way through the sea of stuffed animals. "You broke that screen door?"

Tucker tickled Jason so he made a happy squealing noise. "I wanted to see my son."

"You've got two choices," said the policeman. "Either you leave right now and don't come back, or you go to jail."

Getting a firmer hold on Jason, Tucker stook up. "I was just going," he said. He kissed Jason on the cheek, gave him a hug, then gently set him down again between an orange bear and a donkey.

Jason picked up the pink beagle and said, "Bow, wow, wow."

As Tucker walked out of the room, Miner stepped behind the smaller of the two policemen.

"Boo," said Tucker.

"He's crazy," said Miner.

———

Lowell Perry leaned back against the side of his red Camaro with his elbows on the roof, letting his cigarette dangle so far down from his mouth that it would have fallen if it weren't stuck to his bottom lip with a drop of spit. The five o'clock sun reflected off the display windows of the bookstore and tearoom across the street. Some of the stores were closing and people were getting off work. Mr. Pierce, who ran the insurance company right in front of where Lowell Perry was standing, was just locking his door. It was a warm day and Perry was sweating a little. Although it would have been hard for anyone to look more relaxed, he was nervous and even angry.

After another moment, Cindy came out of Kirk's Drugstore and turned up the street. She wore a blue gingham dress and carried a white sweater over her arm. When she saw Lowell Perry, she paused ever so slightly, then continued to walk toward him.

" 'Lo, Lowell," she said. "Aren't you working?"

Perry dropped his cigarette on the pavement and crushed it with his cowboy boot. "Got off early. You want to go for a ride?"

"I have to get home and fix dinner." Cindy stood in front of him with her hand up over her eyes to shield them from the light reflected from the windows across the street.

"You got a date with Tucker?" He said this flatly as if just asking the time of day.

"What business is it of yours?"

She had gotten angry and it grated on him. He didn't like people angry with him, especially girls. It seemed she should appreciate the fact that he was giving her another chance. "He's no good, that's all," said Perry. "Don't go out with him."

"You mean so I can go out with you instead?"

She didn't expect an answer and he didn't give her one. After another moment, she turned away almost violently and continued up the street. He watched her go, watched how her ass swung back and forth under the blue gingham. He imagined her stretched out naked on the red leather of his new Corvette with her own sweat and body smells mixed in with the smell of the leather and general newness of the car.

Brian's night vision was no good and never had been. He was always stumbling over his feet in the dark. And following Lowell Perry down this dirt road, he kept tripping over rocks, splashing through mud puddles. Why couldn't they have driven, that's what he wanted to know? But Lowell said it had to be a surprise. Brian didn't like surprises. He liked everything clear and manageable. There wasn't even any moon. He knew where he was of course. A couple of times he'd been over here to sell lobsters to Superior Shellfish, even though mostly he sold them in Belfast and not Searsport. It was closed now and the building was dark.

He tripped again and Lowell Perry shushed him. They had passed the lobster place and were going up a small hill toward the water. A faint yellow glow filled the sky to his left where a ship was being loaded or unloaded. Brian began to see a little better. Perry held out a hand to stop him and Brian saw Tucker's truck parked at the crest of the hill. He couldn't think what Tucker was doing and at first thought he must be fishing or even digging for clams, even though that was illegal because of the junk dumped in the water by the chemical company.

Brian looked over the bed of the truck and through the rear window. He saw Tucker, saw he wasn't wearing a shirt. Then he saw someone else sitting up, saw a bare shoulder and long hair that looked like Cindy's hair. Then he saw her profile, even a bare breast against the yellow light from the docks.

She was kissing Tucker. Brian turned away, almost more embarrassed than astonished. He hadn't seen her naked since she'd gotten big.

"You want to throw a scare into them?" whispered Perry.

Brian stared into Lowell Perry's face, trying to read his expression. "Is this why you brought me here?" he asked. It suddenly occurred to him that Lowell Perry was sick. And there was Tucker with Cindy. Everyone was sick.

"You know what he's doing to her?" said Perry with his mouth about an inch from Brian's ear. "You know where he's got his filthy hands and how he's touching her, how he's sticking himself inside her?"

Brian pulled back and again looked at the truck. He didn't speak. Lowell Perry took his arm and Brian jerked it away. Then he allowed himself to be led a few yards down the hill. Brian thought of Tucker making love to Cindy. More than angry, he felt disappointed. And he felt deceived, not just by Tucker but by everything, as if the world had tricked him. And he also felt angry at Perry, for even though he'd suspected this, he hadn't wanted to know for certain. But then something wet brushed against Brian's leg and he realized it was Rooster. Just as he was trying to see where the dog was, Rooster jumped up, planting his feet on Brian's chest, and licked his face. Brian pushed him down, patting his back and hoping he wouldn't bark.

"Is that his damn dog?" asked Lowell Perry. "I got my knife, why don't we kill it."

"Don't talk crazy!" said Brian, more loudly than he had intended.

Rooster galloped off again. Brian took a deep breath and glanced back at the truck. He had the sense of too many things being out of control.

Perry tightened his grip on Brian's arm. "Brian, listen to me, tomorrow night you and Tucker are going out on the bay. There's a salt boat coming up from Brazil." Brian tried to pull away but Perry held on. "Somebody on board will throw a package in the water and you'll pick it up. Do I have to tell you what's in the package? Then you'll come back to Belfast. The only trouble is that Customs agents will be waiting for you."

Perry let go and Brian stumbled back. "You mean the police?" Tucker had explained about the second trip Sunday afternoon. Brian hadn't been happy but the first trip had been so simple that he at last agreed. But the police were something else again.

Perry shushed him. "Sure, they'll all be there."

Although frightened, Brian also felt he had lost two of his friends—Tucker for what he was doing with Cindy, and Lowell Perry for telling him. At that moment he heard Cindy laugh and it was almost as if she was laughing at him, laughing at her foolish brother-in-law. He felt confused and isolated and wanted to hit someone but didn't know who to hit or why it would do any good. He couldn't imagine being arrested or imagine his life any different than it had been for years.

"Why're you doing this?" asked Brian.

"So you won't go out. Let Tucker go by himself. Let him bring in the cocaine alone." He paused. His voice had been hushed and tight like a mechanical thing. Now it got louder. From the dock came a staccato honking as some truck or forklift began to back up. "You know he's been seeing her every night? He brings her down here. He takes off her clothes. I been watching. He just strips her like you'd strip a banana."

Brian was afraid that Tucker or Cindy would hear. He squeezed Perry's arm. The brake lights on the truck flicked red and then went out.

"You don't owe him any favors," continued Perry, lowering his voice. "He's supposed to be your friend and he's corrupting her. She's just a kid. He's making her as filthy as he is. Let him go out by himself. Let the cops take care of him."

———

Pete Talbot didn't like what was happening. He was afraid that Tucker had fucked up and wasn't paying attention. Although he considered Tucker his best friend, he didn't entirely trust him. It was like Tucker could only live in the present and paid no attention to what had just happened or what might happen in the future. It fucked up his sense of cause and effect.

At that particular moment, Talbot was straddling a straight chair backward and drinking a Budweiser as he watched Tucker pack. Tucker was a lousy packer and was just tossing stuff into his bag any which way. It was Tuesday afternoon and on Tucker's kitchen table was a pile of money amounting to forty thousand smackers. Talbot had done well with the cocaine. He'd found a lot of eager noses, especially over in Bucksport and around the docks in Winterport. Even up in Bangor. He'd cut the cocaine with lactose until he had four hundred grams. Even so it had been potent. If Tucker could get the same amount again, then they'd be talking real money. But now something had gone wrong and Talbot didn't think Tucker was being straight with him.

"There're these new guys around," said Talbot, "tough guys. They're asking questions. They know there's a new supply of coke and they want to know where it came from."

Tucker continued packing. "You mean cops?"

Talbot knew that Tucker knew he hadn't meant cops. "Just the opposite."

Tucker turned, holding a wad of socks in each hand. He wore a red sleeveless T-shirt and his arms were thin and muscular. "Tell them it came from Lowell Perry." He tossed the socks into his duffle bag.

"Why Perry?"

"Because he's a twerp and he's been following me around." There was a scratching at the door. Tucker opened it. Rooster hurried in, ran over to Talbot to give him a lick, then ran to his water dish.

"You told me there'd be no trouble," said Talbot, wiping his face. "Now you've gone and made somebody mad."

"You scared?" asked Tucker. He had started rolling several pairs of jeans into a ball and didn't look up.

"These are mean fellows, Tucker." Talbot hadn't seen them but he'd heard about them—two big guys with beards who punched out a guy in a bar down by the water in Bucksport. Then he'd come across them again out at the 10-4 Diner, asking questions about who was dealing cocaine. Talbot didn't like it one bit.

"You have a weapon?" asked Tucker.

"A rifle. So what? This isn't Vietnam. I can't just ambush them." It occurred to Talbot that Tucker wasn't looking at him because he felt guilty.

Tucker stopped packing, took two Budweisers from the refrigerator, tossed one to Talbot and cracked open the other. "I got one more pickup," he said, sitting down on the edge of the table and patting the pile of money. "I'll give you the stuff tonight. Then I'm outta here. You let me take this money and you can keep every penny you make from dealing the cocaine. That'll be another forty thousand. Isn't it worth the gamble?"

Talbot opened his Budweiser. He imagined those two guys with beards sneaking up outside of Tucker's house. "It's not worth getting hurt," he said. "I thought you knew what you were doing but you've just made a mess of things."

Tucker drank some beer, then started taking three or four flannel shirts from a bureau drawer. He shoved them into the bag without folding them. "I needed the cash so I took the chance."

Talbot had been looking out the window. It was raining. The yard looked like a wreck with junk everywhere and those scrawny chickens. "Who are these guys?" he asked.

"I'm not sure but they might be the people who own the cocaine."

Talbot's hands started to sweat. He moved away from the window. "You mean you stole their fuckin' blow?"

Tucker shoved a ragged L.L. Bean sweater into his duffle bag. "I just skimmed a little and replaced it with lactose."

"But they'd test it."

"I guess so, but who's to say it was me? I mean the stuff came up from Brazil. It'd been on a boat for days. There're all sorts of people who could of done it." Tucker fastened the four grommets on the bag with a padlock.

"Yeah, but they'll come after you first," said Talbot. It struck him almost objectively that this was the first time he'd been frightened since the war. "How could you have done anything so stupid?"

"It was just a matter of doing it and getting out."

"What about me? You'll leave and they'll step on me like a bug." Talbot looked at the money on the table, then looked away. He left his beer on the windowsill. He didn't feel like drinking.

"Then quit now," said Tucker casually. "Forget about the money."

"I don't know. Jesus, Tucker, you're amazing. You rip them off and think they won't notice or do anything?" Talbot looked around the room. He couldn't get over how scared he felt. "Where's your rifle?" he asked.

Tucker took the semi-automatic .22 from the closet and handed it to Talbot. "There's a box of shells in the drawer," he said, gesturing toward the kitchen table.

Talbot sat down and began feeding the shells one by one into a tube that ran through the stock of the rifle. "This is crazy, Tucker," he said. But once he got the cocaine, maybe he could just disappear. Then in a month he'd come back, sell the cocaine and make his forty thousand. By that time everything would be quiet. He'd go home and pack, just like Tucker. As soon as Tucker showed up with the blow, he'd hide it and leave. Janet had been asking about a vacation. As for the kids, they could start school late. They'd go up to Nova Scotia or Prince Edward Island.

"If we do it fast," said Tucker, "then they won't catch us." He finished his beer and flattened the can between his palms. Then he poured some kibbles from a fifty-pound bag into Rooster's dish.

"Just like the paintball game," said Talbot. The rifle felt light and too much like a toy.

"Faster than that," said Tucker.

But Talbot still didn't like it. He stood up and put the rifle on the table. He wasn't convinced that Tucker had any good reason for the stuff he thought. "You got no evidence, man," he said. "You're a dreamer, an anarchist and a fuckin' menace."

Harry Nixon didn't want any mistakes. This was the point in the investigation when too often it all fell back on your head. Like you worked and worked and nobody paid attention but if you fucked up just once, then all those lard asses who had control over your future would come down on you like a ton of bricks. Nixon wanted a desk job and he wanted it in Boston. He'd saved some money and he wanted to buy himself a condo someplace in the Back Bay. Now that his kids were grown up and his ex-wife remarried he could afford to treat himself. Maybe he'd even join a singles club. But he didn't want any trouble and he wasn't sure if he trusted this Belfast police chief not to botch the deal.

Nixon was in Chief Foley's office and it was Tuesday afternoon. Ouside it was raining. It was supposed to rain all day and all night. Nixon hated the damp and hated to get wet. It gave him little pains in his joints. He and Foley were bent over a map spread across the chief's desk. Nixon straightened up, then shifted the .44 Magnum that was stuck in the holster at his belt.

"The only trick will be to get them with the cocaine," he told Foley. "Not just Tucker. I want them all."

The police chief moved away to the window and rubbed his neck. His blue uniform was tight and fitted him like shrink-wrap. "I got plenty of men available," he said.

It wasn't a matter of men, thought Nixon, it was a matter of surprise. He wished it wasn't raining. "We'll have to let him think he's getting away with something, then see what happens." If they fucked up, he might never get his condo. He thought of the personals ads he'd seen in the *Boston Phoenix*. All those women looking for someone affectionate and sincere. It'd be a shame to be stuck in Maine.

"Arrest them when they come ashore," said Foley suddenly. "That's the only sure way."

But Nixon wasn't convinced. He wanted a bigger haul. He only wished that Lowell Perry was more trustworthy. It wasn't good to have spies who were ambitious. They always held something back. Nixon looked at the rain banging off the police cars parked behind Montgomery Ward. Perry wanted a Corvette, that much Nixon knew for certain, but there was also something else he wanted and Nixon wished he knew what it was.

thirteen

When Margaret heard someone banging on the front door, she knew it was Tucker and she knew what he wanted. Pulling her bathrobe more firmly around her, she continued to stare at the television where a policeman was chasing a murderer across the rooftops in some big city, Chicago she thought. The banging kept up but she pretended not to hear. It was just past ten and she wanted to be in bed by eleven. And Brian too, she didn't want him out all night. He'd been tired lately and it was that Tucker's fault. When Brian had left around eight, he'd promised to be back early. She didn't know where he'd gone but he'd been upset. Their whole life had been turned upside down since Tucker had shown his face and she couldn't wait for him to run away to his ghost town or wherever. The hammering got louder and Margaret was afraid it would wake the kids.

From the other end of the sofa, Cindy reached out her bare foot and poked Margaret in the leg. "If you're not going to get it, I am," she said. She had on jeans and a blue sweater of Brian's that came down to her thighs.

Margaret got up and again tightened her bathrobe. She

worried about Cindy and the way she kept talking about Tucker. A year ago Margaret still had the control where she could forbid her even to mention Tucker's name. But at seventeen Cindy was making her own rules. She'd even stopped going to church. Margaret felt bad about that, worrying it might be her fault for not spending more time with her.

Walking through the hall, Margaret flicked on the porch light and through the window she saw Tucker holding the collar of his jean jacket and trying to stand out of the rain. Although she had known it was Tucker, just his outline through the glass filled her with dislike. He kept shifting his weight back and forth as if doing a dance step. Margaret opened the door.

"Where's Brian?" asked Tucker. He seemed surprised to see her.

"He's not here." Margaret began to close the door again.

Tucker put his weight against it, pushing it open and forcing her to step back. "What do you mean he's not here?" he said. "He's got to be here." He stepped into the hall.

Margaret stood in front of him, blocking his path. She wished she had a stick to hit him with. "You can't come in here," she said.

Tucker stepped around her as if she weren't there. He went into the dining room and flicked on the light. "Where'n the hell did he go?"

"He didn't say," said Margaret, following him. She wanted to call the police, then decided to let him look around. It would be easier in the long run. In any case, this was the last time Tucker would set foot in her house. She wouldn't stand to be insulted like this. As she followed Tucker into the kitchen, her slippers made a scuffling noise on the linoleum.

Tucker walked back to the hall stairs and looked up into the darkness. "Hey, Brian!"

"Be quiet," said Margaret. "You'll wake the kids." Cindy stood in front of the sofa, watching them.

214

Tucker went up the stairs, turning on lights and opening doors. Margaret followed him, turning off the lights again. It seemed obvious that Brian wasn't here. She couldn't see what Tucker's problem was. At the same time, his disappointment pleased her. He looked hurt and she thought it served him right. He went into the kids' bedroom and flicked on the light, then, with the kids stirring in their beds, he left again, turning off the light as he shut the door.

Margaret stood in the hall waiting for him. This time she'd say what she thought. To Margaret, Tucker was like a ghost, a bad spirit who lived half in the world and half out. She'd felt that when she first laid eyes on him three weeks earlier. He was so caught up with himself and his foolishness that he hardly existed in the world at all. He was just an appetite, a pair of jaws eating everything in its path. And he'd wreck their lives if they weren't careful.

"Tell me where he went," he asked.

"He went out," said Margaret. She was breathing heavily and didn't want Tucker to see how upset she was. If she had been a man, she'd have hit him.

"But where?"

"What business is it of yours?" said Margaret. "I've had about enough of this. You come barging into our life upsetting everything. You bother Brian, you bother Cindy. Why don't you go back to your own nasty life."

Tucker looked at her as if surprised, then pushed his way around her down the stairs to the front door.

Pulling up the collar of his Levi's jacket, Tucker hurried across Brian's front yard to his truck. He didn't want to walk in the rain, but neither did he want to leave his truck on the wharf. He decided to park it near Rollie's. Fast, fast, he wanted things to move fast. The freighter would be coming any time within the next couple of hours and he had to be out on the bay waiting for it. What the hell was wrong with Brian? As he started to climb into his truck, he saw someone running out of the house toward him. It was Cindy.

"Tucker, hey, Tucker, wait." She was wearing a black raincoat and rain hat with her blond hair poking out beneath it.

Tucker pushed open the door on the passenger's side. Rooster began wagging his tail, hitting Tucker in the face. "You know where Brian went?" He felt Brian had tricked him.

Cindy got into the cab of the truck, pushing the dog back out of her way. Beyond her, Tucker could see Margaret standing in the doorway of her house. "Maybe he's down at the boat."

"Cindy, get back here!" shouted Margaret, coming down the front steps.

Tucker started the truck, then revved the engine. One of the cylinders wasn't firing. He had the sense that everything was falling apart. "He was supposed to meet me here," he said. He accelerated down the street, then turned left on High Street. Rooster sat between them. There was no one around, no cars, no people. As he turned, his headlights picked out a gray cat hurrying along the sidewalk, wet and bedraggled, going home.

"He went out earlier," said Cindy. "He didn't say where he was going. He's been acting funny all day. I tried to talk to him but he just ignored me. I thought he might have heard me come in last night. It was pretty late."

Cindy put her hand on Tucker's knee. He patted it but didn't look at her. He passed Clara's, which seemed deserted, then turned right at the light and coasted down the hill. Down to his left he could see a couple of cars parked in front of Rollie's. His windshield wipers went *whap-whap, whap-whap,* smearing the water around on the glass. He'd have to take the boat out by himself.

"What's going on?" asked Cindy.

"Business, that's all." Tucker parked by the gas station

across from Rollie's, pulling the truck around the corner. He was thinking so hard about Brian and the fact that he would have to run the boat that he had hardly noticed Cindy. Taking a small backpack from behind the seat, he got out of the truck, slammed the door, then started down the hill to the wharf. Rooster would have to stay behind. It was one thing for him to drown but he didn't want his dog to drown too. He realized that Cindy was following him.

"What do you think you're doing?" he asked. The wind was blowing hard and he had to raise his voice.

"Coming with you."

"You can't." Her bare feet in her white sneakers looked fragile. He was struck by how much he liked her. It was something he hadn't counted on or planned for. He wanted to touch her, just reach out and take her hand, but there wasn't time. Everything had to be fast. He turned and continued down the hill as she half walked, half ran beside him.

"Don't tell me that," she said. "You plan to run the boat yourself?"

"Why not?" He reached the wharf, then went down the ramp to the float where the dinghy was tied. He was freezing as well as wet and he hoped he'd find rain gear on the boat. The water was choppy and the float bobbed up and down.

"You think you're so clever, Mr. Tucker," said Cindy, hurrying after him. "You're going out to do something illegal. And since Brian's let you down, you're going to do it all by yourself. Is it smuggling? I'm not a baby. Let me come with you. I can help."

Tucker untied the dinghy, then looked up at Cindy. Rain dripped off her face and she wiped her nose on the back of her hand. She looked small and defiant. Out in the harbor, Tucker saw Brian's lobster boat rocking back and forth. He wondered if he could really operate it, get the package and deal with the cocaine by himself. "Get in," he said.

She got into the dinghy, then steadied it against the float

as Tucker climbed in. He handed her the backpack and took the oars. The rain was running off his face and he licked at it. No joking this time, he told himself, you got to be careful. He rowed steadily as Cindy directed him left or right toward the *Margaret*. Tucker looked back at the dock. There were no cars, no one in sight. Even the restaurant was closed. It was a hard rain and his clothes were drenched. In the morning many trees would be showing their fall colors. By then he'd be on his way out of here. He'd pick up Jason and by eight he'd be on a flight heading west. Wouldn't Sarah be surprised when he burst into the house and snatched his kid. He'd have to remember to pull their phone wires, maybe do something to their cars. If he got a half-hour head start, they'd never catch him.

The dinghy bumped up against the lobster boat. Cindy tied the painter to the mooring as Tucker removed the oars. Then he grabbed hold of the *Margaret* and pulled himself over the side. Cindy tossed him the backpack and he gave her his hand to help her up. The boat was rocking and he slipped a little. He tried not to think what it would be like out on the bay. Ducking into the cabin, he took off his Levi's jacket, then found a sweater and a yellow slicker and put them on. In the cooler, he discovered one last six-pack of Budweiser left over from the picnic. He took one, cracked it open and drained half of it without taking a breath. This at least was a smidgen of good fortune. Wiping his mouth, he turned his attention to starting the boat.

Cindy stood in a corner of the shelter out of the wind. Rain drummed on the roof. Tucker flicked the toggle switch and pulled out the choke as he had seen Brian do, then pushed the starter so that it made a grinding noise. Tucker stopped pushing the starter, took a deep breath and blew out between pursed lips. He pushed the starter again. This time the motor caught.

"Hey," said Cindy excitedly.

Tucker pushed the throttle forward very slowly, not wanting to disturb anything. The motor coughed and started to die. He pulled back on the throttle and gave it a little more choke. Then he waited a moment. He could see nothing out in the bay, just blackness. He wondered how he'd find the freighter. He had to remember about the chain steering, that it took a moment for the boat to respond. He pushed the throttle forward and the motor increased its low growl. He pushed in the choke a little. From someplace he heard a shout, then another.

"It's Brian," said Cindy, pointing toward the dock.

Tucker saw Brian standing on the float waving his arms. For a second, he considered going out in the bay without him, but he didn't trust himself with the boat and didn't want to risk losing the money. Also he was worried. He'd been bothered by what Pete Talbot had told him that afternoon about those two guys with beards, and Tucker had a sense of dark forces conspiring around him. He felt like someone winding along the S-curve of a dollar sign, while the enemy moved up the two straight bars to cut him off.

"I'll pick him up," said Tucker. He put the boat in gear but nothing happened.

"We're still tied to the mooring," said Cindy. "I'll get it."

Tucker pulled back on the throttle. It occurred to him that in Vietnam he never forgot anything, was always alert and never fucked up. Maybe he'd smoked too much dope, maybe that was the trouble. Cindy waved to him from the stern. Tucker again pushed the throttle forward and turned the wheel as the lobster boat curved left toward the float. Cindy rejoined Tucker by the wheel, then ducked into the cabin. At first he thought she was cold. Then he realized that she didn't want Brian to see her.

Tucker again drew back the throttle and the *Margaret* drifted toward the float. Brian jumped, then hung for a second on the gunwale before pulling himself over. He too wore a yellow slicker. As Brian recovered his balance, Tucker steered the boat out into the bay and gave it more gas. He felt angry with Brian and he didn't trust himself to speak. Brian came into the shelter out of the rain.

"Where the hell you been?" said Tucker. "We might have missed the freighter." Looking into Brian's face, Tucker saw he was angry as well, but what did he have to be upset about? It was Tucker's plan that would be ruined by his fooling around.

"I wasn't going to go," said Brian.

"Are you nuts? Why not?" Tucker turned the wheel sharply to avoid sideswiping a moored sailboat which he hadn't seen in the dark. Brian took the wheel and Tucker didn't object. He finished his beer, crushed the can and tossed it into the stern. Even above the sound of the motor, he could hear the rain pattering on the roof and making a hissing noise as it beat against the water.

"I just wasn't, that's all," said Brian. He spoke without looking at Tucker.

The cabin door opened and Cindy emerged. Tucker could just see her face in the lights from the control panel. She seemed embarrassed. "Hi," she said.

Brian turned quickly, "What's she doing here?"

"She was going to help me," said Tucker.

"Are you kidding?" said Brian. "She could go to jail. We've got to take her back." They were already out of the harbor and behind them Belfast was disappearing into the rain and fog. The boat was beginning to roll heavily. Tucker had to brace himself against the roof and after bulkhead. Brian began to turn the wheel and Tucker put his hand on his arm to stop him.

"There's not time," he said.

Brian pulled back on the throttle and the boat slowed. Tucker looked out toward Isleboro for some sign of the freighter but could see nothing. The trouble was it could come during the next several hours or next several minutes.

Brian started to speak, then didn't. Cindy was looking at him. Brian shook his head as if to clear it. "The police know about it," he said at last. "The Customs patrol will be at the dock when we get back. It's Lowell Perry. He works for them. He knew about the boat coming up the coast and about the cocaine."

The wind took some of his words and it was hard to hear. At first Tucker thought that Brian was joking. "How'd you know all this?" he said.

Brian turned away from Tucker. "He told me," he said.

"That rat," said Cindy.

"Why didn't you let me know earlier?" said Tucker. Again he thought of dark forces conspiring around him. He knew Perry had been up to something. Why hadn't he paid more attention? "We could have changed our plans."

Brian still had his back to him. "I wanted you to go to jail," he said.

Tucker didn't understand. He grabbed Brian's arm. "What have I done to you?"

Spinning quickly, Brian swung out with his fist. Tucker didn't see it and Brian's fist glanced off his jaw. "You been fooling around with Cindy, that's what!" said Brian.

Tucker stumbled back against a lobster pot and fell to the deck. He lay there as the rain beat down on his face. Brian kept shouting at him.

"I told you and told you to leave her alone! You don't give a damn about anyone! You come into people's lives and just make a mess of them."

Tucker sat up a little. He thought of the police waiting for them. "I like her," he said. He saw Cindy standing in the corner of the shelter, small and drawn into herself.

"She's just something for you to play with," said Brian, still shouting and coming into the rain. Water was splashing over the gunwales.

Tucker got to his feet and steadied himself against the wall of the shelter on the port side. "Hey, man, we're buddies."

"That's not how buddies work!" shouted Brian. "You're just using me. I'm just a guy with a boat and you need a boat."

Tucker started to get angry. "Then why'd you come back if you feel that way?" asked Tucker.

Brian kicked at one of the lobster pots. The boat was rocking a lot and Tucker felt queasy in his stomach. Maybe another beer would make him feel better.

"I don't know," said Brian. "I didn't want you to go to jail."

"It's the money," said Tucker. "You need it as bad as I do."

Brian started shouting again. "I like you. You're my best friend. I've known you all my life." He took another swing at Tucker but missed as Tucker dodged away.

"You got a funny way of showing it," said Tucker. He didn't want to fight with Brian, who could probably beat him with one hand behind his back.

"But we got to get Cindy off the boat."

It seemed to Tucker that they could still go ahead with their plans. "There's no need. We'll pick up the stuff like before and sink it in a lobster pot. Then we'll drop Cindy off and go back to Belfast. When the cops show up, we'll say we been fishing and drinking beer."

"In the rain at midnight?" asked Cindy.

Tucker came back into the shelter. "Sure, I'm a crazy guy. Why not?"

"It's too dangerous," said Brian. "We should go back now."

"Look," said Tucker, "tomorrow morning I pick up my kid and I'm on a plane out of here. I've got to do this. If we pull it off, they'll never find me."

"What about me and Cindy?" asked Brian. He had lowered his voice and Tucker could barely hear him.

"What about you? You'll have ten grand and no worries." Tucker didn't see what his trouble was. The cops couldn't do anything if they didn't find any cocaine. Brian could come out later by himself, pick up the stuff and meet him in Saturday Cove. Then Tucker could take it down to Phillip, grab his kid and be gone.

"You still don't understand, do you?" said Brian.

"What's there to understand?" asked Tucker. The chance of outwitting Lowell Perry made it a whole new challenge. "Come on, man, the ship'll be here anytime. We gotta get going."

Brian made no movement toward the wheel. "I thought if I told you about the cops," said Brian, "you'd just forget about it and we could go home."

Tucker felt exasperated. He guessed that Brian was making trouble because he was still angry about Cindy. Wasn't she old enough to make her own choices? "I don't know what you're talking about," said Tucker. "You want to throw away that money? Jesus, you know your problem? You're sentimental."

Brian took off his rain hat and rubbed his head. "Maybe so," he said. "Maybe that's just what I am."

"And the freighter?" persisted Tucker.

"I don't know."

"Look, I know I've been bad," said Tucker, "but we've only got this tiny bit left to do." He paused, then added, "Come on, Brian, I need your help." Tucker hated saying that, but he did need his help. Without Brian the whole thing would fall apart. Couldn't Brian see that he felt embarrassed?

"You just think I'm a fool," said Brian.

"I need your help," repeated Tucker.

"I'm always helping you," said Brian, taking the wheel and pushing forward the throttle. "And what do I get back?"

Tucker took another beer from the cooler. He didn't want to say anything or argue any more. His stomach still felt queasy. He went into the cabin to get the flashlight. Taking it from the cabinet, he shone it around the small space. A new Coleman lantern, held in place by tension cords, stood on a shelf. Tucker had put it there that morning. He noticed his paint pistol and considered sticking it in his belt, then left it where it was. He drank some beer but it didn't help his stomach. He kept thinking that Brian was right. But it wasn't true that he'd just been playing with Cindy. He liked her, he really liked her. The only way to fix things was to get out. In the morning he'd be gone and Brian and Cindy and Margaret, even Pete Talbot, they could all have their lives back. He drank some more beer. It didn't taste good. That, however, was no reason not to drink it. He found his baseball cap and put it on. As he left the cabin, he put his hand on the cap to keep it from blowing away.

Brian was steering the lobster boat farther into the channel. Tucker could just make out some lights over at Bayside and maybe a house on Isleboro. "Can it get by us without our knowing?" he asked.

Brian didn't answer.

Tucker braced his legs as the boat rocked back and forth, holding one hand against the ceiling of the shelter. He was glad that he hadn't brought Rooster, who would have been sliding all over the place. The rain blew against him even in the corner of the shelter and water sloshed over the gunwales. Tucker wished he could rummage around in the cabin for more clothes. He held the light, ready to flash it when the freighter went by. Cindy stood behind him, using him to block her from the wind. She reached out to take his hand. Tucker looked to see if Brian might notice but it was too dark for him to see anything. Even so, Tucker moved his hand away. He didn't want to think about her right now.

They waited half an hour without speaking. It seemed to Tucker that Brian was trying to make him feel bad. Tucker knew he had used him and maybe he should have let Cindy alone as well, but Brian was still getting ten thousand. That should make up for a lot. But even as he thought it, Tucker knew it wasn't true. The main trouble was that Brian still saw him as he had seen him in high school. Margaret was right, Tucker thought; he was no hero. Not only that but he had no wish to be a hero. Heroes got killed. He'd seen it happen. What you needed was to be someplace where nobody paid attention to you. Shit, that's what it was all about, finding the perfect foxhole.

This time it was Cindy who heard the freighter first. Brian had turned the lobster boat toward the shore so it was heading into the wind. Tucker went to the stern where Cindy was pointing off toward Isleboro and tried to will his eyes to see through the darkness. He could hear nothing over the noise of the lobster boat and wind and rain. Mostly he was hanging on to the side to keep from losing his footing. Then he saw the freighter's forward anchor light high above the lobster boat. It seemed to be bearing down upon them.

"It's going to hit us!" he shouted to Brian.

The lobster boat surged forward toward the mainland, sending up a rooster tail of water. Off to the port side the freighter rose up like a great wall. Way, way above him Tucker could see a sailor looking down. Tucker clung to the gunwales, half ready to dive overboard. He imagined trying to help Cindy make it to shore, wherever that was. The salt spray made it hard to see. The freighter's forward light bathed them in pale smoky light and everywhere the water seemed white and frothy. But then the distance between the two boats increased. The prow of the freighter missed them by twenty feet. The lobster boat was tossed up in its wake and the propeller made a noise like a dentist's drill. A great wave of water splashed over the stern. Tucker grabbed Cindy's arm to keep her from falling. Then they both fell and slid across the deck before

Tucker was able to catch hold of the wall of the shelter. His baseball cap had disappeared. Tucker scrambled to his feet, then helped Cindy. The noise of the freighter's engines drowned out their voices, the rain, even the sound of the lobster boat itself.

As the freighter slid past them, Tucker stumbled to starboard side and got ready with the light. The stern of the lobster boat was bouncing like the tip of a diving board and water continued to slosh over the gunwales. Brian turned the boat across the freighter's wake and Tucker flashed the light. They were surrounded by bubbling white water as the freighter began to pull away from them. Tucker kept slipping on the deck. After a moment, he saw a green light fall from the port quarter of the freighter, making a green arc through the darkness. Brian saw it as well and steered the *Margaret* toward the green Cyalume lightsticks bobbing in the water. Leaning over the side, Tucker grabbed at one of the orange life jackets with the gaff hook. Brian handed him a rope. Tucker slipped it through the life jacket and when it was secure, he called back to Brian, who wrapped the other end around the niggerhead on the pot hauler. The package and the two life jackets rose out of the water. Tucker dragged them aboard, then unfastened the package and threw the lightsticks and life jackets into the bay. Then he carried the package into the cabin. Cindy followed him.

"Just stay out here idling for a bit," Tucker told Brian. "I got to fix this." Brian didn't answer.

Once in the cabin, Tucker took the Coleman lantern, pumped it up, then lit it. The bright light was almost blinding after the dark. Tucker spread some newspapers out on the table and put the package on top. Opening his backpack, he removed the Cuisinart kitchen scale, some measuring spoons, a package of lactose and a dark red aluminum water bottle. He could feel his heart beating hard and he wondered if they had really been in danger. He liked danger, liked how it made everything fast. Cindy sat behind him on a lobster pot.

"What are you doing?" she asked. She was shivering and rubbing her hands to warm them.

"Engaging in a little petty theft," said Tucker. He opened the package. As before it was divided into ten separate packages, each weighing a kilogram. He started to undo them.

"Won't that make somebody mad?" Cindy took off her rain hat and shook free her blond hair.

"People like that are mad all the time anyway."

Carefully Tucker began to take twenty-five grams of coke from each package, putting it into the dish on the scale until he had two hundred and fifty grams. The lobster boat was rocking badly and he was afraid of spilling the cocaine on the floor.

"But it doesn't belong to you," said Cindy. She sounded more curious than concerned. Tucker didn't see why she was bothering about it.

"This is illegal goods. It belongs to whoever has his hands on it." The scale slid to the side of the table and Tucker pulled it back.

"Aren't you afraid they'll come after you?"

Tucker glanced at her and saw anxiety in her face. He realized that even though he was afraid of those two guys with beards, their presence made the whole business more exciting. He put the pilfered cocaine into the red aluminum bottle, then measured out twenty-five grams of lactose which he mixed with the cocaine in the first package.

"Who's to say it was me?" said Tucker. "It could have been the guy on the freighter."

"And Brian," said Cindy, "they'll come after him too."

Tucker reached out to touch her arm, meaning to reassure her, but she pulled away. He went back to measuring the lactose into the packages of cocaine. Her concern almost worried him. Then he shook his head and tried not to get distracted. "What's Brian know?" asked Tucker. "He's just the guy with the boat."

"But do they think that?"

Ten minutes later Tucker had rewrapped the cocaine into two packages and put each package into a lobster pot. He was again wearing his Levi's jacket under the yellow slicker and the aluminum bottle with Talbot's cocaine was in the large inside pocket. Tucker opened the door of the cabin and lugged the two lobster pots out onto the deck. Brian looked at him but didn't try to help. Tucker returned to the cabin for the scale and lactose, which he dropped over the side of the boat. Cindy followed with the wadded-up newspaper which she threw over the side as well. For a second it looked like a great white bird before it disappeared into the dark.

"Probably a dozen cops watching us with binoculars," said Brian.

"What's there to see except rain?" said Tucker. "Swing by your other pots and I'll push these babies over. Make sure you know where it is. You'll have to come back here tonight. Let's hope the plastic doesn't leak."

"What about Cindy?" asked Brian with his back to Tucker.

I'll take her with me, thought Tucker, and make love to her until the steam puffs out of her ears. "We'll drop her off below town near the hospital," he said.

Cindy had dragged the two lobster pots with the cocaine to the stern of the boat. Tucker joined her and took the metal bottle from his Levi's jacket. He was turned away from Brian and didn't want him to hear. He gave Cindy the metal bottle. "Take this," he told her, "and put it under the seat of my truck."

She held it in her hands, looking down at it, a gray shape in the dark. "What if I get caught?" she asked.

Tucker felt angry. Everyone was falling apart on him. "You won't get caught," he said, trying to sound reassuring. "Jesus,

will you stop worrying? If you hear anyone, just heave it."
But don't heave it far, he thought.

It was another thirty minutes before they got back to Belfast
harbor. Tucker stared over the bow looking for any activity
on the town wharf. The two lobster pots had been dumped
over the side and attached to one of Brian's markers near
Brown's Head. Then they had let off Cindy near the road
that led to Belfast City Hospital. Because of the rocks, Brian
hadn't wanted to go in too close, so Cindy had to jump off
about twenty feet from shore where the water was up to her
waist. Tucker was now on his fourth beer. Brian was also
drinking one.

"This is supposed to be a party," said Tucker, "and we act
like ghosts." He had gotten two fishing rods from the cabin
and was letting several mackerel jigs trawl behind the boat.
If they caught themselves some mackerel all the better. Tucker's queasy feeling had vanished and he felt ready for action.

"They're hiding up there," said Tucker. "They're going to
wait for us to make our move, then jump on us, just like the
fuckin' Viet Cong. Trouble is we already done escaped."

Brian pulled back on the throttle and the lobster boat drifted
toward the mooring and the dinghy. "It's not like that," said
Brian. "This is Belfast, Maine. Chief Foley's up there and
some of the others. I've known them all my life."

"So what?" said Tucker. "They can't prove anything and
you're another five thousand dollars richer."

"Not yet I'm not."

"Well, you will be soon. It'll be a breeze. You can meet
me in Saturday Cove and I'll give you the money right there."
Reaching over the side with the gaff hook, Tucker grabbed
the mooring. Brian cut the engine. It was raining harder and
water ran down Tucker's neck. He picked up the fishing poles
and tackle box. No mackerel, not even some seaweed. He
took the last beer for good luck, then climbed into the dinghy.

Brian rowed back to the wharf. Several inches of water sloshed around in the bottom but they didn't bother bailing it out. Tucker didn't think he had a dry place on his body. At least once he got to Talbot's he could put on something warm. Brian wouldn't look at him and Tucker couldn't tell if he was scared or angry or what. They tied up at the float, then walked up the ramp which was slippery and wet. Tucker began to exaggerate his walk, swaying a little. He slapped Brian on the back. Here it comes, he thought, they gonna jump us.

As soon as they reached the parking lot, there was a slamming of car doors as uniformed police and several men in plainclothes surged toward them through the rain. Tucker saw that some were holding revolvers down at their sides but the whole display was so much less than he had imagined that he felt disappointed.

"What the hell's this noise?" Tucker shouted.

Chief Foley had some kind of paper which he was trying to keep from getting wet. One of the plainclothesmen snatched the tackle box from Tucker's hand. "We have a warrant," said Foley, "to search you, the boat and your personal belongings. I must tell you that you have the right to remain silent. . . ."

Tucker swayed back and forth. He guessed they thought the cocaine was in the tackle boxes. How silly. "Not me, man," he shouted, "hear me yell. *Wowowo!*" Tucker laughed to himself and looked around the lot. Over by the fish market, he saw Lowell Perry's Camaro. Tucker would like to trot over there, yank him out of his car and beat the pants off him. Not worth getting shot for, though. Nothing was.

Brian felt humiliated. He was sitting on a stool in police headquarters while a few feet away Tucker continued to make a fool out of himself, shouting and carrying on and acting drunk. Maybe he really was drunk after all that beer. The Customs agents had searched his boat, they'd even gotten a dog over there as Tucker laughed and said the dog would fall out of the dinghy. The big Doberman had looked as nervous and uncomfortable as Brian felt. When they hadn't found anything, they brought Tucker and Brian back to police head-quarters. Then, for the past hour, they'd been going round and round with their questions. Brian shook his head and couldn't bring himself to speak. Tucker appeared to be having the time of his life.

"Fishing," repeated Tucker, "I told you we were fishing. Of course there was nothing else on the boat. What did you think we had? Gold?"

Tucker was sitting and Foley and another man were standing over him, trying to frighten him or threaten him, but Tucker seemed unconcerned. Two other men were standing by the door. One was a local patrolman. Brian knew him pretty well. He had married one of Margaret's cousins and Brian had gone to the wedding. They had given them some blue canisters for flour and sugar and stuff. Margaret had wanted to buy the red ones, but Brian liked the blue better. The patrolman, Jimmy Pendleton, kept looking at Brian like he'd never seen him before.

"What were you doing fishing at midnight in the rain?" asked Foley.

Tucker grinned his dog-like grin. "You caught me. You trapped me in an untruth. Actually, we were drinking and bullshitting, but in order to keep our hands busy we put a line in the water."

Foley was disgusted. He glared at Brian, who ducked his head. Even if they got out of this, Brian thought, he wouldn't be able to look Foley in the face again. Also everybody in town would hear about it. He might even lose his job.

"What'd you catch?" asked the older of the two plainclothes-men. He was a big man in his forties and Brian had heard the police chief call him Nixon.

"Nothing, man," said Tucker. "All the fish was asleep." He

swayed on his stool and shut his eyes as if to show he'd like to be asleep himself. He opened his eyes again. "Fish ain't dumb. Look, we been through this again and again. You been on the boat, your dog's been on the boat, you searched everything. What'd you find? Either charge us or let us go."

"You had drugs on the boat," said Nixon. "The dog smelled it."

Tucker shook his head. "He smelled the beer, man. He smelled my aspirin or cough medicine"—here Tucker coughed—"he smelled my Pepto-Bismol. Either put us in jail or let us go."

Foley stood over by the door. Nixon looked hard at Tucker, then went to join him. They talked for a moment. Brian tried to catch Jimmy Pendleton's eye, hoping to make some apologetic gesture, but Pendleton was watching Tucker as if he expected him to make some sudden movement, which Pendleton intended to stop. Tucker yawned, stared up at the ceiling, then scratched under his arm. It was cold in the room and Tucker was sopping wet but he showed no sign of discomfort. Brian couldn't get over how much Tucker seemed to be enjoying himself.

Chief Foley walked back to them. "Get outta here," he said. Brian jumped to his feet. Tucker got up more slowly and made a little bow. He's going to drive them crazy, thought Brian. Tucker strolled to the door and into the hall, still grinning. Brian followed him. Pendleton stood aside, refusing to look at him. Brian wanted to grab Pendleton's arm and shake it, but he was afraid to.

Harry Nixon shut the office door. He'd like to smack that Tucker one. But it didn't matter. It was even better this way. Make them think they were getting away with something. "We'll get them later," he said.

"You mean just those two?" asked Foley.

Nixon shook his head. He had men outside in cars, men

down at the wharf. Anything that happened, Nixon wou
about it. It was like having a net and he was the big fishe
He'd settle this baby and his stock would go up a hu
points.

"No," he told Foley, "I want them all."

down at the wharf. Anything that happened, Nixon would hear about it. It was like having a net and he was the big fisherman. He'd settle this baby and his stock would go up a hundred points.

"No," he told Foley, "I want them all."

fourteen

Tucker had grabbed another six-pack before the Quik-Stop closed at one. Everything was right. Everything was swell. He had found the aluminum water bottle tucked beneath his front seat and when he and Jason changed planes in Chicago, he'd send Cindy a little trinket from the Windy City. *"Whooee,"* he shouted to Rooster as he shot along 131 toward Toddy Pond where Talbot lived. It was heading toward 2:00 A.M. and a whole new day. This was the day he got outta here. Give Talbot the blow, shoot back to his own place for the money and his bag, then pick up the rest of the cocaine sunk in those lobster pots and head down to Camden. He'd call Phillip from Talbot's house. No need to have him worry.

For a moment, Tucker considered forgetting about Talbot, Brian and Phillip and leaving right now. After all, he had the forty thousand, plus that earlier five from Phillip. But then he felt ashamed of himself. At least let everyone have their money. So what if it made it more dangerous. He wasn't going to cheat his friends.

As for the cops, they might see the boat going out again, but how would they know where Brian and Tucker were planning to join up? They were a real team, bamboozling those boys in blue. Bayside, Temple Heights, Saturday Cove— he'd meet Brian wherever it was easiest. Then he'd be gone. He'd pop Brian his five grand and keep the ten he got from Phillip, then maybe catch a few winks someplace before making his 6:00 A.M. baby snatch. He'd have fifty thousand smackers. His in-laws' house was usually unlocked and anyway he knew where they kept the key. He'd tiptoe through it in his best LURP manner. Mr. Shadow was coming for his kiddo. They wouldn't even know he'd been around. For a moment, Tucker thought again of those dark powers, the ccps or those guys with beards, but he was moving fast now, he was watching his back. They'd have to move like lightning to catch him and nobody, just nobody was quite that quick.

Tucker braked and skidded into the left turn at Nickerson Mills just shy of Robertson Hill. Bouncing a few hundred yards along the dirt road, he looked for the cutoff to Pete's place— a rough track leading into the woods, even more isolated than Tucker's. If you didn't know it was there, you'd never find it. His windshield wipers were making a mess of things and it was hard to see through the rain.

Tucker made the turn, then took another can of beer from the six-pack on the floor. Maybe he should have picked up a six-pack for Talbot but he probably had one already. Tucker jounced along the track toward Talbot's house, bracing himself in his seat so he wouldn't crack his head on the roof. His springs squeaked and the whole truck rattled as he splashed through the mud holes. After another moment, he pulled into the yard and drew to a stop behind Talbot's truck. His house was dark. Everybody snoozing. Tucker got out with the alu-mimum water bottle and the rest of the beer, leaving his lights on so he could see. Slamming his door, he slammed it again when it bounced open. Rooster ran off across the yard, probably looking for Spike. Tomorrow Tucker would leave his truck near the Bangor bus station and take a cab to the airport.

He wouldn't be sorry to see the end of the old hunk-a-junk. At least he wouldn't have to spend any more time staring under its hood wondering why it was acting up.

Tucker hurried up the front path. There were flowers on either side. It was still raining but he didn't care. Couldn't get much wetter than he was already. Tucker bent over, picked some kind of wet flower and stuck it in a buttonhole of his Levi's jacket. Then he trotted up the steps and knocked on the door. No answer. He knocked again. Still no answer. He tried the knob and found that the door was open. He gave it a push with his foot and stepped inside.

"Pete," he called. The lights from his truck shone through the window. Something was wrong.

"Tucker, Tucker, watch out!"

It was Pete's voice. Then there were gunshots—Tucker's own rifle, a quick staccato banging, almost a snapping. At the same moment, someone smashed against Tucker, knocking him back and smacking his head against the wall. Big hands grabbed his jacket and yanked it up over his head. Then he was hit in the stomach. The six-pack flew in one direction, the metal bottle in another. Tucker tried to twist away and was again hit in the stomach. He fell to the floor. The light blinked on. Pete was half crawling, half limping toward the doorway. There was blood on the floor behind him. A big man with a beard pointed Tucker's rifle at Talbot and began firing, pulling the trigger as fast as he could pull it.

"No!" shouted Tucker. He tried to get up but a second man with the beard kicked him back against the wall. The first man fired about six times. Pete Talbot had fallen forward. He wasn't moving.

"Pete!" shouted Tucker.

The second man pulled Tucker to his feet and threw him against a table, knocking it over. Then he picked up the metal water bottle.

"You killed him," said Tucker. He stared at Pete. He wore

a white cowboy shirt and a dozen red holes pocked his back.

"You killed him," said the first man. "It's your fuckin' rifle." He began reloading, feeding the shells into the tube in the stock.

"Pete." Tucker took a step toward his friend.

The second man grabbed him and pushed him toward the wall. He had a revolver stuck in his belt. He unscrewed the top of the metal bottle and looked inside.

"Hey, Seymour," he said, "the soldier was bringing his buddy a little present."

Seymour looked in the bottle, then looked at Tucker and shook his head. His beard was black and bushy but his black hair was cut short. He was a big man with a big beer belly. Both men wore Oshkosh overalls and plaid shirts.

Still carrying the rifle, Seymour walked over to Tucker and kicked him in the leg with his work boot. Then he pointed up at the ceiling. "What's that?" he said.

Tucker glanced up but saw nothing. As he was looking, Seymour lifted the rifle and smashed Tucker in the stomach with the butt. Tucker retched and stumbled back against the wall, hitting something in a glass frame which fell to the floor and broke. Tucker was down on his knees vomiting beer. The glass frame had held Talbot's diploma from the University of Oregon, which he had kept around as a kind of hippy joke.

Seymour reached down, grabbed Tucker's ear and yanked up his head. "Where's the rest of the product?" he said.

Tucker couldn't think what he was talking about. "What product?"

Seymour let go of him and hit him again with the rifle butt, this time on the shoulder. Then he grabbed Tucker's collar and dragged him across the room through Talbot's blood, trying to hit him as he went, swinging the rifle and banging it against Tucker's head and shoulder.

Seymour pulled Tucker to his feet and shoved him into a

straight chair, which fell over backward. Tucker's head smacked the floor.

"Shit," said Seymour. He again dragged Tucker to his feet, righted the chair and pushed Tucker into it, this time more carefully. He slapped Tucker, then left him to walk over to Talbot. Tucker felt dizzy. His ribs and head hurt. He started to get up and the other man pointed his revolver at him. Seymour dragged over Talbot's body, then yanked him up so he was almost standing and set the body into another straight chair which he pushed and jostled until it stood only a few feet from the one in which Tucker was sitting. Talbot's head fell forward until his chin bumped his chest. His eyes were slightly open and he seemed to be staring at Tucker through the cracks. He looked stupid. He's dead, Tucker kept thinking, he's dead.

Seymour took the rifle and shoved the barrel into Tucker's mouth, bashing it against his teeth and shoving the barrel into his throat so the bead tore the roof of his mouth. "Where's the rest of the product?" repeated Seymour.

Tucker couldn't talk. The gun barrel was pressed against his pharynx and he retched. He could hardly breathe.

"Take the gun out of his mouth, Seymour," said the other man. "He can't talk with his mouth full."

Seymour pulled the barrel out of Tucker's mouth and pressed it against his nose so that Tucker tipped back in his chair. "In the bay," said Tucker, "the stuff's in a lobster pot in the bay."

"Go get the car, Mr. Jones," said Seymour. Then he shoved the rifle forward, until Tucker's chair tipped over and he fell to the floor. Talbot still seemed to be looking at him. I'm sorry, thought Tucker. He wanted to say kill me too, but he didn't have the nerve. He thought Seymour would do it. Tucker lay on the floor and tried not to move. If he lay still enough, maybe his body would slip right through the floor, maybe the floor's molecules and his body's molecules would just slide around each other and he'd fall through to the earth below. Then he'd crawl out into the woods and let the rain beat upon him.

Several minutes later Seymour kicked Tucker in his kidneys and his whole spine snapped straight. "Get to your feet, soldier, Mr. Jones is back with the car."

Tucker started to get up. Seymour grabbed his collar and yanked so that Tucker's feet scraped and jittered across the floor like a puppet. Seymour pulled open the screen door and pushed Tucker down the steps into the rain. He tumbled forward and banged against the side of a car, an old Oldsmobile. Tucker slipped in the mud. Seymour came down the steps and again dragged Tucker to his feet. But at that moment there was a furious barking and a black shape rushed past Tucker and fastened itself onto Seymour's leg.

"Yow!" shouted Seymour, letting Tucker go and stumbling back.

Tucker jumped to his feet, meaning to run toward the woods, but then he saw Seymour grab Rooster by the red bandanna, yank him off his leg and lift him into the air. "This is one dead fuckin' dog," said Seymour.

Tucker kicked out at Seymour, then hit him in the face. At the same time, he pulled Rooster away. He saw Jones hurrying toward him. "Run, Rooster, get outta here." Rooster disappeared across the lawn, just as Jones grabbed Tucker and hit him across the side of his head with the revolver. There were half a dozen shots from Tucker's rifle as Seymour fired at the dog, then swung the rifle toward Tucker.

"Get out of the way, Mr. Jones. He's dead meat."

"Marston wants him alive."

"He's not going to get him."

"You want that coke or not? You can finish him later. It'll be a treat for you."

Opening the front door of the Oldsmobile, Jones pushed

Tucker inside. Seymour stood there for a moment with Tucker's rifle, pointing it at Tucker through the open window. Then he reached back and threw the rifle toward the trees before climbing into the rear seat. Tucker didn't move. He wanted to look and see if Rooster was all right but he didn't dare to. Reaching forward, Seymour grabbed Tucker's hair and yanked his head back against the headrest. Then he shoved something hard and cold against Tucker's ear.

"Let's go, Mr. Jones," said Seymour. "The chief's waitin'."

Jones fishtailed across the grass, then bumped onto the dirt track, giving it the gas so the car leapt forward, spinning its tires. At the end of the track he turned without slowing and the Oldsmobile again fishtailed down the dirt road toward Route 131, which it slid onto sideways. The Oldsmobile slewed around toward the trees, then straightened itself out, heading toward Belfast. Tucker couldn't move and didn't know what he'd do if he could. These are the forces of darkness, he thought. But he knew it wasn't so simple. All that time Pete had been careful in Vietnam just to get shot down in Brooks. And now they'll kill Brian, thought Tucker. He pulled his head forward half hoping that Seymour would kill him too.

Seymour slapped the side of the face with the barrel of the revolver, then yanked his head back. "Don't get restless, soldier," he said.

It took fifteen minutes for Jones to reach Brian's house. As the Oldsmobile drew to a stop, Seymour got out and stood waiting in the rain. Tucker started to sit up, then felt a sharp pain in his left side as Jones shoved a revolver in his ribs. By the light of the streetlight Tucker saw that Jones was grinning.

Brian's front door opened and Brian stumbled down his front steps and fell to his knees on the sidewalk. A tall man in a tan London Fog raincoat and a dark fedora came down the steps after him. He prodded Brian with his foot and Brian got up and walked toward the car.

"Hey, chief," said Seymour, "the stuff's . . ."

"He already told me, Seymour," said Marston. "Let's go."

Lowell Perry saw the gray Oldsmobile drive onto the wharf and stop at the ramp. Four men got out and Perry recognized Brian and Tucker. Of the other two, one looked like a wood-cutter and the other looked like a cop. A second man with a beard remained in the car. He saw the woodcutter give Tucker a shove toward the float. Then they all walked down the ramp and one of the men began untying Brian's dinghy. Lowell Perry was slouched in the front seat of his Camaro just barely looking over the top of the steering wheel. He knew who the men were, although he hadn't seen them before. But he'd heard about those two big men with beards. He knew they were the ones who owned the cocaine, or thought they owned it.

Lowell Perry hoped they'd kill Tucker, just shoot him and throw his body in the bay. And it'd probably be for the best if they shot Brian too. He'd told Brian to pay attention. He'd told him what would happen and Brian ignored him. Lowell Perry had given Brian the choice between him and Tucker, and Brian had chosen Tucker. Well, he'd pay for that. He'd get himself killed. My, wouldn't Lowell Perry enjoy paying his respects to the grieving widow and her sister. He'd ask if there was anything he could do to help. He'd stop by often. He wouldn't be pushy, but he'd become the friend they couldn't do without. And sooner or later Cindy would ask to go for a ride in his new Corvette. He wasn't sure if he'd say yes right away. He'd have to see how he felt.

The four men could barely crowd into the dinghy. The woodcutter did the rowing while Tucker and Brian sat in the stern. Lowell Perry had his sniperscope on them now. Tucker's face had been cut up some and Perry liked that. He wished he'd seen it happen. Then the Oldsmobile started up again, made a U-turn in the parking lot and came back up the hill.

Perry ducked down in his seat. When the car had passed, he started his Camaro and after another moment he made a U-turn, following the Oldsmobile. The dinghy had almost reached the lobster boat. As Lowell Perry shifted into second, he again thought of the square gearshift knob on the Corvette, how the little points of the square would press against his palm.

The Oldsmobile turned left onto High Street at the light. Perry figured they would all join up someplace down the coast after the other guys retrieved the cocaine from wherever Tucker and Brian had hidden it. Perry slowed at the light. Before turning, he flicked his high beams at a patrol car parked in front of the Grasshopper Shop. The patrol car flicked its lights back.

Brian was sitting on the deck in the stern of the lobster boat. It was wet and he was wet and the rain kept beating on his head. Tucker was sitting beside him with his face in his hands. The man called Seymour was at the wheel of the boat which rose and fell in the waves. The other man, Marston, stood just under the roof of the shelter with a pistol in one hand and a flashlight in the other, pointing both at Brian and Tucker. Brian had first thought he was a cop, since that's what he said he was, and apparently he'd followed him home from the police station. He guessed Margaret and Cindy still thought he was a cop. At least they hadn't gotten hurt, thought Brian. He was so scared he was afraid he'd pee himself and, inconsequentially, he was glad it was raining because it would keep anyone from seeing he had done it. His pants were sopped already. Brian hated to be scared. He hated the trouble they were in. And he felt sorry for Tucker, who was crying and trying to hide it.

Brian worried about Tucker and that too seemed an inconsequential thought since it looked like they would both be shot and then it wouldn't matter that Tucker was miserable and crying and seemed half crazy, muttering to himself and talking about his friend Talbot. Tucker looked up at Brian and blinked in the light from the flashlight. The raindrops on his cheeks had run together with the tears so it was impossible to know which was which. Brian touched his arm, squeezing it. It seemed that for three weeks he'd been trying to help his friend and really he'd done nothing.

"They killed him," said Tucker. "They killed Pete."

Marston took a few steps toward them, then stood with his legs wide apart to keep his balance. It was hard to see him behind the flashlight. "What the fuck did you expect?" he said.

Tucker stared up at him. "He was my friend."

"So what?"

"They murdered him." Tucker had raised his voice and Brian again reached out to touch his arm.

Marston moved back under the shelter in order to light a cigarette. "I hate fuckers like you," he said, raising his voice over the sound of the motor. "You feel you can upset everything and steal my merchandise and nothing's going to happen? It was mine, soldier. You think I'm dumb, that I won't test it? You think I'm just a crook so why not rip me off?"

Brian didn't know what Marston was talking about. At first he had thought that Marston was out to steal the cocaine from Tucker, but now it seemed that Tucker had stolen it from him. All he knew for sure was that Tucker had gotten them both in a mess.

Tucker kept shaking his head. He started to speak again and Brian squeezed his shoulder. "*Shh,* don't talk anymore."

"That's right," said Marston. "Keep him shut up or I'll put him into the water right now."

"What are you going to do?" asked Brian, feeling scared. Tucker had crouched down and again had his head in his hands.

Marston pointed the flashlight down at the deck. He wore

black wingtips and they were muddy. "We'll pick up the product," he said, "then meet Mr. Jones in Bayside."

"What about us?" Brian couldn't see Marston's face, only his tan raincoat and shoes.

Marston didn't speak for a moment and Brian was about to repeat his question. "We'll have to see what happens," said Marston. "Where're your pots?"

Brian knew what that meant. He knew they meant to kill him. Then he thought it would never happen, life wasn't like that. But sure it was. All over the world it was like that. He hated how scared he was. But even though he was scared for himself, he also felt scared for Tucker. It seemed awful for Tucker to get killed before getting himself straightened out. He was lost in his life and now he'd die lost. Brian was almost amused by his concern since he too, presumably, would die. But he loved his life, loved his children and family, while Tucker knew only dislike and disappointment.

Brian stood up to see if he could spot his markers. The wind cut through his wet clothes. They had passed the mouth of Little River and were approaching Brown's Head. The only lights were the buoys out in the channel. Marston was shining his light up past the bow. "Right up ahead," said Brian. Maybe his buoys were another hundred yards farther on. He kept waiting for the flashlight to pick out their orange Day-Glo paint.

"They're going to kill us," said Tucker in a loud vice, "just like Pete."

"Don't get over-excited, soldier," said Marston, "or I'll tell Seymour to cool you down." He continued to shine his light forward over the bow while turning back now and then to keep an eye on Tucker. "Which buoy is it?" he asked. The water was rough and pockmarked with the rain.

Brian saw two of his markers off to starboard, then saw a third and fourth. "The third orange one," he said.

Brian kept thinking about Tucker, or perhaps not exactly about Tucker but about why he should be thinking of his friend when his own life was in danger. But Brian had had a good life. That didn't mean he was ready to let it go but Tucker had had no life at all; or rather, he'd had what struck Brian as great promise. That's what he had through high school: great promise. Then came the army and drifting around afterward and that great promise just slipped away. And now he was going to get himself shot and he'd have no more promise than a squashed ant.

Marston joined Seymour at the wheel and pointed out the orange buoy. Brian crouched back down on the deck. Tucker again had his head in his hands. "You gotta stay quiet," whispered Brian. Tucker made no sign of having heard.

Seymour slowed the boat, then stopped. "Hey you," called Marston, "drag up those pots."

Brian went forward, leaned over the side, caught hold of the rope with the gaff hook, slung it over the davit and wrapped it three times around the niggerhead. His fingers were stiff with cold. The first lobster pot broke the surface, then the second. Marston watched from the shelter as Brian dragged them onto the washboard, then threw them onto the deck. The light reflected off the black plastic inside the lobster pots.

Marston shoved Brian back toward the stern. "Go join your friend," he said.

Brian crouched down next to Tucker as Marston opened the pots and took out the packages of cocaine. Resting his hand on Tucker's shoulder, Brian continued to wonder why he had done what he had done, and he found himself thinking about the gap between what a person was and what he could be or wanted to be. In his own case, he didn't think there was a gap, while in Marston's case there must be a huge one, unless he was born to be a drug dealer and murderer. But in Tucker's case there appeared to be only a little gap and it had seemed that with a small effort Brian could help put him on the right road again. Tucker had called him sentimental and Brian guessed he was right. He had wanted to help Tucker become better than he was, to step above himself even if it meant living in a ghost town. Wasn't that chance worth the risk?

But even as he thought this, Brian wondered if it was true. He had wanted it to be like old times. He wanted Tucker to like him, to be his buddy again. And his wish for that had kept him from seeing clearly. Also he wanted the money. It wasn't simply a matter of helping Tucker. He wanted the freedom that ten thousand dollars would give him. No more night work, no more pickup crews.

Marston opened the two packages to look inside. Then he rewrapped them and shoved them over by Seymour's feet. Picking up the two lobster pots, he threw them in the water. For some reason, that act more than any other made Brian think that Marston meant to kill them, as if he and Tucker were as expendable as those lobster pots.

Marston was looking down at them again. "I can't believe you wanted to steal this stuff from me," he said. "What'd I ever do to you?" He turned back to the shelter. "Let's go, Seymour."

The lobster boat surged toward Bayside, the engine roaring so loudly that Brian was afraid he'd crack the block. Marston kept the flashlight pointed at Brian and Tucker. Brian shielded his eyes. He wished he was a better swimmer, since he thought that he could probably get over the side before Marston had a chance to shoot. But he didn't want to leave Tucker and still hoped he'd have a chance to help him.

After several minutes, Brian got up on one knee and saw the lights of Bayside over the starboard bow. The houses were dark, but he could see the light on the dock, then several streetlights by the common. The white gingerbread cottages seemed to glisten in the rain. Brian stood up and Marston motioned to him with his pistol to get back down. Parked near the foot of the common, Brian caught a glimpse of the gray Oldsmobile and Jones walking toward the wharf.

Seymour pulled back on the throttle and the engine went silent as the lobster boat slid through the water toward the wharf. Taking a line, Seymour threw it to Jones, who wrapped it around a piling. The *Margaret* bumped up against the pier.

"On your feet, boys," said Marston.

Seymour carried the packages of cocaine and climbed over the gunwales onto the dock. Marston stood back to let Tucker and Brian follow. Glancing quickly at Brian, Tucker whispered something. Brian had no idea what it was and Tucker had already lowered his head before Brian could indicate his confusion. He started to feel scared again. Backing along the dock, Jones held a newspaper over his head to keep from getting wet, while keeping his pistol aimed at Brian and Tucker. Marston clambered over the gunwales and came up behind Brian and gave him a shove.

"Move," he said.

All five men walked toward the gray Oldsmobile. Seymour first with the cocaine, then Jones who was half turned and kept looking over his shoulder, then Tucker and Brian, and last of all Marston. As they neared the Oldsmobile, Jones began to dig into his pockets for the keys. Tucker appeared to slip on the muddy path and went down on knee. Brian stepped forward to help him, then realized it was a trick because as Tucker recovered his balance, he threw himself toward Marston, knocking him down.

"Brian, run!" shouted Tucker, rushing back down the path toward the water.

Brian was taken by surprise, but turned and ran as best as he could, kicking his foot at Marston and making him duck. Tucker was already ten feet ahead of him. Brian didn't know what they'd do when they got to the water. Behind him, he heard Marston shouting. Brian was only a few yards from the dock. It was difficult to keep his footing in the mud. He heard a gunshot and it seemed that all his muscles grew hard and cold. Then there was another and something kicked him, throwing him forward. He didn't even start to hurt until he hit the dock flat on his stomach and slid. Then his back and shoulder were on fire. There was another gunshot and a fourth. Looking up, he saw Tucker diving forward and thought he'd been hit as well. Tucker went off the dock and splashed into the water. Brian tried crawling to where Tucker had gone over but all his movements were very slow. It was like crawling through thick mud, one hand, one knee, the other hand, the other knee. He fell forward again onto his stomach. I'll get up again in a moment, he thought. Then he heard footsteps running up behind him.

"Did you get the other one?" shouted Marston.

"I don't know," said Jones. "I don't see him."

"Drag this one to the car," said Marston. "We got to get out of here."

"What about Tucker?" said Jones.

"Well, where is he?" said Marston. "Maybe the stupid bastard's at the bottom. Did you hit him or not?"

"I tell you," said Jones, "I don't know."

"Leave him," said Marston. "Get the other one to the car. Hurry!"

Tucker slid up the far side of the *Margaret*, kicked his feet in the water and caught hold of the gunwales. Then he pulled himself into the lobster boat. Crawling into the shelter, he got to his knees and peered through the window to see what was going on. Jones and Marston were hurrying back along the dock toward Brian, who was lying flat on his stomach. Seymour was running toward Brian from the direction of the car. Just the sight of Seymour made Tucker feel frightened. Then he saw Brian raise his head and try to get to his knees. Jones reached out a foot and pushed Brian over onto his back as one might flip over a turtle.

Tucker stepped into the shadow. He had to get out of here. He'd have to leave Brian. There was no alternative. The cops would show up anytime. The whole thing was a disaster, but he still had the forty-five thousand back at his house. He could still pick up Jason and catch the plane in Bangor.

Tucker again looked toward Brian and saw they were dragging him to the Oldsmobile. He must be alive. Most likely they meant to take him someplace more private to finish him off. Several lights had gone on in the cottages, and up the hill Tucker could see a man standing on his front porch.

Tucker turned away and kicked the bulkhead. "Get out of here," he said out loud, "forget him and get out of here."

Again in his memory he heard Talbot shouting his name and then the gunshots. He looked back and saw that Jones had slipped in the mud and was just getting to his feet. Tucker opened the door to the cabin. Forget him, he kept saying to himself, forget Brian. Crouching down in the cabin, Tucker put his hands over his ears. The light on the wharf shone through the window onto the engine. It was no good. He couldn't do it, he couldn't just leave him. Glancing around, he again saw the paint pistol and his ammunition pouch with the paint tubes on the starboard bunk. Tucker picked up the pistol and slipped a tube into the top barrel. Then he loaded it and cocked it. Fast, he said to himself, this time it's got to be really fast.

Tucker opened the cabin door and went back on deck. Jones and Seymour were carrying Brian and had almost reached the Oldsmobile. It was raining harder and the rain drummed onto the roof and pier. Tucker jumped over the gunwales onto the dock. He began to run, watching his feet, making sure not to slip. He had never run so fast. He held the paint pistol out in front of him so everybody could see it. This was what he liked. He jumped from the dock and ran up the path after Seymour and Jones, crouched down, moving so fast the rain never touched him.

It was Marston who saw him first. "He's got a gun!"

Seymour and Jones spun around, dropping Brian and reaching for their own guns as they stumbled back. Jones slipped again and fell on his butt.

"Get away from him before I kill you!" shouted Tucker. He was about ten feet from Brian. Seymour and Marston were backing toward the Oldsmobile. Jones was closest and stared at the paint pistol.

"Hey," he shouted, "that's not a real gun."

"Then you're dead!" shouted Tucker. He fired and a great red flower of paint appeared on Jones's face. Jones yelled and fell back, digging his fingers into his eyes. Both Seymour and Marston had their guns in their hands, but instead of shooting they stared at Jones, rolling on the ground and yelling, smearing the red paint across his face. Seymour ran back toward the car.

Tucker reloaded and recocked the pistol. "Hey," he shouted at Marston, who turned and lifted his gun. Tucker fired first and a great splotch of red appeared on the shoulder of Marston's raincoat.

"*Yow!*" shouted Marston, and then, "it's paint!"

As Marston was looking at the paint on his fingers, Tucker shot him again, hitting his chin so that Marston yelped and slipped in the mud. Then Tucker grabbed Brian and threw him into a fireman's carry. Turning, he ran back toward the dock with Brian over his shoulder, zigzagging a little. Instead of worrying he might get shot in the back, he wondered if someone would ever invent an automatic paint pistol, even a machine gun. Maybe paint grenades. There was a gunshot and he heard the buzz of the bullet. He leapt forward onto the dock. There was another gunshot. Then he heard Seymour shouting something. Tucker reached the boat, vaulted over the side with Brian and fell against the shelter. Brian rolled away. Looking back, Tucker saw six police cars roaring down the hill. Trailing behind them was Lowell Perry's Camaro.

Tucker jumped up to untie the line. Then he started the boat, taking care not to flood it, giving it just enough gas. As he pulled away from the dock, he saw Seymour running toward the woods and Marston climbing into the Oldsmobile. Jones was on his feet and staggering around, still trying to wipe the paint out of his eyes. Neat shot, thought Tucker.

Lowell Perry wished he had a gun, a Magnum. He had one at home of course but Nixon had told him not to bring it, saying he was here strictly in an unofficial capacity. That's not the way Lowell Perry saw it. He was the pro. These other guys were just piddling around. Several of the police cars slid to a stop and cops started piling out and getting wet. At that moment the gray Oldsmobile at the bottom of the hill burst out of the parking lot and across the grass of the common, spinning its wheels and kicking up mud. Two police cars swerved to cut it off. Lowell Perry parked his Camaro behind the other police cars and jumped out. He was wearing one of those waterproof running suits, green with a yellow stripe, so he didn't give a damn how hard it rained. Glancing around, he thought there must be a way to benefit from this circus. A big man with a beard was running toward the woods. Another big man was wandering in circles with some kind of red stuff all over his face. If it was blood, then he should be dead. Perry began loping toward him.

The Oldsmobile hadn't a hope of getting away. One of the police cars bounced toward it, then sideswiped it, forcing it toward the trees so that it banged off one and smashed into another, coming to a stop with the whole car tilted up on its side. A man in a raincoat crawled out and started to run. The second police car slewed sideways through the mud behind him and a blue-clad arm reached out and grabbed the man's collar, pulling him down. Four other cops and plainclothesmen were on top of him almost before he hit the ground.

There was a gunshot, then another. The big guy with the

beard who'd been running toward the woods had turned and fired, and one of the cops fired back. Now lots of cops were firing and the big guy was only able to get off another round before he was hit. Popping caps, said Lowell Perry to himself. If he'd had his Magnum, he would have popped the big guy, no question. He wouldn't have missed first time either. The man had dropped his gun and was on his hands and knees as a bunch of cops ran toward him.

Perry was about fifteen feet from the third man, who seemed harmless. With one hand he kept wiping his eyes, with the other he held some kind of bottle. The rain had washed the red stuff all down his beard and coveralls. Perry realized it was paint. A young Belfast cop came barreling toward him across the common and tackled the man so they both slid across the muddy grass. The bottle flew out of the man's hands, then hit the grass and rolled. Lowell Perry took a few steps toward it and picked it up. It was one of those reddish aluminum bottles that people take camping. Perry opened it and looked inside. White stuff. A whole lot of white stuff. Closing the bottle, he unzipped his running jacket and slid the bottle inside. It was like he was holding a miniature Corvette right next to his heart. He walked back toward his Camaro, not too fast, not too slow. Even though he'd never liked music, he felt like singing. Shit, he'd have sung "The Star-Spangled Banner."

Reaching through the open window, he dropped the metal bottle on the floor behind the seat. Then he looked back to see if anyone had noticed. All the cops were busy handcuffing and dragging and pulling, being professionals. Lowell Perry felt as happy as a mean man could feel. Way out in the water he saw Brian's lobster boat heading toward Belfast. Maybe Tucker wasn't on it, maybe he was dead.

Tucker was being very careful. He knew he could easily park the lobster boat on some rocks and make an additional mess of everything. So he took it slow, heading along the western shore toward Belfast, watching for lobster buoys and keeping his eye out for the lights. Brian was propped up in a corner of the shelter. He was bleeding and the blood mixed with the rain and seawater on the deck. Tucker thought he was hurt pretty bad, although Brian was ignoring it. Instead, he kept complaining about Tucker.

"I tell you," said Brian, "I can get back all right. Just leave me."

"No, man," said Tucker.

"Why not?"

"I fucked up my friends." He was surprised how easy it was to say it. He'd fucked up everything. Like he'd been stupid, he hadn't been paying attention.

"You made a mistake," said Brian.

"It was worse than a mistake," said Tucker. "I was stupid and arrogant." He still couldn't see how he'd let it happen. If this were football or baseball, he could watch the replay and see where he'd gone wrong. But even that was a stupid thought. It had nothing to do with the real world. Talbot had said something like that. It was his fault Talbot was dead and he should pay for it. He didn't deserve to have a kid or anything decent.

"Look, you saved my life," said Brian. "I'm okay, I'll be fine now." His voice sounded weak and muffled, like he was talking through a sock.

"You're bleeding to death," said Tucker, peering through the rain at the shore.

Brian tried to get up and slipped back down. "You got to get outta here. They'll arrest you. You got to catch that plane."

"I've changed my mind," said Tucker.

"What about your kid?"

"He can visit me in jail."

Instead of being frightened, he felt almost glad about going to jail. He wouldn't have to think or worry about anything.

Maybe he'd read a lot. And baseball, he'd heard they played baseball in prisons. Then he stopped himself. I'm still having stupid thoughts, he said to himself. But maybe he'd get himself straightened out. But what about Brian? He'd messed him up too.

It was raining harder than ever but he was already so cold and wet that the rain felt warm. Tucker was looking for that part of the shore where Brian had dropped off Cindy. The street from the hospital came right down to the beach and at the foot of the street was a light. He had the sense of starting a new adventure and had to stop himself to ask what kind of adventure it would be. Jail, he repeated, not a happy place. Would Phillip be in jail too? And Seymour and those guys, would they all be in jail with him? He tried not to think about it.

"Where're you taking me?" said Brian.

"The hospital." Maybe the police wouldn't be looking for him. Maybe he could leave Brian right at the hospital door and sneak away. But the money was at his house and his truck at Talbot's and Rooster was God knows where. He'd have no time. They were sure to catch him.

"Are you crazy?" said Brian. "You'll be arrested. You know what the cops will do to you?"

"Yeah, they'll show me what it's like to be a grown-up. That's what it says on the gates of prison, you know that? Welcome to the adult world. Maybe I can start a rebellion." Then Tucker saw the streetlight and turned the boat. The water was flat and there was no surf. It was already high tide; if he could beach the boat, then someone could get it later. Most likely the cops would impound it. Maybe he should just wreck it. But that was dumb thinking again.

As the boat drifted forward Tucker knelt down beside Brian to get him ready. Brian tried to sit up but he was too weak. He apparently had been shot in the shoulder and the bullet had exited through his lung. When he breathed, he made a wheezing noise. Tucker found himself thinking they'd have to fly him to a hospital in Japan.

"You can still get away," said Brian. "You can make a new life."

"Who the fuck wants to live in a ghost town?"

"You never listen to what I tell you."

"Shut up," said Tucker, lifting Brian into his arms and standing up. "Maybe for once I know what I'm doing."

I'll be a first offender, thought Tucker. Deserted by my wife, decorated in the war, just a poor slob who got mixed up with the wrong people. I could get off with a couple of years. But what about Brian? Jesus, what will his position be after two years in jail? What about his kids and his family and his job? It seemed to Tucker that he would never learn about his life and that even if he did learn, he would still choose the fantasy. He even questioned the grief that now swept through him.

"Brian," said Tucker, "you got to say I forced you to do it, that I tricked and bullied you into it, that it wasn't your fault."

But Brian hadn't heard. He seemed unconscious. Jesus, thought Tucker, I've got to get him to the hospital quick. He held Brian as he stepped back to the wheel. The boat was drifting parallel to shore about ten yards out. Brian didn't feel heavy. Cradling him in both arms, Tucker glanced into his face. In Vietnam, he'd carried guys like this, sometimes wounded, sometimes dead.

Tucker stared toward the streetlight, trying to determine the best place to beach the *Margaret*. One place seemed as good as another. Maybe he could hitchhike out to Brooks or take Brian's car. But it was too late for that, too late for anything. He turned the wheel. The light glittered on the water where it broke against the rocks.

Epilogue

The trouble with Rooster when you got him on a regular leash was that he pulled. The dog had never been properly trained. Cindy planted her heels on the sidewalk, trying not to slip in the snow. Reluctantly, Rooster came to a halt, sat down and began scratching himself. With the post office on her left and the bank on her right, Cindy could see all the way down Main Street to the harbor. It was still snowing and the wheels of an old Chevy pickup whined and spun as the driver tried to make it up the hill.

Cindy had just come from trying to see Tucker in jail but they hadn't let her so she had just left off some cigarettes. The trial had finished yesterday and sentencing was set for next week. This had been the third or fourth trial, Cindy couldn't keep track, but anyway it was the only one she cared about since it was Brian's and Tucker's. Rooster pulled her forward again to the crosswalk at Church Street. It was mid-afternoon and already getting dark. Cindy could never get used to its being dark so early. The sky and the water and the streets were all the same metallic gray. She tucked her red scarf up over her chin and gave Rooster a little yank on the leash just to show she meant business.

Although Brian and Tucker had been found guilty, the trial had not gone as the prosecutor had hoped. For one thing, the police had never located one of the smugglers who had been living in Camden. For another, everyone had been sympathetic to Brian for getting shot. Some people even called him a hero. For a third thing, Tucker had testified that Brian had known nothing about what was going on. And finally, some kind of other evidence hadn't materialized. Cindy didn't know what it was but she thought it had something to do with Lowell Perry, who hadn't gone to any of the trials, not even one day. Tucker's role was also confused and it hadn't been proved that he was any more than a kind of courier. Also, he had testified that he'd seen the two men, Seymour Wright and Henry Jones, shoot and kill Peter Talbot, which had become the prosecutor's major interest. They had already received life sentences, while Marston had been given twenty years.

Actually, Brian's lawyer thought that Brian might get off with a year. Tucker would get more but probably not much. Tucker's wife had refused to come to the trial, had already moved down to Boston. It made Cindy furious to think about it. She knew that Tucker grieved for his son. When they hadn't let her see Tucker, she had led Rooster around behind the jail and made him bark just so Tucker could hear him. Rooster had barked until a policeman came out and shooed them away. Cindy had almost felt that Rooster was talking and even that Tucker could understand. It had been mean of them not to grant Tucker bail like they had for Brian. But of course Tucker hadn't been shot and Brian said that Tucker had made Chief Foley so angry that he'd made sure bail was denied. Also there was some question about some missing money. Cindy didn't understand it. Anyway Tucker didn't seem to mind being in jail except for not seeing his son, or so Brian claimed. Apparently he was trying to invent a new board game like Monopoly which he was calling "Don't" and which would make him a fortune. He was also talking about learning French.

Cindy began to step off the curb when she noticed a car slowing down on her right. It was Lowell Perry in that pretty red Corvette. Sometimes she felt he drove around town all day just so he could bother her. She hated to see such a nice car wasted on such a jerk. Perry drew up in front of her and rolled down the window.

"Why don't you tie that ugly dog to a post and we can go for a ride?" he said, leaning across the seat.

"No thanks. Aren't you 'fraid the snow will hurt that car of yours?"

Perry winked just to show he knew she was making a joke. "What about dinner," he said. "I'll take you down to Camden."

"I'm afraid I'm busy."

"What about tomorrow?"

"I'm busy then too."

Perry's face got tight and red like he was trying to blow up a balloon. "You owe me one, Cindy. If it weren't for me, Brian and Tucker would've gone to jail for years and years."

"Then why didn't you testify?"

"Just to help you out. Brian's my friend."

Rooster was tugging at the leash and growling. Cindy wondered if there were some way she could make the dog bite Lowell Perry, not hard of course but just so he'd disappear. "Brian said you were hiding something," she said, "that you were afraid of getting caught. He said Tucker told him all about it."

Perry grinned but Cindy knew he didn't find anything funny. "That don't change the fact that you owe me."

Rooster chose that moment to jump up and stick his head through the window of the Corvette.

Perry tried to push the dog away and Rooster barked. "Pull that damn dog off!" shouted Perry. "He's scratching the paint."

"Then you better get moving, Mr. Perry, or I'll tell Rooster to climb right inside next to you."

Lowell Perry gave her a mean look and she pulled Rooster back just as Perry hit the gas. His tires spun in the snow and the Corvette fishtailed around the corner and down Main Street—a pretty piece of red plastic. For a moment Cindy considered taking a ride in it, but no, she had to look out for Rooster. She had to take good care of him till Tucker got out of prison.

Cindy stepped off the curb to cross the intersection. Down the hill she saw the traffic light turn red and the Corvette slide to a stop. It was December and the cheap plastic Santas and Christmas lights were up and twinkling above the few shoppers. Past the city wharf the harbor was just a blur as the snow grew thicker. She couldn't see the other side, just an increasing grayness. She hated the winter here, how it kept your body always tight and rigid. It was like being locked in a freezer. She stuck out her tongue and caught a snowflake. Then she gave Rooster an affectionate tug. She felt bad about Tucker. By the time he got out, she could be anywhere. Even married, even a mother. For a moment that future seemed to stretch clearly before her, but then it too got confused and mixed up with the snow and cold until it seemed to disappear into the gray sky above the harbor.